FLINTLOCK: GUT-SHOT

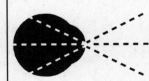

This Large Print Book carries the
Seal of Approval of N.A.V.H.

FLINTLOCK: GUT-SHOT

WILLIAM W. JOHNSTONE
WITH J. A. JOHNSTONE

THORNDIKE PRESS

A part of Gale, Cengage Learning

GALE
CENGAGE Learning·

Farmington Hills, Mich • San Francisco • New York • Waterville, Maine
Meriden, Conn • Mason, Ohio • Chicago

GALE
CENGAGE Learning®

LIBRARY OF CONGRESS CATALOGING-IN-PUBLICATION DATA

Johnstone, William W.
    Flintlock : gut-shot / by William W. Johnstone with J. A. Johnstone. — Large print edition.
      pages ; cm. — (Thorndike Press large print western)
      ISBN 978-1-4104-7249-6 (hardcover) — ISBN 1-4104-7249-3 (hardcover)
      1. Large type books. I. Johnstone, J. A. II. Title.
PS3560.O415F594 2014
813'.54—dc23   2014044931

Published in 2015 by arrangement with Pinnacle Books, an imprint of Kensington Publishing Corp.

FLINTLOCK: GUT-SHOT

CHAPTER ONE

Sam Flintlock smiled and figured the living was easy.

He'd made up a bed of soft pine needles where he could later spread his blankets, the fire burned well, bacon sizzled and the coffee was on the bile.

Then demented Dave Glover called to him out of the darkness and spoiled everything.

"Git up slow, like you got the rheumatisms, and keep your hands where I can see 'em," the old man yelled.

Flintlock got to his feet, his hands away from his sides.

"Turn into the firelight so I can see you," Glover said. "Show yourself now. I can't abide a bashful man."

Then, after a few moments passed, "Hell, you're Sam'l Flintlock."

"Of course I'm Sam Flintlock."

"I heard you'd been hung or shot or

some such."

"Who the hell are you?" Flintlock said.

"Dave Glover, standing right here as plain as could ever be."

"Now I know who you are, state your intentions."

"If you're the ranny who stole my sawn lumber, my intentions are to shoot you down quicker'n scat and take it back."

"Dave, you're still the crazy old loon I recollect from the old days."

"Crazy is as crazy does, Sam'l. And remember that this here Henry is both wife and child to me and she's ready to do my talkin'. If sich is necessary, like."

"I didn't take your damned lumber. I got no need for it. Ah, hell, look what you've done. Now my bacon's burning."

"You're low-down, Sam'l, everybody knows that for a natural fact. Are you a thief as well as a hoodlum?"

"Never in my life wanted anything bad enough to steal it, Dave."

"It's a low-down thing to lift a man's lumber, especially from a ranny you know."

"Dave, I heard you was shot dead by Banjo Tom Lister in a saloon up Denver way."

"Maybe I was."

"So why would I steal a dead man's sawn

lumber?"

"You tell me."

"Well, I wouldn't, that's all."

"You heard wrong about Banjo Tom, Sammy. He couldn't shade me on his best day. I put a bullet in his brisket an' that served him right. I'm coming in. You stay right where you're at."

"The bacon will burn."

"Then take it off the fire, boy. I'm sharp set."

Dave Glover, leading a Missouri mule, parted the darkness like a sable curtain and stepped into the orange glow of the campfire, his Henry in his gun hand.

"Damn you, Dave," Flintlock said. "If my bacon had burned I'd have plugged you fer sure."

"Big talk, Sam'l. Take a heap of doin' though."

Flintlock shook his head. "Everybody's right. You are a demented old coot."

"Hah!"

"What's 'hah'?"

"That's a lot of noise comin' from a feller who carries an old Hawken squirrel gun, hunts for his long-lost mama so she can give him a name, talks to the ghost of his mean ol' grandpappy and has a big bird tattooed across his throat."

9

For a few moments Glover watched Flint-lock salvage the bacon, then he said, "Wagon tracks go right past your camp. I seen that."

"They were there when I got here," Flint-lock said.

"Is that a fer sure?"

"Yeah, it's a fer sure. I figured it was a supply wagon headed for town."

"Town is that way," Glover said, pointing east. "The tracks are headed that way," he added, pointing west. "Didn't old Barnabas teach you how to read sign?"

"How are you so damned certain?" Flint-lock said, irritated.

"Because the hoss goes in front of the wagon and not vice versa. At least that's how it's done around these parts. And the hoss's tracks are headed west, as any damned fool with half an eye can see."

"Hell, you're starting to sound like old Barnabas," Flintlock said.

"Sam. He should've taken a stick to you when you were a younker," Glover said. "I'd say that much is real obvious."

"He did, plenty of times."

"You deserved it."

"Then after I got big enough and mean enough to kick his ass, I guess Barnabas decided I didn't deserve it no more."

"That I'd have to see for my ownself.

10

Barnabas could whup his weight in bobcats an' he was meaner than a lobo wolf, and sneaky with it."

"Well, it happened," Flintlock said. "Just like I said it did."

"I never trusted a mountain man to be out of the fight until after I skun him and tanned his hide for a shirt."

"I just showed Barnabas the error of his ways."

"So you say," Glover said.

He was a skinny old man with a gray beard and an eagle feather in his hat. He wore beaded buckskins that were new when Davy Crockett was a younker and Nez Perce moccasins.

Flintlock let his annoyance simmer for a while then said in a reasonable enough tone, "Tether your mule over yonder by my buckskin then set an' eat."

"I always say that there's no better grub than sowbelly bacon atween two slices of fried sourdough bread," Glover said, wiping grease off his mouth with the back of his hand.

"That's what you always say, huh?" Flintlock said.

"Sure do."

Glover accepted the makings from the

younger man and began to build a cigarette.

Then, without looking up, he said, "I don't think you stole my lumber."

"Well, that's good to know," Flintlock said. "Kind of makes a man feel good all over. Don't it?"

The old man tossed the makings back to Flintlock.

"I'm building a house, Sam'l," he said.

"What kind of house?"

"Big house."

"How big?"

"Two stories tall with a parlor and maybe three bedrooms."

Flintlock used a brand from the fire to light his cigarette.

"That's how come your sawn lumber got stole."

Glover nodded. "That's a real brilliant deduction, Sammy. Yup, stole from right under my nose up on Rock Creek yonder, south of the Sans Bois."

"You're a crazy old coot, Dave, letting folks steal your lumber for a house you shouldn't be building in the first place."

"How come that, Sammy?"

"Why are you building a house where there never was a house afore and probably never will be again?"

"Except for mine," Glover said, behind a

12

blue coil of cigarette smoke.

"I know I'm going to regret this, but tell me why," Flintlock said.

"Why, what?"

"The reason you're building a big house in a damned wilderness."

"All righty then, Sammy, but first let me say something," Glover said. "An' I don't want to hurt your feelings, mind, but you ain't gonna like this, you being so sensitive an' all."

"I don't get hurt easily."

The old man sighed, as though he was real sad about what he had to say.

"Well, see, you just ain't attractive to women, so there are some things you just don't understand. I'm sorry, but that's the way of it with you. I mean, you got that great big beak of a nose and a mustache hanging under it like a dead rat an' —"

"I catch your drift," Flintlock said, testy as hell.

"Glad you do."

"Why are you building a house? My question in the first damn place."

"Me, I'm a handsome feller, Sam'l, an' when I cut a dash the ladies go wild. The thing is though, I'm plumb tired of fighting them off, so I plan to settle down with just one woman, a nice fat gal who'll take good

13

care of me and be the queen of my . . . castle on the creek."

Glover stared at Flintlock, his eyes glittering in the firelight.

"That's how it's gonna be, Sammy."

"Dave, how old are you? Seventy? Eighty?"

"I don't rightly know."

"Well, you're too old a tomcat to be playing around with kittlins."

"Miss Maybelline Bell don't think so."

"Who the hell is she?"

"Lady I got all picked out already and she's more'n willin'. Miss Maybelline was happy to take my gage l'amour, a nice silver ring with a blue stone on it."

"How old is she, this gal who's tetched enough in the head to accept a love token from a loco old coot like you?"

"Oh, seventeen I guess, and as pretty as a fresh-painted Studebaker wagon."

"You said she's fat. How fat?" Flintlock said.

"Oh, I guess she'd dress out around three hundred."

"She'll crush your poor old bones to a powder, Dave."

"Way to go though, huh?"

Flintlock poured himself coffee and when he'd raised the cup to his lips. Glover said, "D'ye mind Black John Miles, Sammy?"

14

Suddenly Flintlock was wary.

"Yeah, I recollect him," he said. His voice was slow as he took time to think.

"I shot him off'n you that time. Now where was that?"

"In the New Mexico Territory down in the Twin Butte country," Flintlock said.

"Is that right? So that's where it was."

"You mind fine where it was. At the time we were runnin' with Billy Bonney and that hard Lincoln County crowd and you haven't forgotten that."

"Black John would've cut your suspenders fer sure that day. Had you on your back with a Green River pigsticker at your throat."

"I could have handled him."

"Hell, you was drunk."

"So was Black John."

"Your old Hawken was back at camp and you fell on your Colt and couldn't get the damned thing shucked. You mind that? You squealin' like a piglet caught under a gate, a-tuggin' an' a-haulin' at your iron an' Black John standin' over you like the very wrath of God."

Flintlock opened his mouth to speak, but Glover's laugh cut across his bow.

"I recollect Black John told you he was gonna cut you to collops then carve the big bird off your throat and get it tanned to use as a hatband."

"He dreamed big, did John."

"He was a thumper an' a moonlight howler, warn't he?"

"Most folks said that. I didn't."

"Anyhoo, when he threatened the cuttin' an' you lying there all scared an' big-eyed, like —"

"Black John didn't scare me, old man. Then or ever."

"I upped my Henry and scattered his brains all over creation. I was fearin' for your life, like." Glover cackled and slapped his thigh. "Good times, Sam'l, huh?"

"Yeah, well, I don't know about that. After all was said and done and the gunsmoke cleared, Billy was dead and so were Tom O'Folliard, John Tunstall and Alexander McSween, all fellers I liked."

He stared bleakly at Glover. "We sure picked the wrong side in that fight."

"Billy teached you what gunfightin' was all about, though, Sammy," the old man said. "It was what schoolmarms call a learnin' experience."

He motioned for the makings again. "I mean, that's why you're such a success in your chosen profession."

"Bounty hunting isn't a profession," Flintlock said. "It's like cow punching, a

16

job a man does when he can't do anything else."

Glover's hair was as long and luxuriant as Wild Bill Hickok's, but gray as a badger. Now, before he spoke again, he tied it back with a rawhide string so it hung down his back like a horse's tail.

"You owe me, Sam," he said, his voice a whisper. Another sigh, deeper this time. "But then, these days a man doesn't recollect what other folks have done fer him in the past. That's progress, I guess."

"You're calling in the favor, huh?" Flintlock said, frowning.

"I don't want to push it, Sammy," said the old man. "It ain't polite."

Flintlock let out his own dramatic sigh. "All right, you read the tracks. How many of them?"

"Three. One of them could be Jake Ruskin. I ain't saying it's so, but it could be."

"Ruskin never leaves the Brazos River country and nothing can budge him," Flintlock said. "And he ain't one to steal a load of timber either, not while he can earn gun wages, he ain't."

"He's got kin here in the Oklahoma Territory," Glover said. "Ol' Jake might be visiting and doing them a kindness, like."

17

"Well, if you say some fellers stole your building wood, and I guess they did, one of them wasn't Jake Ruskin."

"You don't reckon so?"

"No, I don't. So forget the idea."

"Well, if it is Jake, I'll deal with him," Glover said. "I got my hair all tied back fer gunfightin' and he'll know it."

"You can't shade Ruskin in a straight-up gunfight," Flintlock said.

"I reckon not. Kin you?"

"I sure don't want to make a trial of it."

The old man rose to his feet, tall, grim and sinewy in the fire glow.

"Good, then we're agreed that we're both afeared of Jake Ruskin. So let's go get 'er done, Sammy."

"If it is Ruskin, you could get us both killed," Flintlock said. "He ain't much of a one for taking prisoners."

"I ain't reckoning on that," Glover said. He thumped his chest with the palm of his hand. "Hell, I got a house to build and a fat young filly to bed."

CHAPTER TWO

Moonlight lay among the pines like winter frost as Sam Flintlock and Dave Glover followed the wagon tracks west across rolling hill country. For an hour the only sound was the creak of saddle leather and the steady thud of their mounts' hooves on grama grass.

Then Glover said, "Tracks swinging south."

"I see them," Flintlock said.

"A couple of settlements that way. They plan to sell my lumber, the damned rogues."

"How much is it worth?" Flintlock said, already missing his soft bed of pine needles.

Chasing after three small-time thieves was a diversion he didn't need, not when he was on his way to a good-paying job.

"To me, a whole lot," Glover said. "On the open market, fifty or sixty dollars. Call it sixty because they stole a keg of tenpenny nails besides."

"Split three ways, that's twenty dollars each," Flintlock said. "Them boys are sure going to a lot of trouble for twenty dollars."

"The hoss and wagon was mine as well," Glover said.

All at once Flintlock's mood got a lot grumpier.

"They stole your hoss and wagon? What the hell were you doing when all this was going on?"

"Sleepin' off a drunk."

"Damn it, you know you can't drink whiskey."

"It was gin. I made myself up a batch of gin punch with hot water and lemons. Celebrating my upcoming nuptials by wetting the bride's head, like."

"She was with you?"

"Yeah. And that little gal snores when she's been drinkin'."

Glover abruptly drew rein and his mule tossed its head in annoyance.

"Smell the smoke?" he said.

Flintlock turned, lifted his head and his great beak of a nose tested the wind.

"I sure do," he said. "And it's close. We'll go the rest of the way on foot."

The old man's store-bought teeth gleamed in the darkness.

"Bringing your Hawken?"

"Hell no. I only shoot her on Sundays."

"This is Sunday."

"Then it's every other Sunday."

Flintlock swung out of the saddle and slid his Winchester from the boot.

"This is your kind of business, Sammy," Glover said. "How do we play it?"

"Take them alive if we can, kill them if we can't."

"You ain't a man who gives out too many options, Sam."

"No, I ain't." Then, suddenly irritable, "Let's get the damned thing over with. Shooting scrapes in the middle of the night don't set well with me."

Flintlock and Glover made their way through the pines, following the orange glimmer of the robbers' campfire.

The moon had drawn a veil of gray cloud across its face like a mournful ghost and in the distance a hunting pair of coyotes called to each other. The air was cool and thin and smelled of dust. Lime green frogs plopped into a nearby rain pond and old Glover jumped and swung his rifle on them. Then he muttered to himself and walked on.

When Flintlock was close enough to the camp to make out three men lying close to the fire under blankets, he motioned Glover to separate from him. When the old man got ten yards away he held up a hand and stopped him.

Flintlock had no worries about the old-timer holding up his end of the bargain. He'd stand firm and get his work in and he'd killed more than his share back in the olden days when Billy was still above ground.

Gun-savvy geezers like Dave Glover were always dangerous men in a fight. They knew they were too old for a knock-down-drag-out, so they just killed you.

Straightening from his crouch, Flintlock waved Glover forward and walked into the camp, a fire-splashed clearing in the trees where a nearby stream babbled as it bubbled over a pebbled bottom. Somewhere a startled owl questioned the night and rustled a tree branch with restless wings.

"On yer feet, you thieving scum!" Glover yelled, his rifle at the ready.

Flintlock swore. It was a way, but it wasn't his way. He'd planned on getting closer to give the robbers no chance of drawing iron. But Glover had gifted them a margin and the three men took advantage of it.

All at once all hell broke loose.

As men who live their lives on the scout do, the thieves woke instantly. They tangled out of their blankets and jumped to their feet, cursing, guns in hand. But there was a split second delay as the outlaws sought targets in the amber gloom.

It was enough time when killing was to be done.

Flintlock's and Glover's rifles roared at the same time, shots aimed from the shoulder.

But they'd both picked the same man, a big fellow with a black, spade-shaped beard who cried out as he went down, sudden red roses blossoming on the front of his shirt.

"Sam Flintlock!"

Peering through a veil of smoke, Flintlock saw Jake Ruskin standing at a distance, his hand away from his gun.

"I'm out," Ruskin said. He was a medium-sized man who affected the elegant dress and manners of the frontier gambler.

A bullet tugged at the sleeve of Flintlock's buckskin shirt and beside him he heard the thud of lead hitting bone and Glover gasped and went down on one knee.

"This man's getting married to a fat young gal!" Flintlock yelled, outraged. "You can't shoot him like that."

The third robber, a lanky towheaded kid with the eyes of a carrion eater, advanced on Flintlock, triggering two Colts held high at eye level.

He'd heard of such before, but Flintlock had never met a two-gun man face-to-face.

Henry Brown, the famed Missouri gunfighter, once told him that shooting two hard-bucking revolvers at the same time was a grandstand play calculated to get a man killed.

"Only Hickok ever pulled it off with any success," he'd said. "And then only when he was drunk and seeing double anyway."

Now the towhead proved Brown's words.

He walked steadily toward Flintlock, the muzzles of both Colts starring scarlet flame.

To his credit, the kid's bullets came close. Lead split the air around Flintlock's head and kicked up startled exclamation points of dirt at his feet.

But the young gun scored no hits.

However Sam Flintlock was not a man to miss with a rifle at spitting range.

Rapidly levering the Winchester from the hip, his .44-40 bullets tore great holes in the towhead's chest and belly.

Hit hard, blood already making a scarlet gash of his mouth, the man staggered, tried to raise his guns but found that he no longer had the strength.

Finally the youngster raised up on his toes, arched his body like a man does after rising from sleep, then fell, his features drained of all expression. His face crashed into the flames and glowing coals of the campfire and a shimmering shower of crimson sparks cascaded into the air.

Flintlock pulled the dead kid from the flames, then rounded on Jake Ruskin, a named man said to be faster and deadlier on the draw and shoot than John Wesley Hardin.

"You decided to make a play yet, Jake?" Flintlock said.

"You got a rifle on me, Sam, and there's distance between us," he said. "Seems like I'm facing a stacked deck."

"Seems like," Flintlock said.

Ruskin shrugged. "This isn't my fight. The towhead was my cousin, so he was kin, but he wasn't too bright and it was he who brought me to this unfortunate pass."

"Jake, did you put him up to stealing the wagon and lumber?"

"Sure didn't. But I told him to kill the old man or he'd come after him. He said he wouldn't shoot a sleeping man. More fool him. Fellers in our profession don't make such fine distinctions. Do we, Sam?"

"Most times, I guess not," Flintlock said. "Now if you shuck that gun belt and let it fall at your feet I'll be greatly obliged."

He centered his rifle on the gunman's chest.

"Just keep in mind that I'm a nervous man and when I get nervous bad things tend to happen."

Ruskin smiled and did as he was told.

"Step forward now, Jake," Flintlock said. "Easy as you go. Just stride off ten yards of git between you and the iron."

Again the gunfighter complied.

Then Ruskin said, "Mind if take a look at the old buzzard?"

Glover was still on one knee and blood stained the front of his shirt.

The old-timer grinned and said, "That's white of you, Jake. I'm sorry I didn't have the honor of swapping lead with you, but the young feller over there put me out of the fight right quick."

Ruskin smiled. "Maybe some other time, if you ever visit the Brazos country. I'd be pleased to meet you on the field of honor."

"Thankee. The name's Dave Glover an' I'll look forward to it."

After telling Glover to sit, Ruskin stripped off the old man's shirt and undervest.

"Here, Jake, have you done this afore?" Glover said. "Not that I'm doubting a man of your reputation, mind."

"During the war I was a doctor's assistant," Ruskin said. "Hell, I was only a younker then but I saw wounds that still waken me from sleep at night."

He smiled at the old man. "Seen a lot of broken collarbones too, which is what you got."

"Damn, so that's where the bullet hit. I couldn't lift my gun hand. Damn that kid fer a scoundrel who couldn't shoot straight."

"Well, Willie's bullet busted up the bone pretty good then went on through," Ruskin said.

"Will I be able to take ahold of my gal?" Glover said, his face worried.

"Yeah, with your left arm."

The old man's worried expression spread to Flintlock's face like a contagion.

"Hell, Jake, you can't splint a man's shoulder," he said.

"No need for that," Ruskin said. "Strip the holsters off Willie's gun rig and bring me the cartridge belt."

Flintlock did as the bounty hunter asked.

Ruskin buckled the cartridge belt around Glover's neck then, as gently as a woman, eased the old man's arm into the sling it created.

"When you get home, get that gal of yours to make a better sling out of one of her unmentionables or something," he said.

The gunman smiled. "You're a tough old coot, Dave, but don't try to move that arm for three, maybe four weeks. Understand?"

"I'll mind every word that was spoke, Jake," Glover said. "But I got to tell you, boy, it's punishing me like hell."

"Then drink plenty of whiskey."

"How about hot gin punch?"

"It'll do the same thing," Ruskin said. "Make you numb."

"Damn it all, Jake, but you're true-blue," Glover said. "I'm glad Sammy didn't plug you out of sheer spite. He does that kind of thing, you know, and he ain't to be trusted."

"Nor am I," Ruskin said.

Flintlock smiled. "I ain't over this yet, so see you don't push it, Jake," he said. "As Dave says, by times I can be a spiteful man."

Dave Glover said that Jake Ruskin had acted the white man and as they were both Masons the gunman was allowed to bury his dead and ride out of camp.

Flintlock drove the wagon to the old man's partially built house, a frail skeleton of angled timbers and one boarded-up gable wall. Behind the rickety structure was a large outhouse. Flintlock couldn't make up his mind whether or not it was a two-holer, a rare luxury on the frontier at that time, or

28

if Dave had built it oversized to accommodate the derriere of his intended.

Behind the wall stood a large brass bed with billowy white pillows and a patchwork quilt.

Glover had rigged a canvas tarp over the bed and Flintlock reckoned the old coot would be snug enough beside his fat gal if it didn't rain too hard.

Maybelline Bell made a fluttering fuss over her wounded husband-to-be, and then gave Flintlock a bear hug that was perhaps more enthusiastic than was strictly necessary.

He enjoyed it though.

CHAPTER THREE

Sam Flintlock was thirty-nine years old the day he rode into the town of Open Sky, a thriving settlement in the Blue Mountain country of the Oklahoma Territory.

He was short, stocky and as rough as a cob. A shock of unruly black hair showed under his wide-brimmed, much abused hat and his eyes, gray as a sea mist, were set deep under shaggy eyebrows. His mustache was full, in the dragoon style then fashionable on the frontier. He walked with the horseman's stiff-kneed gait, and, if he'd felt inclined, he could have sold his clothes, including his scuffed, down-at-heel boots, for at least a dollar. Flintlock was tough, enduring, raised hard by hard men for a wild, unforgiving land. But there was no cruelty in him. He had much honesty of tongue, a quick, wry sense of humor, and his word was his bond.

He liked whores, children and dogs and

was kind to all of them.

He'd killed a dozen men, three as a lawman, the rest since he entered the bounty-hunting profession, and none of them disturbed his sleep o' nights. The only ghost he ever saw was that of the grandfather who'd raised him, wicked, profane old Barnabas the mountain man who'd been following the devil's buffalo herds this past ten years and more.

Barnabas was enough of a haunting for any man.

Open Sky was prospering from the cattle and lumber trades and could afford its own law, a man Flintlock knew only by reputation.

Marshal Tom Lithgow had been a guard for the Butterfield stage line, a railroad bull for the Southern Pacific and for a spell a Texas Ranger. Back in '79 he'd killed Clyde Westbrook, a gunfighter out of El Paso that nobody thought was a bargain, and there were rumors that he'd put lead into Wild Bill Longley, the fast-drawing Texas badman. But that was never proved.

Stores, offices, warehouses and lumber yards lined both sides of Open Sky's wide main street and there were cattle pens outside of town, but no railroad. The town boasted a fine hotel, two dance halls, six saloons and a four-chair barbershop. A big local attraction, Miss Maisie May, the New Orleans Nightingale, sang and danced nightly at the Rocking Horse Bar and Pool Room and some admirers said she was a better turn than the divine Lillie Langtry.

Open Sky had snap. The stores were filled with luxury goods, the boardwalks crowded and freight and brewery drays trundled along the dusty main street day and night. Though the sporting crowd was still asleep, even the respectable matrons had bold, knowing eyes and their hats were as tiny, their bustles as large, as any Flintlock had seen in Denver or San Francisco.

But Sam Flintlock was there on business, not pleasure, and his business was with the law.

He swung out of the saddle under a pale blue sky, a few white clouds drifting aimlessly like water lilies on a pond. The air smelled of dust and horse dung.

The marshal's office was a robust log building, out of place in the midst of so many painted false fronts. But the grim edifice had been built as a jail and a place of refuge during the turbulent Kiowa and Apache raids of just a few years before. The logs still showed the pockmarks of bullets and a rusty Comanche strap iron arrowhead had defied all attempts to remove it from the pine.

The door stood open to catch the morning coolness and Flintlock stepped inside.

A big, bearded man reading a newspaper sat behind a desk. Without looking up, he said, "What can I do for you?"

Flintlock pulled a sweat-stained dodger from inside his buckskin shirt and slid it between the lawman and the paper.

"Is he here?" he said.

His irritation showing, the marshal slammed the newspaper onto his desk and the dodger fluttered to the floor.

Without a word Flintlock picked it up, tossed it onto the desk and said again, "Is he here?"

"Is who here?" Tom Lithgow said.

"Read it," Flintlock said.

The marshal raised cold eyes to Flintlock, taking in at a glance his worn blue pants and the buckskin shirt, shiny black at the armpits and chest from ancient sweat and the black and red thunderbird tattooed across his throat. Then his stare lingered on the Colt in his waistband, its walnut handle worn from much use.

Lithgow didn't like what he saw. To the marshal, the younger man was what he seemed, a frontier tough and ruffian, prob-

33

ably with a gun rep.

"What's your name, mister?" Lithgow said. He made no move to pick up the dodger.

"Sam'l Flintlock, as ever was. I know yours."

"Then you know I'm hell on bounty hunters. I don't like them, seed, breed and generation. If it was up to me, I'd hang the whole bunch."

"Ah, then your obvious distaste tells me that you've heard of me, huh?" Flintlock said.

"Some. None of it good, I assure you."

Flintlock said nothing.

"Last I heard you was running wild with Abe Roper and that outlaw crowd. Some kind of hunt for buried Spanish treasure an' the like."

Flintlock shook his head. "Sorry. It doesn't ring a bell."

Lithgow sighed and picked up the paper.

"Wanted, dead or alive for rape, robbery and murder," he read aloud. "Hack Weight. Three-thousand-dollar reward. Warning: This man is armed and should be considered dangerous."

"Dodger says it all, don't it?" Flintlock said. "Whoever wrote that was a crackerjack writer like that Charlie Dickens an' them."

"Hack Weight alias Frank Wilson alias Denny Smart." Lithgow held up the dodger. "But it doesn't say that here."

"He was using the name Hack Weight when I tracked him to Open Sky," Flintlock said.

"State your intentions, Sam'l."

"I figure to take Weight to Fort Smith to be tried and then hung at Judge Parker's convenience."

"He's in town," the marshal said.

"The hotel?"

"I'll take you to him."

"This is between me and Weight," Flintlock said.

Lithgow rose to his feet.

"I said I'll take you to him."

The lawman lifted a shotgun from the gun rack, checked the loads then snapped it shut again.

"Lithgow, I want him alive," Flintlock said. "You know what a damned nuisance a dead man is on the trail?"

The marshal nodded but said nothing.

When he reached the door, he said, "After you, Sam Flintlock. I don't cotton to a man like you at my back."

Flintlock was about to make his usual protestations that he'd never shot a man in the back and never would, but he knew his

35

words would fall on deaf ears so he held his tongue. Tom Lithgow had made up his mind about the kind of man Flintlock was and nothing in the world would change his opinion.

"You must think I'm a real desperate character," Flintlock said.

"And aren't you?"

"Only to people I don't like."

"I'd say that takes in a heap of territory," the marshal said.

Flintlock and Lithgow stepped along the boardwalk, their spurs ringing, a couple of hardened fighting men with little liking for each other.

The marshal smiled and touched his hat to the respectable housewives and fashionable belles he passed, and they simpered shyly in return.

But their smiles melted like snow off a brick wall when they caught sight of the menacing, stocky Flintlock. The ladies pegged him for a dangerous frontier ruffian, and later in the privacy of their silken boudoirs they'd shiver in delightful remembrance, like Roman matrons after a chance encounter with a scarred and famous gladiator.

Flintlock was aware of the impression he

made on the fairer sex, both good and bad, but he seldom studied on it. He expected women to take him as he was, just as dogs did, and he was a tender hand with both.

The boardwalk came to an end at an undertaker's emporium on the very edge of town. Away from the saloons and dance halls this was a gloomy part of town where the sun shone a little less bright and the birds sang more melancholy songs. Or so Flintlock imagined.

Lithgow stepped down into open ground and turned to his left. Flintlock followed. The lawman led the way across a grassy area, the view of what lay beyond obscured by piñon, juniper, thick stands of prickly pear cactus and a colorful riot of wildflowers.

"A couple of months after Open Sky was founded, they found the bones of a big animal in this meadow," Lithgow said, displaying unexpected civility.

"What kind of animal?" Flintlock said, his pale eyes probing the distance ahead of him.

"Nobody knows. But one of its leg bones was as tall and big around as me. Later they dug up a jaw with a row of teeth that were six inches long. Teeth like that could bite a man in half, and maybe they did back in the olden days."

"Where did the bones and stuff go?" Flintlock said.

"Some fellers with spectacles and long beards came in from a museum in New York City and took all the bones and teeth away."

"Maybe folks had some mighty big coyotes, back in the day," Flintlock said.

"Maybe so," the marshal said. "And maybe the folks themselves were giants."

Flintlock stopped in his tracks.

"What the hell?" he said.

"You wanted to meet Hack Weight. Well, he's in there. You could offer to shake his hand but I doubt if he'll hear you."

Ahead of Flintlock stood open cemetery gates and arching above them a wrought iron sign that read: REST YE AND BE THANKFUL.

"I really cotton to a peace officer with a sense of humor," he said.

"Follow me," Lithgow said, grinning.

Hack Weight lay in a fresh, unmarked grave. Someone, no doubt one of the town's more charitable matrons, had placed a small bunch of pink wildflowers on the mound of sandy dirt.

Flintlock's face was bitter.

"You sure it was him?" he said.

Lithgow nodded.

"It was him all right."

"How do you know fer sure?"

"Before ol' Hack passed, he confessed to his many crimes and said he'd die sure in the knowledge that the Good Lord had forgiven him his sins."

"Yeah, well I haven't," Flintlock said. "He was worth three thousand dollars to me. Who the hell plugged him, Lithgow? You?"

"Nobody plugged him. He died of consumption and I buried him myself ten days ago. Weight didn't have much weight to him by then."

"Funny, Lithgow. Real funny."

The big marshal grinned.

"You could always dig him up, put a couple of bullet holes in him and take him to Fort Smith and claim the reward."

"And send you half, huh?"

"If you felt so inclined."

"I'm not inclined to dig up a man who died of consumption and has been in the ground for ten days."

"If you'd told me you were coming, Flintlock, I'd have kept him longer. But this is summer and the town doesn't have much ice, so I don't know about that."

"I never took you fer such a humorous man, Lithgow," Flintlock said.

"I'm not. I just wanted to see your face

when you realized that three thousand dollars was gone . . . phhht . . . just like that."

Flintlock opened his mouth to speak but Lithgow turned on his heel abruptly and walked away, still grinning.

"You're an idiot, Sam'l. I always thunk that and now I know it."

Flintlock knew the voice and followed it to the top of a piñon tree where old Barnabas sat peeling an apple, a coil of bright green skin hanging down like an overstretched spring.

"I don't need you to tell me that, Barnabas," Flintlock said.

The old mountain man sliced a piece of apple and stuck it in his mouth. He wore buckskin with fringes on the arms and legs fully two feet long. There was no wind, but Barnabas's long hair tossed around his face.

"You found your mama yet?" he said.

"Not yet."

"She needs to tell you the name of the gambling man that spawned you on her. How many times do I have to tell you that?"

"I'm still looking. I'll find her."

"You'd better. A man should have a name."

"You gave me a name."

"Damn you, boy, Flintlock ain't a name, it's a rifle."

"Then why did you give it to me?"

"Because it was all I could think of at the time."

"Ma is your daughter, Barnabas. You could have given me your name."

"I ain't your pa, Sam'l, thank God. You need to take the gambling man's name. That's how it's done."

"Always before you came to me in a dream, Barnabas. What the hell are you doing in the top of a tree where the squirrels live?"

"Sam'l, only an idiot like you would take advice from a dead man who comes to you in a dream. That's why I'm here."

"Where's Ma, Barnabas? Tell me."

"I figure down Louisiana way in the swamps. But I could be wrong."

The old man chewed on another piece of apple, then said, "I'm not here because of you, Sam'l. I was bored was all."

"How the hell can hell be boring?"

"I can't tell you that, but it is. Hear that sound?"

"I don't hear a thing."

"It's Old Scratch sounding his horn, calling us back. I got to go."

"Barnabas, is Ma really in the Louisiana swamps?"

"I think so . . . maybe . . ."

Barnabas faded like morning mist until only his voice, now thin, distant and echoing, remained.

"Sam'l, bad times are coming down," he said, a whisper in the sunlit morning. "Now don't you walk into no shooting scrapes and get yourself gut-shot . . ."

After Barnabas vanished, for a while Flintlock stood alone in the sun, a wild oak casting dappled shadow around his feet. From somewhere close he heard the buzz of bees. To his right was an aboveground tomb where mourning angels, each as tall as a man, stood on either side of mildewed bronze doors. The angels had never shed a tear from their stone eyes, but their expressions were suitably anguished as though both suffered from a bad case of dyspepsia. A crow perched on the peak of the tomb's Greek temple roof and regarded Flintlock with mocking eyes that were black with mortal sin.

"Bad times coming down, bird," Flintlock said. "But for who? Me?"

If the crow cared about the question it didn't let it show. It cawed, flapped its wings then sat hunched, its eyes slowly opening and closing, planning deviltry.

Flintlock turned his back on the bird and stepped back to the grave.

"Damn you Weight I should dig you up and shoot you out of spite," he said.

The crow thought that funny and cackled.

CHAPTER FOUR

The meadow was, in the opinion of retired physician Dr. Isaac D. Thorne, an ideal habitat for the elusive *Papilio multicaudata* butterfly, popularly known as the two-tailed swallowtail.

With a wingspan of five inches at maturity, the yellow and black Lepidoptera would make a most welcome addition to his collection.

In addition to a host of wildflowers, Dr. Thorne's keen eye detected thistles, milkweed, buckeye and lilac, from which the swallowtail sipped such exquisite nectar. Ah, indeed the creature must be here, flitting like faerie queen from blossom to enchanted blossom, waiting to pop into his net.

The doctor wore a tweed suit, stout leather ankle boots and a deerstalker hat that he'd purchased in London's Savile Row from a tailor's shop once patronized by the great Lord Horatio Nelson, butterfly collector and sailor.

In addition to his net and muslin collecting bag, Dr. Thorne carried a British howdah pistol of the largest size, a necessary precaution in a land abundant with bears, bandits and belligerent Indians.

After an hour of search, *Papilio multicaudata* continued to elude the physician and given the heat of the late morning and a growing appetite for lunch, he took shady refuge under the wild oak where he'd left his picnic basket.

Dr. Thorne smiled and rubbed his hands together. Mrs. Grange, his housekeeper, had done him well, God bless her. Fried chicken, a slice of boiled ham, a pork pie and a bottle of mineral water would settle, one atop the other, very nicely.

The physician tucked a blue-and-white-checkered napkin under his several chins and raised a chicken leg to his open mouth.

But the tasty morsel was stilled and Dr. Thorne's mouth remained open as he caught a glimpse of a yellow flutter close to the tree line to his left, an area he had not yet hunted.

Could this be it? The two-tailed swallowtail was too rare a prize to ignore.

The physician reluctantly tossed the chicken leg back into the basket, grabbed

45

his net and with amazing agility for a man of his portly girth jumped to his feet. He ran in the direction of the trees, the net poised above his head like a rotund David about to decapitate Goliath.

But a moment later Dr. Thorne knew he'd made a mistake.

It was an error that would haunt him for the rest of his life.

A girl's slender body sprawled in the grass, the hem of her yellow sundress lifting in the wind. Her arms were outstretched, as though in supplication, and blades of grass threaded through her hair. Her blue eyes, wide open, gazed without expression at a sky she could no longer see.

"My dear child, are you asleep?" Dr. Thorne said, his now florid face concerned.

The girl did not respond, and he took a knee beside her.

Waves of yellow hair cascaded over the girl's slim shoulders and on the middle finger of her left hand she wore a silver ring with a red stone.

Dr. Thorne picked up the girl in his arms and then jerked back in alarm.

Why, it was Polly Mallory, the school-teacher.

Over the years Dr. Thorne had seen death, his mortal enemy, in many guises, from a native water bearer savaged by a Bengal tiger to a British soldier lying gut-shot and screaming on a bloody stretcher during the Bhutan War of '65.

And the physician again recognized his adversary's work.

By the bruises on her throat, the girl — he placed her age around twenty — had been strangled, her trachea crushed, by someone with immensely powerful hands. As far as Thorne could tell, death had come quickly and the girl had not put up a desperate struggle. There were no shards of her assailant's skin under her fingernails and no blood.

After a quick examination Dr. Thorne saw no evidence of sexual assault. It seemed that someone, probably a man judging by the girl's injuries, had met her in the meadow and coldly and casually murdered her.

The physician stood and rubbed his chin with a forefinger. It was possible Polly knew her assailant because of the lack of evidence of a struggle prior to her death.

"Perhaps my arrival may have scared away the murderer after he'd concluded his devilish task," Dr. Thorne mused aloud. "Hello, what's this?"

He bent and picked up a small, metal object from the grass.

"What the deuce!" he said. "Now this is passing strange . . . but it may be a clue of the greatest moment."

A plain silver cross, about an inch high, lay in the palm of his hand. It had a pin at the back and Dr. Thorne knew he'd seen it before, affixed to the lapel of a young man's coat, the chap who worked at the bank.

The doctor shook his head, shocked by his own terrible thought.

Could Jamie McPhee, the owner of the cross, have committed such a terrible crime?

It was unthinkable. He was such a mild, shy, retiring creature who wouldn't say boo to a goose. Yet the evidence in his hand was proof of the young man's guilt, torn from his coat during young Polly's last despairing moments.

It was a two-mile walk back to town and the girl's body would have to remain where it was until Marshal Lithgow investigated.

Dr. Thorne's round face assumed the steely-eyed, stalwart look that English gentlemen always adopt when they're determined to do their duty for Queen and Empire.

He left his butterfly net where it was and returned to the wild oak.

Anticipating a need for sustenance during his expedition back to Open Sky, the physician filled his pockets with fried chicken, then pork pie and mineral water in hand, he set forth.

Soon a vicious criminal would be brought to justice or by the lord harry, his name wasn't Isaac D. Thorne.

CHAPTER FIVE

"This is where you found the cross, Doc?" Marshal Tom Lithgow said.

"Yes. Right there where I indicated," Dr. Thorne said.

"Any idea how long she'd been dead?"

This from Pike Reid, a sour-faced man who was one of Lithgow's deputies.

"No more than an hour," Dr. Thorne said.

"Time of death?" Lithgow said.

"I arrived at the meadow around ten o'clock and embarked on a hunt for *Papilio multicaudata* —"

"A Mex?" Reid said.

"No. A butterfly," the physician said, his face stiff.

"Go on, Doc," the marshal said.

"Well, after an hour my prey had eluded me and I stopped for light lunch. That's when I saw poor Polly's dress stirring in the wind."

"So she was murdered some time before

50

ten in the morning?" Lithgow said.

"Shortly before would be my guess," Dr. Thorne said.

The pork pie, eaten on the march, had given him dyspepsia and he felt most uncomfortable.

"Hell, Tom, we know who done fer Polly," Reid said. "That damned milk-drinking sop Jamie McPhee."

"We don't know that for sure."

"Everybody knows him and Polly Mallory were walking out together."

"It could be his cross all right," Lithgow said. "Or one like it."

The big marshal stood head bowed in thought for a few moments, then said, "Let's go talk to McPhee and see if he's still got his cross."

"I know what happened," Reid said. "McPhee lured Polly to this meadow and tried to have his way with her. Rather than face a fate worse than death, she refused and he killed her. Simple as that."

"You don't know what happened, Pike. And I don't know what happened either. But I aim to find out," the marshal said.

He nodded in the direction of Dr. Thorne. "Hell, the doc here could've done it. He was in the right place at the right time."

Dr. Thorne was not in the least fazed by

the marshal's statement. It was perfectly logical after all. Any decent London barrister would have raised the point in court.

"I could have," he said. "But I believe that a young, healthy girl like Polly Mallory would make short work of an old man like me with two bad knees and an unfortunate tendency to gout."

"Stranger things have happened," Reid said, his reptilian eyes malicious.

Dr. Thorne's choleric anger flared. "What an infernally nasty man you are, Mr. Reid," he said.

"You've noticed, huh?" Lithgow said, grinning.

"Indeed I have, Marshal. I perceived at once that Mr. Reid has a most singular protuberance of his skull's supraorbital foramen, which I'm very much afraid denotes a person of a dull and brutish nature and volatile temperament. As a keen student of the science phrenology that is my diagnosis and I will not budge an inch from my position." He glared at Reid. "I say not an inch, sir."

Reid blinked a few times, then said, "Hey, Tom, have I just been insulted."

"Beats the hell out of me," Lithgow said.

"Well, when you study on it, let me know," Reid said.

"You're a bounder, sir," Dr. Thorne said. "There, that should be insult enough for any man. Old though I am, I'm willing to meet you with either pistol or saber, or both, if that be to your liking, on any field of honor you care to name."

The fact that the physician had served with the British army in India gave Reid pause. And so did the large pistol at the physician's waist, a lethal monstrosity with two barrels that looked like it could blow a man apart. It was a gun to be reckoned with.

In addition, Pike Reid was not particularly brave and he was happy enough to let matters drop when the marshal asked his help to lift Polly Mallory's body into the spring wagon.

The wagon with its sad burden immediately attracted a gaping crowd when it stopped outside the marshal's office.

Pike Reid immediately sought the limelight.

"Murder!" he yelled. "Polly Mallory has been done to death." Then, like a man enjoying the sound of the word, "STRANGLED as she defended her maidenly honor!"

This drew gasps of horror from the onlookers, among them Sam Flintlock, who'd been shopping for tobacco and rolling papers.

Tom Lithgow stepped from the wagon seat onto the boardwalk.

"Marshal, is there a murderer among us?" a big-bellied, prosperous-looking man in broadcloth and gold watch chain said. "Or should we form a posse?"

"No need for a posse," Lithgow said.

"Right, no call for that," Reid said.

"And what is your reason, sir?" the prosperous man said.

"Because we know who done it," Reid said. "And yeah, the murdering devil is in this very town and walks among us. Oh he's a sly one, but me and the marshal have taken his measure, lay to that."

A matron, with the stern, lantern-jawed face of a prune juice drinker, called out, "Who is the fiend, Marshal? Are we in terrible danger? I fear for my daughter Ethel's virtue."

"I will make an arrest very soon," Lithgow said. "And your daughter is in no danger. This was a crime of passion."

For her part, Ethel, a scrawny girl who looked somewhat like a turkey, seemed aggrieved by the lawman's last remark.

Several women pushed and prodded Polly Mallory's body, sniffing into tiny lace handkerchiefs like the grieving dwarfs around Snow White.

Suddenly irritated, the marshal yelled, "You women get away from there. Someone bring Silas Strange. He's got work to do."

The undertaker, a small, thin man in a clawhammer coat three sizes too big for him, flapped along the boardwalk like a crow with a broken wing. He took the dead girl away in a reusable canvas coffin carried by two burly assistants, their faces professionally solemn.

Flintlock caught a glimpse of the bruises on the girl's throat and dismissed the murder as indeed a *crime passionnel,* not an unusual occurrence on the frontier when eligible women were few and desires and jealousies ran deep.

In other words, he told himself, it was none of his business.

CHAPTER SIX

"It's your kind of business, Sam," Clifton Wraith said.

Flintlock studied the Pinkerton agent with a mix of astonishment and disdain.

"Where's the profit, Cliff?" he said.

"From me, none. From the young man's lawyer, gun wages. At least for a while."

"What's a while?"

"Until he can get Jamie McPhee out of town."

"Well, I'm just about flat broke."

"I know. Too poor to paint, too proud to whitewash, as they say."

"Yeah, well what they say just about sums it up."

"A man who relights the same cigarette three times and nurses the last inch of Old Crow in the bottle is hurting for the ready. I could see that."

There was only one chair in the hotel room and Wraith sat on it. Flintlock rose from his perch on the corner of his bed and stepped to the window. Day shaded slowly into evening and a night watchman wearing an old Confederate greatcoat lit the reflector lamps along the street one by one. It was payday Friday and across the way a row of cow ponies stood hipshot at the hitching rail of the Rocking Horse saloon. Inside the tinpanny piano played "Old Zip Coon," but the notes lost themselves in the roar of whiskey-drinking men and the laughter of women who coaxed them to buy more of it.

"Polly Mallory was murdered two weeks ago," Wraith said.

"I know," Flintlock said. "You certain McPhee will walk?"

"The circuit judge told me he'll release him tomorrow."

"Seems like McPhee is as guilty as hell," Flintlock said.

"He says he and Polly planned to get married and he gave her his cross as a —"

"*Gage l'amour,*" Flintlock said.

Wraith's raised eyebrows revealed his surprise.

"All the years I've known you, Sam, I never reckoned you were such a romantic."

"I'm not," Flintlock said. "McPhee said he didn't get to his desk at the bank until noon on the day the girl was murdered.

How does he explain being late that day?"

"He gets bad headaches. He had one that morning. The bank manager confirms that McPhee seemed to be in real pain."

"Mighty thin," Flintlock said. "Not much there for his lawyer."

"But then, the evidence of a fifty-cent silver cross isn't enough to hang a feller either."

"Maybe you're right."

"The judge, a man named Drummond, says McPhee has had death threats. Marshal Lithgow finds two or three on the jailhouse doorstep every morning."

"It's the ones who don't make threats that do the deed," Flintlock said. "At least in my experience."

"Polly Mallory was a fine schoolteacher and she was well liked in this town," Wraith said. "As, indeed, was Jamie McPhee."

Flintlock smiled. "Yeah, I've seen lynch mobs string up a man for killing somebody they liked, even if the dear departed was a low-life skunk. One time I saw the Texas draw fighter Wild Horse Harry Dean strung up for shooting a wife-beater and chicken thief by the name of Hoag Blacker. The prosecutor convinced the jury that they liked Blacker just fine and that Harry had murdered a solid citizen. Well, Harry got the drop all right, and a month later the same jury hung Blacker for being a damned nuisance."

"And that's why McPhee needs you as a bodyguard," Wraith said. Then, more convincingly, "As you said yourself, you need the money, Sam."

"You're right about that. I'm close to riding the grub line."

Flintlock turned from the window and stared at Wraith, mild accusation in his eyes. "Why the hell did you become a Pinkerton, Cliff?"

The older man smiled. "It's a story."

"I'll listen."

"Do you recollect Dog Wilson that time?"

"Yeah. As I recollect he set a pack of coonhounds on you, or so I heard. Dog was mean and lowdown, everybody knew that."

"Yeah, well those hounds tore me up considerable until I got a bullet into Dog's brisket, then his curs lost interest. But the damage was done. Later a doc stitched me back together again."

"An angry dog can put a hurting on a man."

"No doubt about that. I remember thinking, 'I killed a man, got set upon by a ravenous pack of hounds and all for a fifty-dollar reward.' "

"So you turned your back on the bounty-hunting business and became a detective."

"More or less, but not immediately. For a while I had a job as a restaurant dishwasher down Austin way. The restaurant was called the Copper Kitchen and at first it was all right."

"But you didn't like that job either?"

"I broke about two hundred o' cup and bowl, got fired and then joined the Pinks."

Flintlock didn't respond and Wraith said, "The pay is good and I enjoy the job."

"Why are you here?" Flintlock said finally. "You investigating the murder?"

"No. Jamie McPhee's lawyer asked for a Pinkerton to keep his client alive. A few of the death threats were serious enough to alarm him."

"Then why do you need me?" Flintlock said.

"I need your gun, Sam, and your cussedness."

"Both are for sale."

"And you step lightly from one side of the law to the other, which gives a man a broader outlook on things. Some say you're a bounty hunter some of the time and an outlaw most of the time. I don't know if that's true or not."

"What's this lawyer's name?" Flintlock

said, ignoring that last.

"Crusty old feller by the name of Frank Constable, rode with General Wade Hampton an' them and won a medal at Trevilian Station. Walks with a cane thanks to a Yankee musket ball."

"He thinks McPhee is innocent?"

"I don't know. But he's a stickler for the law and he says a charge of murder can't be proved against his client." Wraith shrugged. "Which it can't, of course."

"Tell Constable my fee is two hundred a month or any part thereof for my services, plus expenses." Flintlock said. "The first month payable in advance."

"And what do I tell him he gets in return?"

"Tell me what you think of me, Cliff."

"Well, you're a barely civilized savage, mean enough to piss on a widow woman's kindling and you cut your teeth on a Hawken barrel. You've killed more men than I've got toes and will probably go on to kill as many more." The Pinkerton made a show of thinking deeply, a forefinger on his temple. "Let's see, you frequent loose women, by times drink too much, are given to profanity and you've never lived within the sound of church bells in your life."

"Is that all?"

"You're a product of your time and place,

61

Sam, a hard, unforgiving man bred for a violent land. Some say you're low-down and a natural outlaw, but I don't hold with that."

"Then that's what you tell Constable he's getting for his two hundred a month."

"Tell him all of it?"

"All of it."

"That's quite a résumé," Wraith said.

CHAPTER SEVEN

All interested parties, in other words just about everybody in Open Sky, crowded into the courtroom to hear Circuit Judge Altheas T. Drummond deliver his opinion on the guilt or innocence of Jamie McPhee, bank clerk.

Behind the judge's great leather chair that was raised high on a dais, stood United States Marshal Coon McCrystal, a bull of a man who scowled suspiciously at the crowd from under lowered, shaggy eyebrows.

Drummond, by contrast, was a small, sharp-angled man with the bright, intelligent eyes of a house sparrow.

After he gaveled for silence, the judge spoke into the sudden hush.

"Ladies and gentlemen," he intoned, "before we start I need a lighter head to offset my heavy heart. Oh, unhappy day."

McCrystal bent, reached into a drawer in the judge's desk and produced a bottle of

Old Crow and a glass. He poured three fingers and placed the glass in front of Drummond, who downed it in a single gulp.

The little man wiped his mustache and again regarded the crowd.

"Uneasy lies the head that wears the crown," he said.

This caused a puzzled stir of conversation in the crowd and Flintlock, sitting at the back of the courtroom, was as bamboozled as the rest.

"Oh, perfidious fate that compels me to render judgment today," Judge Drummond said. "I must set free a monster, nay, a ravening wolf, to once again walk among you to prey on the womanly virtue of your wives and daughters. Nay, I say to myself, don't do it Drummond, don't free the brute! But, alas, I have no other course. I must work within the law and aye, the sacred pages of Holy Scripture." Then, in a whispered aside, "Hit me again, Coon."

"Where the hell is McPhee?" a man in the crowd yelled.

And another, "You ain't really letting him go, yer honor?"

"I must. I must," Drummond said after he drained his glass. He raised his hands and wailed, "Oh, unfortunate day that this travesty of justice should come to pass."

That last was the fuse that lit the ticking time bomb that is a hostile crowd.

"Shame! For shame!" a woman called out.

"For shame!" Judge Drummond cried, his face miserable. "Yes, dear lady, for shame indeed."

There were more outraged yells, chairs overturned and one half-drunk rooster waved a pair of revolvers in the air.

"Where is McPhee?"

"Get a damned rope!"

"String him up!"

The angry crowd advanced on the dais, cursing their rage and disappointment, thirsting for McPhee's blood and Flintlock told himself that maybe two hundred a month for this job wasn't near enough.

Then Coon McCrystal stepped forward, a huge Colt's Dragoon in each massive fist.

"By God, I'll kill any man who moves closer!" he roared.

The crowd shrank back, stunned.

"Then be damned to ye," a man yelled. "We'll string up the damned judge."

But the baying pack read the signs. The long-haired marshal was not a man to mess with.

Flintlock rose to his feet and slipped out the door. What happened in the courtroom was no longer his concern. But Jamie

McPhee was.

A few steps along the boardwalk took him to Marshal Lithgow's office. But Pike Reid, a star on his vest, lounged against the door and blocked his way.

"What the hell do you want?" the deputy said, his buzzard eyes sullen.

"I'm here on business," Flintlock said.

"Beat it," Reid said.

"Oh dear," Flintlock said.

He grabbed Reid by the front of his pants and pulled him into the short, choppy right he threw from the shoulder. When Flintlock's fist hit, the left side of the deputy's face seemed to crumple like a stepped-on hatbox and he fell in a heap onto the boardwalk.

"I can't abide an uncivil lawman," Flintlock said. "Hell, I can't even abide a civil lawman."

But Reid didn't hear. His tongue lolled out of his mouth and his eyes rolled in his head.

Flintlock stepped inside and met Tom Lithgow as the marshal rushed to the door.

"What happened out there?" he said.

"Your deputy fell down and hurt his jaw, Lithgow," Flintlock said. He closed the door behind him. Then, "Where's McPhee?"

"Back there in his cell. What happened to Reid?"

"I told you. He fell down. Get McPhee out here."

"Why?"

"I'm his guardian angel."

"Flintlock, are you crazy?" Lithgow said. "I can hear the damned crowd from here. Those folks will be coming with a noose and they'll kill anybody who gets in their way."

"When I take a man's money, I ride for the brand," Flintlock said. "Now get McPhee out here."

"Well, I got no reason to hold him," Lithgow said.

"Uh-huh. That's right, you don't."

"Then it's your funeral."

"Tell me something I don't already know," Flintlock said.

Jamie McPhee was a tall, thin, round-shouldered man in his early twenties with a pointy, hairless chin. He had pale hair and eyes and his desk clerk's pasty face now bore a terrified expression.

"Scared?" Flintlock said.

The young man swallowed, his prominent Adam's apple bobbing.

"Yes, I am. Who are you?"

"Name's Sam Flintlock and I'm scared too. I'm being paid to keep you breathing. Lithgow, you got a back door in this place?"

"Hell, Flintlock, it's a jail. No, I don't have a back door."

"Not the best news I've heard today."

Flintlock's face was grim. "Then let's go . . . Jamie. Hell, that's a sissy name to call a man. I don't even like to say it."

"Then you can call me McPhee."

"Good. It sure as hell beats Jamie."

"Flintlock, I heard you got a thing going in your head about names," Lithgow said. "But you're about to get hung in a moment if you don't get the hell out of here."

"Now Sam is a good name," Flintlock said as though he hadn't heard. "Samuel, Sam'l, Sammy, they're all crackerjack. But Robert is good too. Rob, Robbie, Bob, Bobby, and the French pronounce it Robair. The French can make any name sound good."

"Flintlock . . ." Lithgow said.

"Yeah, I know. We're going."

"I can't help you. I got to live in this town."

"It's my job, Marshal. I'll go it alone."

"I feel bad. But you see how it is with me."

"Yeah, I see how it is with you."

"Where will you take McPhee?"

"To my hotel room. If we make it that far."

68

"Good luck, Sam Flintlock."

"You too. Now I got to go."

Flintlock stepped onto the boardwalk in time to see Judge Drummond and Marshal McCrystal lighting a shuck out of town. It seemed that neither man cared to face the wrath of the good people of Open Sky. Flintlock smiled, the situation amusing him, then motioned for Jamie McPhee to follow him onto the boardwalk. The morning was clear, clean and bright as a newly minted penny.

People spilled out of the courthouse and stood in knots talking, their faces grim and determined. Then they caught sight of McPhee and their mood became menacing.

"Get behind me," Flintlock said to the young man. "And don't do anything real sudden like you were reaching for a gun."

"What will they do?" McPhee said. His voice was unsteady.

"What a mob always does," Flintlock said. Then to the crowd, "Stay back. This man is in my legal custody and I'll kill any man who reckons otherwise."

Sam Flintlock was a skilled revolver fighter and such men were always exclamation points of danger in Western towns. The crowd, baying for McPhee's blood, recognized him for what he was and a few already looked uncertain, weighing the costs. To kill McPhee they'd lose some of their own and where was the bargain — or the fun — in that?

It was then a real possibility that Flintlock and his charge could have made it to the hotel unmolested and in one piece.

But every town had its bully, the local gun slick who'd killed his man and figured he was cock of the walk — and usually was.

Hamp Collins was such a man. And only a lowlife like him would carry a hemp noose along with his arrogance.

Big, heavy, dressed like a puncher although he'd never been near a cow in his life, Collins pushed his way through the crowd then stopped and yelled to Flintlock, "You, step aside. I want that murderer."

Sam Flintlock, a seasoned manhunter, looked Collins up and down and saw no real sand, only bluff and bluster. Such men were a dime a dozen on the frontier and none ever amounted to a hill of beans.

"Follow close," he said to McPhee. "We're getting it done."

He stepped from the boardwalk into the dusty street, the morning sun warm on his face. A little calico cat sat on the rail of the hotel porch opposite and with green eyes watched the fun.

"Wait up there tattooed man!" Collins roared. "I'm talking to you!"

He had a massive chest, thighs as big around as tree trunks and looked as though no force on earth could move him.

Flintlock, his face as composed as a nun's in church, walked on, McPhee now stepping in front of him. He looked as beaten down as a whipped pup.

Hamp Collins, aware of the eyes of the townspeople on him, knew he'd been caught flat-footed. The tough-looking man with the strange tattoo on his throat had ignored him and made him look bad.

And that was mighty hard to take.

Collins rolled the dice.

He drew and fired.

Dirt kicked up an inch in front of Flintlock's left boot and his anger, always an uncertain thing, flared.

"Stop right where you are!" Collins yelled, his confidence returning.

Flintlock turned and faced the man, his mouth a hard line under his mustache. "Mister," he said, "I'm getting mighty tired of you."

The crowd behind Collins parted, out of the way of any flying lead.

"I want McPhee," Collins said. "I aim to

hang him. So step aside." He tossed a nickel into the dirt at Flintlock's feet. "There. Go buy yourself a beer."

"You want him, then come get him," Flintlock said, resignation in his tone.

Collins grinned. He'd put the crawl on the ranny with the tattoo and hell, that must look real good to the crowd.

Collins hefted the noose in his hand and walked toward Flintlock.

"McPhee," he said, still grinning, "say your prayers an' git ready to meet your Maker."

Flintlock timed it perfectly.

He waited until the big gunman got within striking distance then pulled the Colt in his waistband. The revolver crashed hard against the right side of Collins's face, completing the fast, fluid motion. The big man staggered, but didn't go down. For a moment, as though the ground heaved beneath his feet, Collins spread his legs, trying to maintain his balance. Like skeletal scarlet fingers, blood poured down his cheek from a deep cut above his eye.

Flintlock moved again, no let-up in him.

His right boot kicked upward, slammed between Collins's legs and smashed into the man's groin. The big gunman's face contorted in pain and he went down like a felled redwood, frantically clutching at his mashed manhood.

A groan went up from the male members of the crowd and even a few of the ladies winced.

Collins writhing and cussing at his feet, Flintlock addressed the onlookers. "McPhee is in my custody and I will protect him with my life. Those are the facts so state your intentions."

A respectable-looking man in the crowd stepped forward and said, "That murderer should be hung."

Others roared their approval.

"The judge thought otherwise," Flintlock said. "You all heard him."

"Judges can be wrong," the respectable man said. "And this time the judge admitted he had to deliver a wrong verdict."

"Right or wrong, this man is under my protection," Flintlock said.

"We'll come for him, tonight," another man said. "You can lay to that."

"Then you'll step over the bodies of your own dead to take him," Flintlock said. "Lay to that."

Collins, bloody and in pain, got up on all fours and began to slowly crawl away.

Flintlock, who laid no claim to being a merciful or forgiving man, kicked the gunman in the butt and said, "You stay right there, boy."

Collins collapsed onto his belly and lay still.

"McPhee, walk to the hotel and step inside," Flintlock said.

His Colt was up and ready and his eyes roamed over the crowd, a little cowed since their Goliath was felled, but still angry.

"Shame on you," a plump woman in a poke bonnet said. "You know that man is guilty."

Flintlock made no answer but backed toward the hotel.

Then he pointed at Collins with his Colt and said, "You folks take care of this man. He's gonna walk funny for a spell."

He turned, crossed the street and stepped into the hotel.

Behind him a rock thudded onto the porch.

CHAPTER EIGHT

Hamp Collins, steeping his hurting parts in a bowl of warm water and brandy, was in a killing rage.

"I'll gun him, Nancy," he said. "I'll shoot him down on sight."

"They say his name is Sam Flintlock," Nancy said, a long-serving whore with a heart of iron. "Funny name."

"It ain't funny to me," Collins growled. "I had to ride in here sidesaddle and it's a long way from town."

The Gentleman's Retreat cathouse was situated a mile north of Buzzard Gap and its back porch gave a fine view of Blue Mountain. Once a stage station, the original building had been burned by Apaches, rebuilt and then extended, an extra floor added. The madam was a four-hundred-pound Frenchwoman named Josette and she boasted a bigger mustache than most of the cavalry officers who visited the place.

Since it was still early in the afternoon the brothel was not busy — the sporting crowd from Open Sky and the surrounding ranches would not arrive until evening.

Boredom, not a concern for Collins's hurting private parts, kept Nancy Pocket in the room with the injured man.

"Feeling better?" she said. "They say brandy works wonder for men in your delicate condition."

"I won't feel better until I kill Flintlock, if that's really his name," Collins said.

"You would've hung that McPhee feller if it wasn't for him," Nancy said. She was a bottle blonde with brown eyes and a wide, expressive mouth.

"If McPhee don't hang, another will in his place. Depend on it."

"What does that mean?" the woman said.

"It means that around here you should keep your trap shut about Jamie McPhee," Collins said. "It might play wrong with a certain person."

"Then I won't mention his name."

"Good. Just remember that."

Collins winced as he shifted position in his straight-backed chair and water slopped over the side of the bowl. "There are them who are a mite uneasy about this man Flintlock," he said. "When I kill him, I'll be in good with some powerful folks."

"Money?"

"When I bring in Flintlock's scalp I'll have enough to keep me in whiskey and whores for a long time."

"Then throw some business my way, Hamp, huh? A working girl's got to make a living you know and a man with busted balls ain't the ideal customer."

"I will, if you treat me right and shut your trap about my balls."

"How well did you know Polly Mallory?" Nancy said. "I thought she was nice."

"Hell, everybody knew her. She was the town schoolteacher."

"She was pretty."

"Yeah, I'd say that. I tried to spark her once or twice but she turned me down flat."

"Ah, that's because she never saw you with your balls in a bowl," Nancy said.

"I'll smack you across the mouth, you sass me like that," Collins said.

Nancy laughed.

"Hamp, you'd never catch me."

"I'm hurtin' here," Collins said, in a surge of self-pity.

"I know you are, Hampy," Nancy said, cooing. "When you're all better again I'll take good care of you."

"Pour me another whiskey, will ya?"

Collins said. "To ease the pain, like."

Nancy passed a filled glass to Collins, then said, "Who really killed Polly Mallory, Hamp?"

"What is it to you?" Collins said.

"Just interested in what goes on in Open Sky."

"Jamie McPhee killed her. And don't you say otherwise or that pretty head of yours could end up on a damned spike."

The door opened and Madame Josette fluttered inside, a concerned look on her face. Her hands were flapping like plump white doves.

"La, la, la," she said. *"Comment sont les testicules du monsieur?"*

"How are your balls?" Nancy translated.

"I caught her drift," Collins said, irritated. He glared at the madam. "They hurt like hell."

Josette clapped and said, *"Plus brandy dans le bol, Nancy."*

Then she turned and swept through the door again, the smell of her French perfume lingering after she'd gone.

"By God, I'll make Sam Flintlock pay for this," Collins said, his face screwed into a mask of pain as he watched Nancy pour more brandy into the bowl. "I'll shoot him in the belly and listen to him scream."

CHAPTER NINE

"Balls," Sam Flintlock said. "All dogs love to play fetch with balls."

"You have a dog?" Jamie McPhee said.

"Used to, a hound who could charm a coon out of a tree with her voice. She's long gone now, chasing rabbits on the other side."

"I'm not catching your drift about the balls, Sam."

"Well, McPhee, you're the ball and then fellers out there in the street want to play catch with you so badly they'll never give up."

"I didn't kill Polly," McPhee said. "I loved her. You do believe that, don't you?"

"I don't give a damn one way or the other," Flintlock said. "I'm paid to stop you getting hung, that's all."

"That's cold," McPhee said.

Flintlock shrugged. "You want a shoulder to cry on, find somebody else's. Damn it's hot in here."

He stepped to the window and lifted it open.

A dozen armed men stood on the opposite boardwalk and one of them pointed.

"It's him!" the man yelled.

A moment later Flintlock realized that the town of Open Sky was as angry as hell and playing for keeps. A fusillade of shots hammered through the window and he dived for the floor as showering shards of shattered glass cascaded around and over him.

"Get down!" he yelled at McPhee.

Showing commendable alacrity, the young man joined him on the floor.

"They're trying to kill us," McPhee said.

"No kidding? That would be my guess too. But they're mad at you, not me."

"What do we do?"

"Stay right where we're at until them fellers tire of taking pots at the window."

McPhee pushed up on his arms.

"I'll talk to them," he said.

Flintlock grabbed the young man by the front of his shirt. "Are you crazy? By the time they're finished shooting holes in you, you'll look like a colander."

"I must convince them of my innocence."

"Them fellers are already convinced . . . that's why they want to hang you."

Still on all fours, McPhee shook his head and teardrops splashed on the floor between his hands. "Oh, Polly," he whispered. "What happened to us? We were so happy."

"You quit that, McPhee, and quit it right now" Flintlock said, his face stern. "Grown men don't cry. I'm downright embarrassed for you. I've never in all my born days seen such a thing, a man crying."

"I don't care," McPhee said. His cheeks were wet, eyes rimmed red. "Polly is gone and I should just surrender myself and get it over with. Just . . . have them shoot me and end my miserable life."

"Damn you, boy, quit that or I'll put a bullet in you myself. I never in all my born days —"

"Hey, you in the hotel!"

The roar came from the street, harsh, loud, commanding.

"What the hell do you want?" Flintlock yelled.

"I want to talk to you! Come to the window!"

"I ain't that stupid," Flintlock hollered.

"I give you my word you won't be harmed."

"And who is you?"

"Trace McCord. I own a ranch hereabouts."

81

"You can trust him, Sam."

This from Marshal Tom Lithgow, shouting from the street.

"Yeah, but can I trust you?"

"You know you can."

"No, I don't."

Nonetheless Flintlock got to his feet and stood to the side of the window. "State your business, McCord," he said. "And your intentions."

"Come now, let's not yell back and forth like savages," McCord said. "Make your way down to the porch and we'll talk like civilized human beings."

Flintlock made no answer.

"Well?" McCord said.

"I'm studying on it," Flintlock said.

"I will be unarmed," the rancher said.

"I'll vouch for that," Lithgow said.

"You're a snake, Marshal. But I'll come down anyway."

"They'll kill you," McPhee said. "It's a trap, Sam."

"Nah. Right now they plan to offer terms. The killing will come later."

Flintlock took a powder horn and ball from his saddlebags and quickly charged the Hawken.

"You're taking that?" McPhee said.

"Yeah. It impresses the hell out of folks,

makes them think of Boone and Bridger an' my old grandpappy Barnabas. A true American won't shoot a man who's carrying his grandpappy's Hawken. It just wouldn't set right with him."

Flintlock settled his battered hat on his head. "McPhee, no more crying like a girl, understand?" he said. "I'm dealing with men here and I don't want you to make me look bad."

"I don't care. My life is over anyway."

"I don't want to hear that either," Flintlock said.

Sam Flintlock stood on the narrow porch in front of the hotel, the beautiful Hawken cradled in his left arm. He was wary, but relaxed, waiting for whatever was to come. He'd deal with it then.

He stared at the man astride a big American stud and saw trouble.

Trace McCord was a tall, wide-shouldered man, big-boned and as handsome as the day is long. But his face revealed a touch of cruelty, even sadism, his arrogant expression born of raw, unbridled power and an ability to ride roughshod over lesser men. A foot taller than Flintlock and fifty pounds heavier, McCord was a man who cut a wide swath . . . a man to be reckoned with, in his own time or in any other.

"So you're Sam Flintlock," McCord said, his eyes wandering to the Hawken. "I said no guns."

"You said it, not me," Flintlock said.

The rancher sat a black, silver-mounted saddle, shined up, a rig no puncher could own even after a lifetime of saving. The stud McCord rode would cost a top hand a year's wages.

The man had wealth and he didn't mind flaunting it.

"You know what I want to talk about," McCord said.

"I can guess," Flintlock said.

"You're harboring a murderer."

"That's what a feller hired me to do."

"Whatever he's paying you, I'll double it."

"You mean to hand over Jamie McPhee."

"To hand over a cold-blooded murderer."

"When I take a man's money I ride for the brand, McCord. So no deal."

Two things angered the rancher about that statement. The first was the refusal itself.

McCord was a man who'd grown used to getting his own way, with tough men or beautiful women, and now Flintlock, an illiterate frontier thug by the look of him, had turned him down. Defied him, by God.

The second was the use of his name

without the respectful honorific.

Everyone in this part of the Oklahoma Territory, rich and poor alike called him *Mister* McCord. He didn't demand it and never had, but he expected it . . . especially from his social inferiors.

This was an affront that could not stand.

McCord turned his head.

"Lithgow!"

The marshal hurried across the street and stood beside the rancher's horse.

"Yes, Mr. McCord?"

From his great height, the rancher stared down at the lawman then said, "I am not in the habit of addressing riffraff and low persons. Talk some sense into this fellow."

"Flintlock, listen to Mr. McCord. Give us Jamie McPhee," the marshal said, his face pleading. "We don't need all this unpleasantness."

"Lynching a man is pleasant?" Flintlock said. "The law says he's innocent and that's where you should stand, Lithgow."

"Tell him five hundred dollars for McPhee," McCord said. "That's more money than a saddle tramp like him will ever see in one place in a lifetime."

"You know he's as guilty as all hell, Flintlock. Mr. McCord is making you a generous offer," Lithgow said. "Tell me you heard him."

"I heard him," Flintlock said.

McCord's thick lips drew back in a vicious, disdainful grin.

"Lithgow, tell him a hemp rope can choke both him and the chicken he's got around his neck," he said.

Flintlock was on a slow burn. He swung the muzzle of the Hawken and centered it on the rancher's chest. "Come use your rope, McCord," he said. "I await your convenience."

Staring into the cold black eye of a .50 caliber muzzle is not an experience a man relishes or soon forgets.

McCord tensed. The big rancher was not afraid, but all at once he was caught flatfooted and that made him wary.

A silence stretched taut between him and Flintlock.

Lithgow, the peacemaker, broke it. "Sam Flintlock, trigger that long rifle and right afterward I'll drop you where you stand," he said.

"I told you no once, McCord," Flintlock said, ignoring the marshal. "No deal. And I won't repeat myself."

The rancher's anger flared. "Why, you sorry piece of white trash, I'll —"

"You'll what?" Flintlock said. His voice

had the honed edge of a steel blade.

For the first time since they met, McCord recognized Sam Flintlock for what he was, not the ignorant frontier thug as he'd first pegged him but a fighting man who would not admit to being second best to any.

He was a man to be reckoned with.

But then, so was Trace McCord.

"Lithgow, I'll waste no more breath here," he said.

"I'm all talked out myself," Flintlock said.

"From this day forward, consider yourself a dead man, Flintlock," the rancher said. "Prepare your winding sheet."

McCord swung his horse away, and after a last, despairing look at Flintlock, Lithgow followed.

"You make some mighty powerful enemies, Sammy."

Old Barnabas sat on the porch rocker, needle and yellow thread in hand as he repaired a tear in the sleeve of a Cheyenne war shirt.

"Seems like I do," Flintlock said.

"Of course, that's because you're an idiot."

"I guess so," Flintlock said.

"Didn't I teach you that you don't jaw with an enemy? You kill him. End the argument right there and then and save all them fancy words."

"Trace McCord is not my enemy," Flint-lock said.

"He is now. The worst one you ever had."

Barnabas tied off his thread then held up the war shirt and studied it with a critical eye.

"Well, that's the best I can do," he said. "Even dead, them Cheyenne dog soldiers get up to all kinds of mischief an' tear up their duds." Then, "Go to the Louisiana swamps, Sam. Swim with the alligators and find your mother."

"When my job here is done."

"I raised an idiot," Barnabas said.

The empty chair rocked back and forth in the wind.

That's all it had been, Flintlock told himself. Just a restless chair stirred by a warm south wind . . .

CHAPTER TEN

"You'll be a man, Steve, even if I have to beat it into you," Trace McCord said.

"I try, Pa," the young man said.

" 'I try, Pa,' " McCord said, mimicking his son's high-pitched voice. "That's the trouble. You don't try. You've never tried and that's why you've failed at everything, you useless whelp."

The big rancher sprawled in a heavy leather chair studded with brass tacks. He refilled the glass in his hand from the whiskey decanter, then said, "Frisco?"

"Don't mind if I do, boss," Frisco Maddox said.

Scowling, McCord poured whiskey into his foreman's glass.

"How could I have spawned that, Frisco?" he said, jabbing his cigar in his son's direction. "Just . . . tell me how. Hell, he doesn't even look like me."

The big foreman hesitated for a moment,

then said, "He's shaping up, boss."

"Damn it, man, he writes poetry," Mc-Cord said. "Who the hell writes poetry and shapes up?"

"I don't know, boss."

"Me neither."

Something mean stabbed in McCord's belly and something mean twisted his handsome face.

"Say us one of your poems, boy. Let Frisco hear it."

Steve McCord was twenty years old but he still looked like an undersized boy with his pale skin and hair and joyless face. His fingers were long and thin and he played the violin quite well.

"I can't remember any poems, Pa."

"Sure you can, boy," McCord said. Then, his eyes slits, "Say us one. Now!"

The youngster swallowed hard, then in a small trembling voice, said, "I rise from sleep and find the whole world gone. Vanished. Overnight. And I am left alone in darkness —"

"Hell, that ain't poetry!" McCord said. "Poetry rhymes. Any fool knows that."

He shifted his attention to his foreman.

"Frisco, say a poetry that rhymes."

"Boss, I —"

"A poetry that rhymes, Frisco. That's a

damned order."

"All right, boss. I remember one from my first time up the trail when I was a younker."

"Then let's have at it," McCord said. "Just so long as it rhymes."

Maddox coughed then said:

Dirty Mary worked in a dairy,
Dick pulled out his big canary.
"Oh what a whopper,
Let's do it proper."

Trace McCord slapped the arm of his chair and roared with laughter.

"Hear that, boy? It rhymes. Now that's what I call real poetry."

Suddenly enraged, he drew back his arm and with all the strength that was in him threw his Irish crystal whiskey glass at his son's head.

The boy ducked and glass shattered against the wall.

"Write poetry! You damned simpering weakling you can't even do that right. Get the hell out of my sight."

The youngster beat a hasty retreat out the door and into the hallway. His boots sounded on the stairway as he rushed to his room. Upstairs a door slammed shut.

McCord shook his head. "Frisco, I'm

young yet," he said. "I must sire another son. This time his mother won't be around to spoil him as Martha did Steve. She turned him into a girly boy, by God."

"Give the kid time, boss," Maddox said. "He's still learning to hold his own as a man."

"He'll never be a man," McCord said. "I need a son who will grow to manhood, and quick."

"It's a pity Polly Mallory didn't work out, boss," Frisco said.

"Yeah. That ended badly. Bitch."

McCord sat in thought for a few moments, his face working.

Then he said, "Once all this falderal over the girl's murder dies down, we'll move against Brendan O'Rourke and the Circle-O. I need that winter grass."

Maddox looked troubled. "O'Rourke is a stubborn old Irishman, boss. He won't move without a fight."

"Of course he won't. That's why we'll drive him out or kill him, whatever is the more convenient."

Maddox bit his lip. He liked the wiry, cantankerous old rancher, and his wife made the best bear sign and flapjacks this side of the Arkansas line.

Frisco Maddox played for time. "You're

right, boss. We'll let the fuss over Polly Mallory go away then make our move. The law is too riled up at the moment and we could attract unwelcome attention."

McCord accepted that at face value, then said, "What do you know about this Sam Flintlock ranny?"

"Ran with some hard cases in his time, including that Kid Antrim in the New Mexico Territory. Sells his gun. Raised by old mountain men and talks to the ghost of his grandfather."

"So he's crazy."

"Yeah. Like a fox."

"We have to see Jamie McPhee hung, Frisco," McCord said. "Better for everybody. There's too much restlessness around and it makes me uneasy."

"Pity Sam Flintlock is in the way."

"Can you take him?"

"He's tough and he's fast."

"Can you take him?"

"On a good day, yeah."

"Make sure all your days are good days until Sam Flintlock is buried."

McCord picked up another glass and filled it with bourbon.

"Get out of here, Frisco," he said. "I need time to think."

The big foreman stepped to the parlor

door, but McCord's voice stopped him.

"Look around, Frisco, see if there's a suitable brood mare I can breed with. No whores, though. I want a gal with good bloodlines."

"Like Polly Mallory?"

"Yeah, but less damned uppity."

"I'll see what I can do, boss."

"And Frisco . . ."

"Yeah, boss?"

Trace McCord's smile was thin. "Remember, no whores or married women. Those will come after I tie the knot."

CHAPTER ELEVEN

The shattered window in Sam Flintlock's room was a source of great distress to hotel proprietor Hans Albrecht and now he hinted darkly of eviction followed by legal action.

"Hell, I didn't break the window," Flintlock said. "Your townies did."

"But they were shooting at you, *mein Herr*," Albrecht said. "That much is clear."

He was a plump, self-important man dressed in checked pants and a collarless white shirt, a kitchen-stained apron covering his front.

Then, to reinforce his indignation, he said, "The whole window must be replaced. *Mein Gott, meine Frau* and *meine Kinder* will starve. Do you know how much glass costs?"

"How much will it cost?" Jamie McPhee said.

The German was horrified when he saw the wanted young man for the first time.

"I don't know you," he said. His eyes popped out of his head. "You're not in my hotel."

"Yeah, he is. He's standing right there in the corner," Flintlock said.

"*Nein! Nein!* I don't see him!" Albrecht said, squeezing his eyes shut. "He's in Timbuktu, not here in my hotel."

"There are none so blind as those who will not see," McPhee said, smiling.

Albrecht looked blindly around him. "Who said that? *Wer sagt das?*"

The little German might have kept up the charade of denying the existence of a guest who was right in the room with him had not a sharp rap on the door interrupted him.

Flintlock pulled his Colt and said, "Who's there?"

"Open up!"

A man's voice. Thin, reedy, but authoritative.

"My next move is a bullet through the door," Flintlock said. "Identify yourself."

"This is Frank Constable, attorney-at-law. Open the door, you mannerless lout."

Flintlock, gun in hand, cautiously pulled the door open and a small, quick, darting man stepped inside.

Immediately Hans Albrecht's attitude changed from stubbornness to one of fawning, bowing servility. "Herr Constable, how pleasant it is to see you," he said. "You honor my poor establishment."

"What's amiss here?" the lawyer snapped.

No one answered.

"Come now, speak up and be succinct," the lawyer said. "I have no time to dilly-dally."

"Herman the German here —"

"My name is Hans, Herr Flintlock," Albrecht said.

"Wants me to pay for the window his cronies shot out."

"I am a poor man, Herr Constable," the proprietor said, spreading his hands. "A window means a great deal to me and *meine Kinder.*" He patted his round belly. "Look at me, fading away from a lack of food."

"Send the bill to me, Mr. Albrecht," the lawyer said. "Speak at once, fellow. Is that suitable?"

"Yes, Herr Constable. *Meine Frau* will be —"

The lawyer clapped his hands. "Go! *Schnell! Schnell!*"

As Albrecht bowed his way out of the door Flintlock kicked it shut and to his joy heard a Teutonic yelp of pain.

"You are the thug I've hired to guard my client," Constable said. "Speak up, man.

Are you?"

"Yeah. I'm the thug."

"You have a neck made for a noose."

"It seems so does your client."

The lawyer was shocked. "No! That will not do! I will not tolerate humor in any form, Mr. Flintlock. I detest it. It is the sign of a weak mind. Jokes should be banned from this country and the people who tell them."

Constable was a tiny, birdlike man and his pale face had splotches of brown all over like a sparrow's egg. He wore a Prince Albert frock coat of the finest broadcloth, a scarlet cravat and carried a silver-topped cane in the shape of a Chinese dragon. The dragon had two fine rubies for eyes.

"Your lives are in the greatest danger," he said. "The doomsday clock is ticking."

"Don't I know it," Flintlock said without smiling.

"It is therefore a matter of the greatest moment that you leave Open Sky just as soon as it's feasible. Do you understand what I'm telling you? Speak up, now."

"But how, Mr. Constable?" McPhee said. "The hotel is under constant watch. There are armed men everywhere."

"Mr. Flintlock is not the only ruffian in my employ," the lawyer said. "I have arranged for horses to be brought to the waste ground behind the hotel tonight."

"When?" Flintlock said.

"At the darkest time of the night when the restless dead walk," Constable said. "Midnight by the clock."

Anticipating Flintlock's next question, he said, "You will be guided to a place south of here named Bobcat Ridge. I have a cabin there that you will find comfortable."

"Grub?" Flintlock said.

"All you'll need. The cabin is well supplied."

"Good fishing?"

"I wouldn't know, Mr. Flintlock. The cabin was a place of business not pleasure and will be again. Besides, you will have no time to fish. You must be on constant guard."

Then, a glint of pride in his eyes, Constable gave Flintlock more information than the moment required.

"I spent my three years in the cabin attempting to perfect an infernal machine, a weapon that utilizes the elemental powers of steam and fire. Oh, it is a terrible weapon."

Realization dawned on McPhee's face. "That's why folks say the ridge is haunted by a fire-breathing dragon."

"Like this one." Constable held up his cane. "Yes, quite so. And it made me happy to hear such stories. They kept the curious and the thrill seekers away."

Like a man warming to a favorite subject, the lawyer said, "A year ago, almost to the day, I had a conference in Paris with the prophet Mr. Jules Verne, that genius of science and the literary pen. He assured me that one day soon, without doubt before the end of this century, the same steam power that drives our great locomotives across the endless prairie will also take us to the moon. Mr. Verne invited me join the first lunar expedition and, gentlemen, such times we'll have."

Tapping his cane on his gloved hand for emphasis, his eyes as wild as those of an Old Testament prophet, Constable was almost shouting.

"By the year 1900, no later, steam shovels will mine the moon's surface, steam hammers will crush its ores and steam interplanetary ships will carry its riches back to earth. Should the miners encounter hostile Moonlings, steam-driven infernal machines like mine, roaring fire, will keep the lunar savages at bay. I believe —"

Constable abruptly stopped talking and blinked a few times.

"But I digress," he said. "In this parlous present, I should not talk of an astounding future."

"Suits me fine," Flintlock said. He angled McPhee a look that said louder than words, *Your lawyer is nuts.*

But Constable seemed to have regained his usual composure. "Before I leave, Mr. McPhee, I must say a word." He took just a single step toward the door, then stopped and removed an envelope from his pocket.

"For you, Mr. Flintlock, a month's wages in advance. I hope you're worth it."

Before Flintlock could answer, the lawyer turned his attention to McPhee again. "Sir, my efforts on your behalf should not be construed as a belief in your innocence. I don't know if you murdered Polly Mallory or not." Constable's thin face was grim. "Do we understand each other?"

The young clerk looked shocked and opened his mouth to speak, but Constable silenced him by raising his cane like a fence picket.

"As a member of the legal profession, I could not remain idly by and see a man railroaded into a noose without proof of his guilt. And there for now matters must stand."

"What about the real murderer of Polly

Mallory?" McPhee said.

"If he or she is to be found, I will find him." The lawyer touched the brim of his derby hat and gave a little bow. "Good morning, gentlemen."

After the lawyer left McPhee said, "He thinks I'm guilty."

"He says he doesn't know," Flintlock said.

"Do you think I murdered Polly?"

"I already told you, what I think doesn't matter."

"I'm sorry I got you into this, Sam."

"You didn't get me into anything." Flintlock waved the envelope Constable had given him. "I'm doing it for wages."

"Well, I swear that I didn't kill her."

"You swore me that already."

"The question is: Who did?"

"And the answer to that," Sam Flintlock said, "is that it's none of my damned business. How many times do I have to tell you that?"

"Until you've convinced yourself of my innocence," McPhee said.

"Now that may take time," Flintlock said. "Providing, of course, we live that long."

CHAPTER TWELVE

Young Steve McCord rode his horse into the pines then swung out of the saddle. He tethered the black to the slender trunk of a sapling and slid a new .44-40 Winchester from the boot.

From now until the job was done he'd go on foot.

The afternoon had not yet started its slow shade into evening and the sky was still blue, now bannered with cloud the color of polished brass. The young man climbed the timbered rise to a bench of shale rock that overlooked the Circle-O home ranch and bellied down to wait.

Old Brendan O'Rourke's place lay among shallow, rolling hills covered with good grass and here and there stands of piñon and juniper flourished. A windmill turned slowly in the languid summer breeze and the horses in the corral grazed on recently thrown hay. The cookhouse fire was lit for supper and rising smoke from its iron chimney tied bows in the air.

The ranch seemed deserted and still, and young McCord's frustration grew. He needed a target. Now, before it grew too dark.

Long minutes passed then the cookhouse door opened and a red-faced, big-bellied cook stepped outside and threw a basin of scraps to the ducks that congregated nearby.

The cook wiped off his sweating face with the bottom of his apron and stared at the sky.

Kill the cook?

The twenty-year-old weighed that option.

Good cooks were hard to find and this one had a lot of gray in his hair and might prove difficult to replace. But would his death be enough to start a war?

Would killing a Circle-O puncher be better? Or putting a bullet in Frisco Maddox's skull better still?

But Steve liked Frisco. The big foreman had always stood up for him when his father went into one of his rages.

Anyway, Frisco was nowhere in sight. But the cook was.

Steve McCord grinned. A bird in the hand . . .

No bacon, beans and biscuits for the

Circle-O hands tonight!

He centered the rifle sights on the cook's broad chest.

The man seemed to be singing . . . or was he calling out to the ducks? Not that it mattered a damn. He was going to die real soon.

Steve McCord took up the slack on the trigger, let his breath out slowly and fired.

The cook took the hit square in the chest. He fell hard, probably dead when he hit the ground.

Now to give them something to think about and keep their heads down.

McCord triggered shots into the ranch house, the bunkhouse and dropped a couple of horses in the corral. The cow ponies dropped kicking and screaming.

He grinned, watching men run hither and yon like disturbed ants, diving for cover, calling out to one another. A few punchers fired shots at shadows but none came near him.

Yee-hah! He'd sure played hob. But now it was time to light a shuck.

Steve McCord scrambled down the slope, mounted his horse and headed at a canter in the direction of Open Sky.

He checked his back trail but saw no rising dust.

It would take the Circle-O a while to mount a chase and by then he'd be long gone. Besides, he was riding across rough and broken country just north of Limestone Ridge and it would take an Apache to track him.

The youth rode into Open Sky just as dusk fell and both sides of the street were ablaze with light that cast orange and yellow color so vividly on the boardwalks that Steve fancied he was riding past spills of wet paint. He reminded himself to include that allusion in his next poem. Maybe an ode about killing a man and how good — no, satisfying — it felt.

Oil lamps glowed behind the windows of the First Bank of Open Sky as the boy drew rein and looped his horse to the hitching rail.

A tall, gangling youngster dressed in dusty range clothes, he took the steps up the bank and walked inside. A bell jangled above his head.

A teller looked up from a ledger and said, "He's expecting you. Go right inside."

Steve McCord opened the gate at the end of the counter and walked to the back office.

"Come in," a man's voice said to the

youth's knock.

The massively obese man behind the desk smiled. He looked self-satisfied and as sly as the serpent in the Garden of Eden.

"Close the door behind you and sit yourself down, Steve," he said. "It's good to see my old friend and business partner again."

After McCord closed the door behind him, he parked in an uncomfortable wooden chair opposite the banker and said, "Well, I did it, Mr. Tweddle. It's started."

Lucian Tweddle placed his linked hands on his great belly, and his thick, fleshy lips twisted into his repulsive reptilian smile.

"What did you start, dear boy?" he said.

The youth giggled. "Killed the cook. Gunned the Circle-O biscuit shooter, by God."

Tweddle took time to absorb this, his piggy little eyes thoughtful. "That will hurt them," he said finally. "A hungry man is an angry man, or so I'm told."

"Damn right it will. The fat is well and truly in the fire."

"Steve, how did you make it clear that the shot came courtesy of the McCord ranch?" The banker's voice was low, almost menacing.

McCord was taken aback. "Well, I . . . I didn't. I mean, I figured my father will be the number one suspect. He's got everything to gain by a war with the Circle-O."

"Really? Then I'm totally confused. A missed shot from a deer hunter. A passing Indian taking a pot just for the hell of it. A disgruntled ex-employee nursing a beef with the cook. One of the Circle-O's own punchers for a similar reason. A vengeful and scorned lover. There's all kind of motives for a murder like that, and not all of them point to Trace McCord."

The youth looked crestfallen and he hung his head.

"I never thought —"

"Don't think, Steve. Write your poetry, dream of the day the ranch will be yours and leave the thinking to me."

"I'm sorry, Mr. Tweddle."

"No real harm done. But don't make any further moves against the Circle-O until you hear from me."

He steepled his fat fingers, gold signet rings on all of them save the thumbs.

"Is that perfectly clear?"

The youth nodded.

"Good. Then go home and I'll be in touch."

"My father's home is not mine," Steve McCord said.

"I know. But with my help it soon will be."

■ ■ ■ ■

Tweddle waited until the boy was clear of the bank, then uncomfortably shifted his huge bulk in his red leather chair. His face, blue-chinned and pendulous in the jowls, revealed his anger. The McCord boy was an idiot, but he'd just discovered a hidden talent, that of cold-blooded killer, and it could make him hard to handle or a valuable asset, or both. Tweddle allowed that Steve was right about one thing, though. There must be war to the finish between Trace McCord and old Brendan O'Rourke.

After the violence was over, the boy would inherit the smoking ruins of both ranches.

And then, Tweddle smiled, it was all too simple. He'd get rid of Steve McCord and pick up the pieces.

His business contacts in Washington had assured him that the railroads planned to lay tracks this way and soon the land would become immensely valuable. There was a fortune to be made for a man with the guts and vision enough to reach out and grab it all.

And Lucian Tweddle considered himself such a man.

CHAPTER THIRTEEN

By Sam Flintlock's watch, the nickel case knife-scarred on the back where a drunk Navajo renegade had near gutted him, it was twenty minutes to midnight when Clifton Wraith tapped on the door.

"Good way for a man to get himself shot," Flintlock growled as he let the Pinkerton inside.

"You always were a welcoming man, Sammy," Wraith said. He nodded, acknowledging McPhee.

"What's the latest?" Flintlock said.

"You know the latest. You leave at midnight then head for Frank Constable's old place over to Bobcat Ridge."

"I don't cotton to riding night trails. He said we'd have a guide."

"You have, a Pawnee breed by the name of O'Hara."

Wraith smiled. "I'd like to say he's a nice feller, but he isn't."

"Does he know the trail to Bobcat Ridge?"

"He surely does."

"Then he's a nice feller," Flintlock said.

"Mr. Wraith, did you learn anything yet?" McPhee said, hope in his voice.

"Only that a lot of angry people want you dead, Jamie," Wraith said. "But then you already know that."

"It seems Polly Mallory was a popular lady," Flintlock said. "I've never seen a town this riled up over a school ma'am's death."

"Apparently, but to me that's very strange."

"Why is it strange?" Jamie McPhee said.

"Because Polly Mallory was popular, but she wasn't that popular," Wraith said. "From what I've been told she was more than a mite standoffish and her students didn't like her much. Their parents didn't care for her either, especially the mothers."

The Pinkerton rubbed his chin. "But she was a looker, every man in the town agrees on that."

"Maybe a jealous wife or girlfriend killed her," Flintlock said.

"Maybe, but I doubt it. It took a lot of strength to crush the girl's throat. A man's strength."

"Then it's all up with me," McPhee said. "I'm surely doomed."

Not for the first time Flintlock was struck by what a colorless, timid man the clerk was. What the hell had a skirt-swisher like Polly Mallory seen in him?

But aloud he said, "What happens after Bobcat Ridge?"

"I'll arrange for Jamie's transportation to Texas," Wraith said. "I've got a friend in Amarillo where he can stay until he makes plans. And he'll be safe there. My friend has five tall, fighting sons."

"Wish you had them here," Flintlock said.

"Indeed. Even for a few days."

Wraith consulted his watch.

"Better get ready, Sam. O'Hara will have your buckskin and a horse for Jamie. Be warned, he doesn't talk much and he's standoffish, at least to white folks."

"Where will you be, Cliff?" Flintlock said.

"Around."

"You aren't armed."

"Got me a derringer in my pocket."

"That ain't much good in a gunfight."

"There won't be a gunfight. O'Hara will see to that."

"You got more confidence in the Pawnee than I have," Flintlock said.

He shoved his Colt into his waistband then picked up the Hawken and Winchester.

"Let's get it done and over with, McPhee,"

he said. The youth looked scared, green around the gills.

"One more thing, Sam," Wraith said. "Frank Constable has some kind of infernal machine at his place. Stay away from it. From what he told me the damned thing is dangerous and you could get your fingers burned."

"Yeah, he told us too," Flintlock said, stepping to the door. "At length."

"That French feller Jules Verne filled Frank's head with all kinds of nonsense," Wraith said. "Flying machines, horseless carriages and a big bomb that can wipe out an entire city."

"Sounds like ol' Jules drinks too much of that there French wine and Green Fairy," Flintlock said.

"That would be my guess," Wraith said. "Ha! Flying machines. What far-fetched nonsense will Frank spout next?"

The witching hour had come and Open Sky slumbered in darkness.

Only the Rocking Horse saloon showed lights where the local chess club drank coffee and pondered their next moves.

The night desk clerk, paid off by Constable, studiously ignored Sam Flintlock and McPhee as they silently descended the stairs and walked to the back door.

Flintlock motioned McPhee to stop and handed him both rifles. He then drew his revolver and slowly opened the door.

A tall, slender man emerged from the darkness like a gray ghost and stepped toward him.

"O'Hara?" Flintlock whispered.

"Who asks?"

"Flintlock, damn it. Who else would ask?"

A grunt. Then a wave of the hand.

Flintlock motioned McPhee forward and followed the breed.

O'Hara wore a buckskin shirt, elaborately beaded and much finer than Flintlock's own, U.S. Cavalry breeches and boots and a traditional Pawnee otter fur turban covered his head. He carried a battle-worn Spencer rifle.

Flintlock followed the man into the gloom, McPhee holding close to him, to a patch of open ground where the horses were tethered under a gibbous moon.

Without a word O'Hara swung into the saddle and waited until the others had done the same.

Finally Flintlock broke the silence. "Lead on, Mr. O'Hara."

To his surprise the breed answered. "Barnabas walks with us," he said. O'Hara held a forefinger to his lips and said, "Shh . . ."

The night was full of insect chatter and timid, gibbering things scuttled in the long grass. Juniper, piñon and sagebrush bestowed their scents on the breeze.

O'Hara led the way and Flintlock followed. Jamie McPhee's face was as white as parchment in the somber darkness and he sat his saddle with all the grace of a junior bank clerk.

Shadowed eyes that seethed with a murderous hatred watched Sam Flintlock ride into the night. Hamp Collins left the darkness of the parked freight wagon behind the store adjacent to the hotel, then collected his horse from the alley between the two buildings.

He grinned as he swung into the saddle. This was perfect. Flintlock and McPhee were together and he could kill them both at his leisure.

McPhee represented money, but Collins had a more exquisite plan for Sam Flintlock. Thanks to the butcher's knife in his belt, the man's dying would not be quick, easy or painless. In fact, it would be horrific.

CHAPTER FOURTEEN

There was no trail where the Pawnee rode, just a deer path between the trees. Apart from the creak of saddle leather and the soft pad of the horses' hooves on a carpet of pine needles there was no sound.

The wan moonlight lit the way and the ozone smell of lightning tinged the air.

After an hour O'Hara drew rein and pointed into the distance ahead of him. "Frank Constable's cabins are close," he said. "Over the rise."

"Glad to hear it," Flintlock said. "It's getting up to rain."

"Thunderstorm by and by," O'Hara said. He fixed Flintlock with a stare, his black eyes glittering. "Barnabas says you are an idiot," he said.

"Sounds like him," Flintlock said. "Barnabas has a way with words."

"He say go find your ma and your name. He says you should kill McPhee and then leave here."

"I stopped listening to Barnabas as soon as I stood taller than a Hawken rifle," Flintlock said. "Best move I ever made."

"Then more fool you, Flintlock. There is evil in this wind. Its chokes me like the smoke in my grandfather's lodge."

O'Hara kneed his horse into motion as a few fat raindrops ticked among the pine canopy. Ten miles to the north lightning flashed over the peaks of the Sans Bois Mountains and thunder rumbled like a dim distant drum. The air was cool, edged, but Flintlock could sense no evil on the wind, but then he was a white man.

As the moon hid its face behind clouds, he could barely make out the buildings ahead of him. A cabin and two larger structures for sure and probably three or four smaller shacks.

O'Hara led the way directly to the cabin. The rain was heavier now, the thunder closer.

He pointed to one of the large buildings.

"Barn, Flintlock. Put your horses there. O'Hara goes now."

Without another word or a farewell wave, the breed swung his horse and rode away into the teeming, glittering night.

"Right sociable feller," Flintlock said to

117

McPhee, rain drumming on his hat.

"I'll take the horses to the barn," the young man said. Then, "I guess he figured his job was done."

"I guess you're right," Flintlock said. He looked around him. "But I think mine is only beginning."

He swung out of the saddle and stepped into the darkness of the cabin. After allowing time for his night vision to adjust, Flintlock made out a table with an oil lamp in the center of the floor. A box of lucifers lay close by. He lit the lamp and its orange glow spread throughout the cabin but angled shadows remained in the corners where the spiders lived.

Imagine a genteel Victorian parlor, relentlessly middle class, set down in the middle of the wilderness and that was Frank Constable's cabin.

A prime indicator of social status at a time when clutter meant class, the cabin was packed with vases, lamps, china ornaments, lace doilies, tea services and, what old Queen Vic herself considered the ultimate display of good taste and breeding, several stuffed birds and small animals under glass domes.

A portrait of a very young soldier in Confederate gray struck a somber note, draped as it was with black crepe, and a dark red curtain adorned with a Chinese dragon cunningly wrought from colored, metallic threads separated the parlor from the kitchen. The room was cozy enough but a little threatening, as though a murder had been committed there.

Flintlock found the shelves amply supplied with canned and dried food and by the time McPhee returned, the stove was lit and coffee simmered.

"You've been gone a long time, McPhee," Flintlock said.

The young man was white to the gills. "You'd better come see this, Sam," he said.

Something in McPhee's expression stilled the question on Flintlock's lips. The man was thoroughly spooked, his lips pale from fright.

"Lead the way," he said.

The barn was a spacious building with eight stalls and it smelled clean. McPhee had lit a lantern and it sat on an upturned barrel at the door. "There's plenty of hay and I found some oats," he said. "Well, as much as the rats had left."

"Is that what you wanted to show me? Oats?" Flintlock said.

"No. Come follow me."

119

The young man led the way to the last stall and held the lantern high. "When I was looking for oats I discovered this."

"What the hell is it?" Flintlock said. He peered through the dim orange gloom at a charred object on the barn floor.

"Can't you see? It's right in front of you."

"McPhee, are you showing me a burned tree trunk?"

"No. It's human, or it was. Look closer. You can see the teeth."

Flintlock took the lantern from McPhee's trembling hand and bent over for a closer look. "My God," he said. "It is human. I think."

"It's human and he, she, whatever it was, died a terrible death," the younger man said.

"Uh-huh. You got that right. Burned to a crisp."

Teeth gleamed white in the blackened skull and the body's right hand was raised as though in defensive posture. Most of the skin had burned from the fingers so that yellow bones showed. The entire body looked as though it had been transformed in an instant from a living, breathing human being into a cylinder of black, carbonized flesh and bone.

Flintlock looked around him and instinctively his hand strayed to the handle of the

Colt in his waistband. Restless rats rustled in the corners, but there was no other sound, only the steady munching of the horses.

"How did it happen, Sam?" McPhee said.

In the lantern-splashed gloom the young man's eyes looked like black buttons sewn on to a flour sack.

"How the hell should I know?" Flintlock snapped. His fear made him irritable.

"I think I know," McPhee said. "It was the infernal machine."

Flintlock stared hard at the young man. "You don't believe all the crap that Constable told us, do you?" he said. "About men in the moon and sich."

"Yes. Yes, I do."

"The only infernal machine I ever saw was back in '64, a Gatling gun that executed a bunch of black Yankee prisoners down Alabama way," Flintlock said. "When the damned thing started to shoot it sounded like a rusty iron bed dragged across a knotted pine floor." He nodded to himself. "Now that was an infernal machine."

"A Gatling gun shoots only bullets, Sam. Mr. Constable said his infernal machine hurls bolts of fire, and fire harnesses the power of hell."

Rain slanted across the open barn door

121

and lightning seared and flashed and shimmered like sheets of polished silver. Immediately thunder crashed, as though angry at the lightning for stealing the show.

"Let's get out of here," Flintlock said. He glanced at the charred body. "Maybe he —"

"Or she."

"Was struck by lightning."

"Not a chance," McPhee said. "This person was roasted by hellfire."

The way to the cabin lay past another barnlike structure, but a chain and a massive iron padlock secured its double doors. The building had an air of foreboding about it, like a crypt in a story by Mr. Poe.

"I bet the infernal machine is in there!" McPhee yelled above the roar of the storm and the serpent hiss of the relentless rain. "That's why the place is chained and padlocked."

"It's not bothering us, so we'll leave it alone," Flintlock said. Lightning shimmered around him and the rain pounded.

"Don't you want to see it, Sam?" McPhee yelled above the storm.

"Hell no, I don't. And neither do you."

"It could be interesting. I think it killed the poor soul in the barn."

"Maybe so, but I'm not messing around

with infernal machines, McPhee. Keeping you alive is hard enough without any distractions."

"Roasted him or her alive it did. One moment a human being, the next a charred, lifeless corpse."

"Quit with that, McPhee," Flintlock said. "Now you're spooking the hell out of me as well."

"It's a terrible weapon. Mr. Constable told us that."

"Maybe you're thinking about wiping out Open Sky with it, huh?"

"No, but it's an idea."

"A bad idea. I'm sorry I said it." Sam Flintlock shook his shaggy head like a coon dog with a bug in its ear. "Damn it," he said. "What is that?"

"What is what?" McPhee said.

"Something on the back of my neck like a cold breath . . ."

Then he knew it for what it was.

Out there in the darkness something or someone watched him.

CHAPTER FIFTEEN

Hamp Collins felt sorry for himself.

He'd hoped to have had a shot at Sam Flintlock by now, drop him with a bullet to the belly then let his knife take it from there. But he hadn't reckoned on a damned summer thunderstorm.

Huddled under the thin cover of the pines, he studied the cabin. It looked snug and dry behind the chain-mail fall of the rain and Collins believed he smelled coffee and frying bacon.

Damn. He *could* smell coffee.

Flintlock was still tormenting him, belittling him like he'd done in the middle of the street in Open Sky. And in front of everybody! That made Collins's blood boil.

He rose to his feet, his Winchester in hand. Now was the time to interrupt the tattooed man's cozy little dinner party. Let's see how Mr. High and Mighty Flintlock enjoyed seeing his balls floating in a bowl.

For a moment Collins hesitated and ran through a plan in his head. He was a slow-thinking man and he laid it out in his mind . . .

Step by step.

One: Kick the door in.

Two: Shoot Flintlock first. Hit hard enough to put him down but not too hard. He'd have to live for two or three hours while the knife did its work.

Three: Kill McPhee.

Four: Time to geld Flintlock, slice by slice. Do it slowly and tease him, torture him, let him know what terrible thing was happening to him.

Five: Piss on Flintlock's dead body, do a happy dance and then get some coffee.

Collins held up his hand. Five fingers. Five steps. He wouldn't forget. It was a good plan. A crackerjack strategy that he knew would work.

But then happy Hamp Collins got his throat cut and it spoiled everything.

The cut was as thin as a whisper, but deep.

Hamp Collins thought it strange that initially he felt little pain.

But then blood filled his mouth, his breathing choked off and he realized what had happened to him. Luckily for Hamp he

125

was already dying at this point and knew only a few fleeting moments of terror.

O'Hara held him fast and hissed a vision of hell into the gunman's ear.

Hamp tried to scream, but mercifully when the breed let go of him and his body slumped to the ground, he was already dead, his wide, terrified eyes staring into a fiery eternity.

His long black hair plastered to his head and shoulders in tight ringlets, O'Hara stripped Collins of his rifle, gun belt and knife. Then he scalped the dead man and hung the dripping trophy on a pine branch so that the soul of this enemy would not come back to haunt him.

He used Collins's own knife to cut off the gunman's head and then dragged the body deeper into the trees.

After he collected Collins's horse, O'Hara mounted his own paint and rode close to the cabin but remained hidden in darkness. As thunder roared and lightning lit up the land around him the breed chanted his war song, his voice rising and falling in the complex Pawnee cadence.

When the song was over, O'Hara stood in the stirrups and yelled, "Flintlock!"

A few moments passed . . .

The cabin suddenly went dark and the

door creaked open.

"Who's there?" Sam Flintlock called into the teeming rain.

"Flintlock! From now on do your damned job!"

O'Hara yelled a war cry and kicked his horse into a gallop. As he rode past the cabin door he threw something at Flintlock's feet that bounced once in the mud then rolled.

Taken by surprise Flintlock took a step back into the cabin. He caught an ephemeral glimpse of a rider on a paint horse . . . then only rain-lashed darkness.

"Who was that?" McPhee said.

"I think it was that crazy breed, O'Hara. He threw something."

Flintlock stepped into the downpour and pushed a round object with the toe of his boot.

Illuminated by a flicker of lightning, Collins's stark, staring upturned face glared at him.

It was unexpected and Flintlock instinctively jerked away.

"What is it?" McPhee said. His voice sounded scared, an octave too high.

"Hamp Collins's head," Flintlock said. "And it's been scalped."

From somewhere out in the torn night,

Sam Flintlock heard someone's derisive laugh.

O'Hara or old Barnabas?

He couldn't tell.

CHAPTER SIXTEEN

When Clifton Wraith rode up to the cabin at Bobcat Ridge the thunderstorm was yesterday's memory and the morning sun shone bright in the cloudless blue bowl of the sky.

The Pinkerton was in time to watch Flintlock and McPhee throw the last shovels of dirt on two graves, side by side in open ground at the edge of a line of pines.

Flintlock leaned on his long-handled shovel and looked up at the rider. "To what do we owe this honor, Cliff?"

Wraith stared at the graves, then, "You been killing folks, Sammy?"

"Nope. Your man O'Hara killed one and Frank Constable left us t'other as a welcome to my home gift, I suppose."

Flintlock smiled. "You ain't catching my drift, huh?"

"O'Hara killing somebody doesn't come as a surprise. Who was it? Do you know?"

"Sure I know. It was Hamp Collins, the feller I had some cross words with back in town. I reckon he followed us out here and O'Hara done for him."

"That was your job, Sam," Wraith said, his tone mildly accusing.

"Yeah, O'Hara already made that pretty clear."

"The other?"

"You tell me."

"Coffee?"

"It's on the bile."

"I'm a bearer of bad news, Sam."

"Just the kind of visitor I need first thing in the morning," Flintlock said. "Light and set."

After Wraith settled himself with coffee at his elbow and a cigar going, he said, "Describe the dead man you found."

"Ol' Hamp or t'other?" Flintlock said.

"Frank Constable's dead man. I know who Collins was."

"I can't. I don't even know if it was a man or a woman."

"The body was completely incinerated," Jamie McPhee said.

Wraith stared hard at the young man and he seemed about to say something but abruptly changed his mind. To Flintlock he said, "You're thinking what I'm thinking, Sam. An accident with Frank's infernal machine."

"I wasn't thinking that, but it could be," Flintlock said. "Why didn't he bury the body?"

"Maybe it happened in winter when the ground was hard," Wraith said. "Frank hasn't been back here in months."

The Pinkerton's eyes moved back to McPhee. "You been around the Circle-O recently?" he said.

"Brendan O'Rourke's place? No, I haven't."

"Steve McCord said he saw you in the area right after the ranch cook was shot. He says you were riding fast and carrying a Winchester."

McPhee's face didn't register shock, only an odd dejection as though yet another heavy load had been laid on him. "That's a lie," he said.

"I know it's a lie," Wraith said. "The story is you begged the cook for grub, he refused and then you laid off a ways and plugged him out of hard feelings, like."

"I wasn't even near the ranch."

"I know, but that's the way everybody has it figured."

"Can't you tell them that Steve McCord

131

is lying?" McPhee said.

"It's his word against yours, and you aren't exactly popular in these parts."

Wraith raised his cup and stared at McPhee over the steaming rim. "The word is out that you're to be shot on sight. Trace McCord says you're a mad dog, and it seems Sheriff Lithgow agrees with him."

Wraith shifted his attention to Flintlock. "Sammy, you've got your work cut out for you," he said.

"I've got a job to do and I'll do it," Flintlock said.

"We've both got a job to do, Sam," Wraith said. "But if it comes down to gunplay, you're better equipped than I am."

Flintlock read the other man's eyes. "What have you heard, Cliff?"

"Gossip. That's all. Probably not a word of truth to it."

"Tell it."

Wraith drew on his cigar until the tip glowed bright red, then he said, "I get around, Sam. I talk to folks, listen to what they have to say, poke my nose into all the dark corners. It's the way of the Pinkerton."

"And you heard what?"

"It's hearsay, Sam. The small-town rumor mill working overtime."

Flintlock banged the table with his fist.

"Damn it, Cliff."

"All right. I heard that somebody has sent for Beau Hunt."

"Another lie?" Flintlock said.

"A couple of placer miners were talking at the bar and swear they saw him in Tuskahoma down in the Choctaw nation. A man like the Beau is easy to spot."

It took Flintlock a few moments to recover from that. When he finally did, his eyes were unbelieving. "Beau Hunt comes dear," he said. "He doesn't live with Indians and he doesn't sell his gun to rubes."

"He might, if the dollars are enough. And there's money talk around town," Wraith said. "I mean big-money talk."

"Spill it."

"The rumor is that a couple of railroad companies are battling it out in Washington to get the right to lay rails north of here with a depot in Open Sky."

"And that means?"

"Think, man. It means the Circle-O and McCord cow pastures will be worth a fortune when the railroad goes through."

"If any of this is true, my money is on Trace McCord as the one hiring Beau Hunt. It would make sense if McCord plans a range war to take over the Circle-O," McPhee said.

"From what I've seen of Trace McCord he's the kind of man who'd figure he can handle the shooting end himself," Wraith said. "Why would he need an expensive, big-name draw fighter?"

"Then who does?" McPhee said.

"Old Brendan O'Rourke," Wraith said. "He doesn't have the guns to go up against McCord and he knows it. Beau could tip the balance."

"Maybe the cook was the first victim of a range war or maybe he wasn't," Flintlock said. "But my gut instinct is that you've heard some wild talk. How many rundown, hick towns built depots for rails that never arrived? I'd guess I've been in a dozen."

"Well, wild talk is all it could be," Wraith said. "Sam, you ever met Beau Hunt?"

"Yeah, a few times. We've always touched hats and stepped around each other in the street."

"Is Beau as fast with a gun as they say, huh?"

"The best there is," Flintlock said. "He hasn't killed many, but the ones he has were all named men. That's why the price for his services starts at ten thousand and goes up from there."

McPhee, at an impressionable age, whistled between his teeth.

"Yeah, you should whistle," Flintlock said. "Beau buys his suits and linen in Rome and New York, smokes cigars made in Turkey and maintains an account at a London gunsmith. Every round he shoots is made by experts. Add beautiful women, French champagne, fine restaurants, the best horse-flesh money can buy plus a professional gambler's uncanny luck and you got Beau Hunt as ever was."

Flintlock's mouth tightened under his ragged mustache. "He watches your eyes, so if you meet him in a gunfight don't blink. That's all the time Beau Hunt needs on the draw and shoot."

Wraith thought that through. "Ah well, railroads, range wars, draw fighters, after all is said and done maybe it's all just idle gossip," he said finally.

"Idle talk enough to scare the hell out of me," Flintlock said. "Even a rumor of Beau Hunt on the prod is a thing to keep a man staring at the ceiling o' nights."

"Well, it's settled one thing, Sam," Wraith said. "You and Jamie will leave the territory today and flap your chaps all the way to Texas. If I learn anything further about the murders, I'll be in touch."

"No, Mr. Wraith, I'm not running," McPhee said.

The Pinkerton was taken aback. "Did you hear what I said, young man? The order is out to shoot you on sight."

"I've done nothing wrong," McPhee said. "Why should I run?"

Flintlock, as surprised as Wraith, said, "State your intentions, McPhee."

"My intention is to stay right here in the Oklahoma Territory until I clear my name. I didn't murder Polly and I didn't shoot the ranch cook and one day the truth will come out."

"If you live that long," the Pinkerton said.

"I will not flee to Texas, Mr. Wraith. I'm an innocent man and I plan to prove it."

The Pinkerton gave Flintlock a despairing glance. "Sam, talk some sense into him. He's gone loco."

Flintlock shook his head. "Man doesn't want to run, then that's his right. He's not a stubborn child I can spank on the butt and throw on a horse."

"Jamie, by this time I know more about Polly Mallory than most men in Open Sky. She was only as good as she had to be and she was stringing along a number of men, including you."

McPhee opened his mouth to speak, but the Pinkerton talked over him. "Dr. Thorne says she was three months pregnant when she was murdered. Did you know that?"

"Doctors can be wrong," McPhee said, but he sounded uncertain.

"Polly asked Nancy Pocket if she could be with child, and Nancy, being a whore and experienced in those matters, told her she was."

"Did Polly name the father?" Flintlock said.

"No. Nancy asked her but she refused."

"True or not, it makes no difference," McPhee said. "I'm not running, now or ever."

Wraith sighed deeply and said, "I give you and Sam about a week to live. No longer than that. I don't know yet who is, but somebody with a lot of influence in Open Sky wants you both dead."

"Trace McCord, at a guess," Flintlock said.

"He's a possibility."

"No matter, Cliff," Flintlock said. "I took a man's money to guard McPhee and that's what I'll do."

His rugged, sun-browned face was suddenly grim, and, not for the first time, Wraith saw the deadly resolve of the gunfighter in him. Flintlock's next words confirmed that impression.

"Cliff, you let it be known in Open Sky

that if a hanging posse comes after Jamie McPhee I'll pile their dead high."

"You would do that, wouldn't you?" Wraith said.

"Bet the farm on it," Flintlock said.

CHAPTER SEVENTEEN

Sam Flintlock spent a couple of uneasy days at the cabin and he never strayed far from his rifle.

Jamie McPhee's determination to remain close to Open Sky and clear his name didn't waver but he was as tense and troubled as Flintlock.

On the morning of the third day, Flintlock saddled his buckskin. "Stay close to the cabin, McPhee," he said. "I'm heading out to scout around."

"You think we're in danger?" the young man said.

"I know we're in danger," Flintlock said. "The question is, how close is it?"

"Take care, Sam," McPhee said. "Remember that shoot on sight warning."

"I surely will," Flintlock said.

Thirty minutes later Flintlock rode west of Dripping Vat Mountain, a low peak set down in the middle of forests of broadleaf trees, mainly oaks, with some scattered juniper and piñon. The land around him was vast and empty, echoing silence, and, as far as his eyes were good, Flintlock saw no movement.

He swung west and followed the south bank of a creek through treed, rolling hill country and got a good view of the entire sweep of Bobcat Ridge and saw no human activity or rising dust. The day was hot and arcs of sweat showed in the armpits of Flintlock's buckskin shirt and stained his back. He saw nothing, heard nothing, only the insects making their small sounds in the grass.

He headed south again and fetched through a shallow valley, following a dim game trail that wound between piñon and extensive stands of sagebrush and bunchgrass. The valley gradually opened up into an area of open ground where old Barnabas sat on the seat of a ruined wagon and played catch with a browned skull. Any other man would have been startled by the sight of a ghost but Flintlock was used to it.

"Lookee, Sam," Barnabas said. He held the skull out for inspection. "Tomahawk wound right there. It scattered his brains, all right."

"Who was he?" Flintlock said, drawing rein.

"How the hell should I know? But he was a sodjer fer sure."

"Hell of a place to die," Flintlock said.

"Anywhere is a hell of a place to die." Barnabas studied the skull for a few moments then tossed it away. "I got advice for you, Sam," he said, wiping his hands with a yellow cavalry bandanna.

"I'm always willing to listen, Barnabas."

"You listen but don't act on my wise counsel, Sam. That's why you're an idiot."

"I'm listening now."

"Well, here's how it goes. I was talking to" — Barnabas quickly glanced around him — "you-know-who, and he says the best thing you can do is put a bullet in the McPhee kid, then hightail it for Louisiana and find your ma. Of course you-know-who says you should torture McPhee first, pull out his fingernails, stuff like that, but then he's a tad that way inclined toward folks."

Flintlock said nothing. His horse tossed its head, the bit chiming.

"Well?" Barnabas said.

"Well maybe it's time *you* stopped listening to advice, Barnabas, especially from Old Scratch."

"Shh . . . don't say that. He hates that name."

"I've been hired to save Jamie McPhee's life, not kill him, and that's what I intend to do. Tell him so."

Barnabas slowly turned to mist but his eyes still burned like blue sapphires and his laughter echoed.

"Like you saved Billy?" he said. "You could've taken that damned scarecrow Pat Garrett any day of the week, any hour of the day. You damn well know you could."

"Excuse me, Barnabas, but you know I'd lit a shuck by then," Flintlock said. "I was in Texas."

"You could've come back, Sam. Saved poor Billy Bonney but you didn't. Same way as you ain't gonna save Jamie McPhee."

A wind sprang up from nowhere and shredded the mist and then Flintlock saw nothing but land and sky.

He sat his saddle for long moments, head bowed, deep in thought. Then he said, "I couldn't save you, Billy. I couldn't change what fate intended for you."

He swung his horse away from the wagon, his expression solemn.

Laughing, loving Billy was five years dead and lying cold in his grave.

Lord God Almighty, that was still hard to believe.

Jamie McPhee saw Sam Flintlock ride past the cabin on his way to the barn.

He ran outside brandishing something in his right hand. "Look, Sam! I found the key!"

Flintlock drew rein. "The key to what?"

"The padlocked building. It was hanging on a hook in the kitchen."

"Put it back, McPhee. It's got nothing to do with us."

"I bet that's where the infernal machine is."

"And that's where it should stay."

Flintlock kneed his horse forward.

"You see anybody, Sam?" McPhee called after him.

"Not a living soul," Flintlock said.

After he took care of his horse, Flintlock's plan was to return to the cabin, drink coffee and convince McPhee that he should high-tail it out of the Oklahoma Territory and never come back. But the wide-open door of the large building stopped him in his tracks.

"Damn you, McPhee," he yelled. "You'll get us all killed."

The young man appeared from inside, grinning. "Come take a look, Sam. It's a modern-day wonder."

Flintlock laid his Winchester against the building's front wall and thumbed back the hammer of the Hawken.

"If the damned thing cuts up nasty, this here long gun will blow it apart," he said.

"The machine is asleep, Sam. There's no danger."

Flintlock stepped to the barn door and his eyes got as round as coins. "What in God's name is that?" he said.

"Isn't she a beauty?" McPhee said. He was dancing with excitement. "She's steam driven with a separate mechanism for the fire thrower. Amazing to think that Mr. Constable and Jules Verne will take her to the moon."

"You sure this contraption ain't ready to blow?" Flintlock said.

"Nah. You'd need to fire up the boiler to get her started and I don't know how the flame gun works. But I plan to find out."

"It's an unholy thing," Flintlock said. "It don't belong in this century or any other."

"Now don't go touching off that blunderbuss, Sam," McPhee said. "You could damage her. She's got very delicate mechanisms."

"I doubt it I could damage it," Flintlock said. "That thing is as solid as a house."

The infernal machine got its motive power from what looked like a tiny steam locomotive with a cabin large enough for only one person. A pair of dark goggles dangled from behind its thick glass window. The boiler, painted bright red, was covered in shiny brass tubes and in front of that was a complicated machine consisting of more brass tubes, pistons and vessels of differing sizes, some polished bronze, others of tin-plated iron.

In front of this machine was a flat Studebaker wagon with massive yellow wheels. Four brass cylinders in the shape of recumbent dragons lay side by side on the wagon bed, their gaping, snarling mouths blackened by soot and flame.

Flintlock, raised by superstitious mountain men, figured that Lucifer and his fallen angels used a weapon like the infernal machine when they fought their rebellious war against God.

McPhee read the stunned look on the other man's face, and said, "And lookee here what I found. It's to Frank Constable from the government's War Department, no less."

Flintlock made no move to take the letter,

145

so McPhee read it to him:

"Dear Sir: I am instructed to inform you that my department will make no further tests of your fire machine and, unfortunately, there the matter must end.

"The weapon lacked sufficient range and had an unsettling effect on cavalry horses. It also did not perform well on rough terrain and is quite unsuitable for anything but urban warfare. This hardly justifies the weapon's price and the high cost of transporting it to the battlefield.

"Thank you for your service to our great nation.

"I remain, Sir, Your Obedient Servant, Michael J. Maxwell, Captain, United States Army.

"Kind of puts a damper on things, doesn't it?" McPhee said. "And a letter from a general would have been more polite."

"Where did you get that letter?" Flintlock said.

"From the little box there on the wagon."

"Then put it back and lock this thing up again."

McPhee shook his head. "I'm going to get it running, Sam."

"Are you crazy, McPhee? I don't know how much noise that thing makes, but I'd guess it's as loud as a steam locomotive.

You'll draw posses like wasps to honey."

"Remember the talk about Bobcat Ridge being haunted by a fire-breathing dragon? A posse takes one look at the infernal machine and they'll scamper."

"I wouldn't count on it. Too many hard cases who want you dead ain't afraid of dragons."

Flintlock held up a hand for silence. "And while I'm on the subject, we're getting out of here. Tomorrow at first light."

"I'm not leaving, Sam. I told you that and I told Wraith that," McPhee said.

"How are you going to prove you didn't murder Polly Mallory? Or the Circle-O cook?" Flintlock said.

"The first thing I plan is to talk to Steve McCord and ask him why he lied about me."

"How will you manage that?"

"Ride over to the McCord ranch and wait my chance."

"You'll get yourself killed. You're a bank clerk. Have you ever shot a gun?"

"Sure. A lot of times."

Flintlock took the Colt from his waistband. "Here, pick a target and cut loose."

"Noise could draw a posse. You said that yourself."

"Not today. There's nobody around. Now

let me see you shoot."

"See that little pine tree over there," McPhee said.

"Yeah. It's a good ten paces. Sure you don't want to try something closer?"

"I'll hit the trunk."

"It's only two inches wide."

"I know."

"Then let me see you get your work in," Flintlock said.

CHAPTER EIGHTEEN

After the smoke cleared, Sam Flintlock said, "The safest place in the whole territory was right here beside you."

"I didn't hit it with five shots?" Jamie McPhee said.

"I don't know where the bullets went, but none come near the pine."

McPhee was crestfallen. "Geez, I thought for sure I'd hit it."

"Anybody ever tell you that you close your eyes when you pull the trigger?" Flintlock said. "And you hold the Colt like a maiden aunt?"

"That bad, huh?"

"Maybe the worst I've ever seen and I've seen plenty of bad, most of them dead now."

McPhee swallowed hard. "Could be it was the gun," he said. "Can you hit with it, Sam?"

Without a word Flintlock took the Colt and reloaded with rounds he took from a deerskin pouch that hung on his belt.

He raised the big revolver and fired.

Thinking back on it later, McPhee couldn't remember hearing individual shots, just a continuous roll of gun thunder that lasted a second or two.

The pine jerked, splintered and then fell over.

McPhee whistled between his teeth then did a little dance. "Huzzah for the man in the buckskin shirt! I've never seen the like."

"And me only half trying," Flintlock said.

"Five shots just like —"

"Six. I loaded six. So it wasn't the gun."

"Just like, like lightning. Can you teach me how to shoot like that?"

"I can teach you how to hold and shoot a firearm, but I can't teach you how to do it like me. It's a skill you're born with and maybe one man in a thousand has it."

McPhee shook his head in wonder. "Then you're just a natural-born shootist."

"Something like that and I'm glad you appreciate it. Now let me tell you something, Mr. Bank Clerk, I'm scared right now of the hard times coming down, so imagine how scared you should be."

"I can take care of myself. I'll manage," McPhee said, his face stiff, defensive.

"No, you won't manage. You'll die. You

heard Wraith, this thing hasn't even begun yet. Understand me? I think the wheels will be set in motion real soon."

Flintlock read the young man's eyes and decided McPhee wasn't catching his drift.

"I believe you didn't kill Polly Mallory," he said. "For one thing, I don't think you've got the nerve for it. But the man who did has plenty of nerve and he'll make his move soon. He has to kill you, McPhee, and he needs to make a show of doing it legally."

"Then he'll know where to find me," McPhee said.

CHAPTER NINETEEN

Horn Tate and Willie Litton were blunt instruments, and thus they suited Lucian Tweddle's purposes perfectly. Dull, brutish, violent and drunken, the pair killed with the lead-filled sap, the billy club and their own bare hands.

"Glad you could come, gentlemen," Tweddle said, slightly amused that the last word of his sentence was so badly misused. "I trust your recent business trip out of town was a successful one."

Tate, whose coarse black hairline began just above his eyebrows, grinned. "Successful enough, boss. But robbing two by twice sodbusters don't return much of a profit. You need a killing done?"

"Not quite. But it is a distinct possibility for the future," Tweddle said.

He sat forward in his chair, his great belly hanging between his thighs like a sack of grain. He looked like a great bullfrog.

"I want you to set a fire," he said.

"Burn down this stink-hole town?" Willie Litton said. "I'm all for that."

"No. Not Open Sky, you idiot," Tweddle said. "My business interests are here."

"Nobody likes me in this town," Litton said. "They hate me, especially the women."

His black eyes were never still and when he stood, as he did now, his hands hung in front of him, the thick fingers curled like meat hooks. "Miss Polly never liked me," he said.

"Yes. She was lacking in good taste, that one," Tweddle said, his face straight.

"I liked her a lot," Litton said. "But she wouldn't give me the time of day."

He was four inches over six feet and his shoulders and chest were massive.

"What do you want burned, boss?" Horn Tate said.

"A barn, I think. Yes, that will do nicely, a barn full of hay and horses."

"Where?"

"At Trace McCord's home ranch."

Tate winced like he'd been punched. "Boss, Trace McCord is a hard man. If we get caught he'll hang us."

"I know," Tweddle said. "That's why the job is worth a thousand dollars."

The banker let the two thugs stew on that

for a while. He reached into his desk and produced a bottle and glasses. He poured the cheap rye he kept for low-class guests and smiled at them like an obese cherub.

"Well, Mr. Tate? Mr. Litton? Have you reached a decision?"

"Boss, why can't we just kill somebody like we done the last time?" Tate said. "Break somebody's neck for you, huh?"

"You can and you will. But burn the barn first. A thousand dollars, gentlemen. How much whiskey and whores does that buy?"

Tate rubbed his mouth, his eyes working. Finally he said, "All right, we'll do it."

"Do you agree, Mr. Litton?" Tweddle said.

"Sure. Why not?" Litton said.

"Indeed, why not?" Tweddle said.

He glanced out his office window and smiled when he saw dear Mrs. Barrett on the opposite boardwalk, pretty as a picture with sunlight tangled in her corn-silk hair and a shopping basket over her arm. Her shapely body moved with that languid elegance only the true Southern belle possessed and when she smiled at friends and neighbors, her white teeth flashed. The girl had traded Tweddle mattress time for his promise not to foreclose on their mortgage, with her husband's blessing, he supposed.

The banker's smile faded. He still planned

to foreclose.

The young lady had lacked a bed partner's necessary enthusiasm and inventiveness. That was as unfair as it was unforgivable. Tweddle felt cheated. Mrs. Barrett had promised much and delivered little and that was so unjust. The uppity bitch had taken advantage of him.

"When do you want it done, boss?"

"Huh?" Tweddle said, his mind still in bed with Mrs. Barrett.

"When do you want the barn fire?" Tate said.

"Oh, tonight will be fine," Tweddle said.

"That soon?" Tate said.

The banker's eyes hardened. "I said tonight will be fine. Is there anything about that simple sentence you don't understand?"

Tate took a gulp of his whiskey. "Whatever you say, boss. Whatever you say."

"Now we'll move on to the next item on the agenda," Tweddle said. He leaned his elbows on the table and clenched his fists, an aggressive posture that Tate believed could only signal a killing. It did.

"This Jamie McPhee person has to die, Horn," the banker said.

"The one that done fer Miss Polly?" Willie Litton said.

"Are there two men by that name in this

town?" Tweddle said.

Litton had proven himself to be a reliable dark-alley killer, but sometimes the man's stupidity irritated Tweddle.

"I liked her," Litton said. "I called her my Miss Pretty."

"Yes, we know, Willie," Tate said. He laid his empty glass on the desk. "Where is McPhee, boss?"

"I don't know. But that O'Hara breed is hanging around town, so when you leave, send him to me. He'll find McPhee for you. He says he can smell a white man at a mile."

"Sounds easy, boss," Tate said.

"No, it ain't easy. A gun by the name of Flintlock is with him."

Horn's eyes widened. "Sam Flintlock, the bounty hunter? Got a tattoo of a big bird on his throat?"

"I've only seen the gentleman at a distance," Tweddle said.

"And that's a good place to keep him," Litton said. "He's pizen."

"He scare you that badly?" the banker said.

"He's as mean as a teased rattlesnake, boss," Tate said. "And he steps from one side of the law to t'other as it pleases him an' he picked up some right unfriendly habits along the way."

"And he's good with a gun I take it?" the banker said.

"Chain lightning with the Colt's gun. Yeah."

"So you're afraid of him and don't want to take the job?"

"I didn't say that, boss. Me an' Willie ain't met a man yet we can't kill."

"Can you kill Flintlock?"

"Sure we can. May take a day or two longer, is all."

"My main concern is with McPhee. He's the one I want dead first," Tweddle said. "Don't waste too much time on the kill."

"We'll get him," Tate said. "You can depend on Willie and me."

The banker lit a cigar and leaned back in his chair. He looked smug and self-satisfied, a man who knew how to operate.

"One more thing," he said. "I presume you'll kill McPhee and Flintlock at a distance, yes?"

Tate nodded. "We have our ways, me and Willie. An' that's one of them."

"That's all good and well, but I want one of you to take a bullet," Tweddle said.

"Huh?" Tate said, surprised.

"Make it look good, you understand?"

"Boss, I ain't catching your drift," Tate said.

"You and Willie, just a pair of innocent sportsmen, were deer hunting when McPhee bushwhacked you and shot . . . well, one of you," Tweddle said. "Wounded, you had no choice but to return fire and kill him." The banker smiled and squeezed his cigar. "Nobody's going to ask questions after that. No second-guessing. The young man's guilt will be obvious, his death cut-and-dried and I'm well out of it."

"But why do we need to get shot?" Tate said.

"To make it look good, of course, Mr. Tate."

The man blinked, his mouth hanging open. "Well, I can understand that," he said. "I guess."

"Only one of you, Mr. Tate," Tweddle said. "It doesn't have to be a serious wound. I suggest you simply lay the muzzle of your rifle against the meat of Willie's shoulder and pull the trigger. All we need is a grazing wound." He waved a dismissive hand. "A mere scratch you understand."

"Why me? Why not Horn?" Litton said. "How come I always get the dirty end of the stick?"

"Because I'll pay you a thousand dollars for the kill and extry five hundred dollars for the inconvenience of the wound, Willie.

I can't say fairer than that. Think of the whores, man."

"Why do you want this man McPhee dead so bad, boss?" Litton said. "Were you sweet on Miss Polly?"

Tweddle's anger surged. Cigar smoke flared out of his nostrils and mouth like incense pouring from the statue of a fat Oriental monk.

"That's none of your business, damn you!" he said.

"We'll take on both jobs, boss," Tate said, real quickly. "The McCord barn goes up tonight and then we go after McPhee. Ain't that right, Willie?"

Despite his size and hulking presence, Litton was intimidated. He knew how deadly Lucian Tweddle could be if he took a dislike to a man.

"Sure we will, boss," he said. "The barn goes up tonight and when we kill McPhee I'll take the wound for the extry five hunnerd."

"Good, then we're in agreement," the banker said. "Now get out of here, both of you. And when you see the breed O'Hara tell him I want to talk with him."

After the pair left, Tweddle sniffed. Damn, they stunk up the place.

159

CHAPTER TWENTY

The *Territorial Times* was the most widely read newspaper in Open Sky and the news of the McCord ranch barn blaze made front-page news.

ARSON IN THE NIGHT

A Dastardly Deed at The McCord Ranch

EIGHT HORSES DEAD IN BLAZE

Empty Coal Oil Can Found at Scene

Marshal Lithgow Vows To Arrest Culprit

THE TIMES asks the question boldly and fearlessly: Was last night's barn fire at the McCord ranch more revengeful mischief perpetrated by that ravening wolf in the

clothing of a white man, to wit, the murderer of

MISS POLLY MALLORY?

How else to explain the tragedy that took place?

Could anyone else but the monster Jamie McPhee commit such a crime? We think not. And to damn McPhee further, the fire was set only days after young Steve McCord saw the man shoot Max Bender, the Circle-O ranch cook, and leave him dying and

WELTERING IN HIS BLOOD.

Oh, how McPhee, that callous killer, must have laughed when the witching hour approached and he heard the screams of eight fine

THOROUGHBRED HORSES

as they burned to death in the devouring flames that engulfed the McCord barn, aye, and for a while threatened to spread to the very ranch house itself. After the flames were quenched it was seen that the barn was a total loss and our intrepid reporter found Mr. Trace McCord and his loving, supportive son

Too Upset to Speak.

But our bold local lawman, Marshal Tim Lithgow, was much more vocal as he condemned the crime as "the wanton act of a desperate criminal out for revenge." When asked by our scribe if Jamie McPhee — oh, how we need to rinse out our mouths whenever we mention that vile name — was the offender, the marshal said, "There can be no other. It was he who used

Deadly Coal Oil

to set the blaze and within a very few minutes burn the barn to the ground." Marshal Lithgow says McPhee is in the company of a

Desperate Character

who goes by the name of Samuel Flintlock and is well known to law enforcement agencies throughout the Territory. But be warned: Both McPhee and Flintlock are armed and dangerous, so let Marshal Lith-

162

gow and his gallant deputies handle their arrest and bring them in to face the "tender mercies" of the hangman.

THE TIMES raises our collective hat to our lionhearted lawmen and we declare most fervently, "Up and at 'em, lads!"

Two men read the newspaper that morning, one with anger, the other with growing concern.

Lucian Tweddle was enraged.

He sat behind his desk and squeezed his morning cigar, his small, yellow teeth bared in a snarl. Damn it! This was not at all what he wanted. The stupid newspaper should have placed the blame for the fire squarely on Brendan O'Rourke and his Circle-O, obviously a savage act of retaliation for the killing of their ranch cook. But since O'Rourke was a wealthy and influential man, the nonentity Jamie McPhee was an easier and less litigious target for the rag's editor.

However, despite his frustration, Tweddle knew he'd overreached and made a bad mistake. He'd acted way too hastily.

Trace McCord wouldn't link the burning barn to O'Rourke either. Why should he?

Tweddle knew he should have cast more shadows of suspicion into the minds of both ranchers before he'd made his move. Better if he'd ordered Tate and Litton to kill a Circle-O drover out on the range somewhere, then a few days later burn the McCord barn.

That would have been . . . what was the phrase? . . . oh yeah, a casus belli, a justification for war, and then McCord and O'Rourke, each blaming the other, would have at it.

Tweddle cursed under his breath. Yes, he'd made an amateur's mistake. He would not make another.

The banker had trouble moving his massive bulk and it took him several tries before he managed to heave himself out of his chair.

Life was unfair to him, always had been, and now with this setback Tweddle felt he needed a shoulder to cry on. He needed Nancy Pocket. Whores slept late, but he'd wake her.

Nancy had been in the profession long enough that she didn't care if he abused her. She knew he needed a release from his business worries and if he slapped her around a bit, well, she understood. God knows, he paid her plenty to take a few bruises.

Tweddle smoothed his fussy little waxed

mustache and was about to take his hat from the rack when the office door opened and a clerk stuck his head inside.

"There's a person named O'Hara here to see you, Mr. Tweddle," the man said.

Irritated, the banker said, "Show him in." Then, when O'Hara appeared, "You should have been here yesterday."

The breed made no answer.

"Did Horn Tate tell you what I want?"

"He did. How much?"

"Fifty now. Fifty when Jamie McPhee is dead."

"Hundred now. Hundred when McPhee is dead."

O'Hara's face was impassive as though carved out of mahogany like a cigar store Indian. He wore two guns, butt forward in flapped cavalry holsters, a buckskin war shirt, beautifully braided and beaded, and over that a black frock coat, frayed at the collar and cuffs.

"I could hire another damned Indian for fifty cents a day," Tweddle said.

O'Hara nodded. "Then hire one."

The breed turned to leave but Tweddle stopped him.

He'd already made one hasty mistake and didn't want to make a second.

"All right, O'Hara, a hundred now and

the rest when McPhee is dead."

"In gold," O'Hara said.

Tweddle sighed and waddled to the office safe. He opened the steel door, removed a box and, his hand like a pudgy bear claw, scooped out a few coins. He piled the five double eagles on his desk then used a wooden pointer to slide them toward O'Hara. Touching a breed's hand would have horrified him.

O'Hara, well used to such things, smiled slightly as he picked up the coins.

"How will you play this, O'Hara?" Tweddle said. "Well and soon, I hope."

"I told Tate where to meet me," O'Hara said.

"Spare me the details. Just make sure he finds and kills McPhee."

O'Hara turned and left.

The breed would do his job, Tweddle knew that, so now it all depended on Tate and Litton. He smiled and saliva gathered at the corners of his wide mouth. It was high time to wake Nancy Pocket.

Clifton Wraith folded the newspaper and placed it on the table beside him, his appetite for the bacon and eggs on his plate suddenly gone. He stared intently at the cascade of headlines about the barn burning, as though by sheer willpower he could change them.

But the Pinkerton recalled a verse he'd memorized about such a thing, penned by the poet Mr. Edward FitzGerald:

The Moving Finger writes; and, having writ,
Moves on: nor all thy Piety nor Wit
Shall lure it back to cancel half a Line,
Nor all thy Tears wash out a Word of it.

What was done was done and he couldn't undo any of it.

"It's just a terrible business, isn't it?"

The teenaged waitress, the belle of the Longhorn Café, glanced at the newspaper as she refilled Wraith's coffee cup.

"I hope they catch that awful Jamie McPhee," she said. "He always looked shifty to me, hunched over at his desk in the bank from dawn to dusk, never seeing the light of day."

"It is indeed a terrible business," the Pinkerton said. "All those fine horses killed. A real tragedy."

The waitress, Wraith believed her name was Evangeline, held the pot in front of her like a shield and said, "A most singular thing is that McPhee danced in the flames with demons as the horses burned and there were devil horns on his head. A customer told me that."

Evangeline fluttered her beautiful blue eyes, then, "I'm so afraid."

"I'm sure you'll be quite safe in town, young lady," Wraith said. "Marshal Lithgow and his deputies are standing a most vigilant guard."

"Oh, I do hope so," the girl said. "But all the same I'll sleep with my holy rosary under my pillow tonight."

She carried her sooty coffeepot to another table and left Wraith to his worries.

Of course it was nonsense that Jamie McPhee had burned the McCord barn. He was with Sam Flintlock, a man who came straight at an enemy with a gun in his hand. He wouldn't sanction something as . . . treacherous.

The Pinkerton poked at his eggs with his fork. But how about the crusty old Comanche-fighter Brendan O'Rourke? No. The rancher was cut from the same cloth as Flintlock. If he had a beef with Trace McCord he'd come a-shooting. Then who?

Wraith let go of his fork and heads turned in his direction as it clattered onto his plate. He didn't notice. The Pinkerton was deep in thought, sure the murders of Polly Mallory, the Circle-O cook and the barn fire were related. His gut instinct told him that one man was behind all three events, and it wasn't Jamie McPhee. The young man wasn't smart enough and he didn't have the sand for such violence. Wraith figured he must look for a man who was ruthless, a born killer with a cool, calculating, scheming mind without conscience, a man who'd much to gain if this part of the territory erupted into open war and terrorized the population . . . people like Evangeline with her rosary.

"You don't like your breakfast?" the girl asked him.

The Pinkerton blinked like a man waking from sleep. He smiled. "It's just fine. I'm not hungry, I guess."

Evangeline nodded, and put her hand on Wraith's shoulder. "We're all upset," she said. "This town won't be the same again until Jamie McPhee is caught."

"Until somebody is caught," Wraith said.

CHAPTER TWENTY-ONE

The afternoon sky tinted red when Horn Tate and Willie Litton met O'Hara on the bend of a small creek midway between Dripping Vat Mountain and the eastern slope of Bobcat Ridge.

"We seen your smoke just like you laid it our fer us, O'Hara," Tate said. He shoved a pint bottle of whiskey in the breed's face. "Want a slug or three?"

The breed grunted, ignored the bottle, and poured water from his canteen over his small signal fire.

"You will kill McPhee and Flintlock today?" he said finally.

"Just lead us to them," Tate said. "We'll get the job done."

"It should be easy. They're sick," O'Hara said. "Both very sick."

Tate frowned. "Sick with what?" he said.

O'Hara shrugged. "Bad food, maybe. Tainted water. Both bring on the fevers."

O'Hara's fingers moved to his throat. "Flintlock has a thunderbird here. The thunderbird is the messenger of God and it carried bad medicine to him, maybe so."

"Here, it ain't catchin', is it?" Litton said, his simian face worried.

"No. But now you can kill McPhee and Sam Flintlock as they lie abed."

"They're asleep, like?" Litton said. "Down with the fever?"

O'Hara nodded. "Asleep all the time. You can cut their throats" — he drew a forefinger across his neck and smiled — "and they'll never wake up."

Tate and Litton exchanged glances.

"We caught us a break, Horn," Litton said. "Now we don't need to stake out the cabin until we can get a shot."

"Injun, are you sure Flintlock is sick?" Tate said. "You wouldn't be joshing me now, would you?"

"He will die soon, and McPhee with him," O'Hara said.

Tate's gaze searched the breed's face, but the man's features were set and hard, like chiseled stone. "Then let's get it done," Tate said. "We can be back in Open Sky by dark and hit the saloons one by one."

"With two thousand dollars to spend,"

Litton said. "Man oh man, we'll be like kings."

"Add another five hundred added to that, Willie," Tate said.

"You be real careful when you do it to me, Horn," Litton said. "I don't want to get plugged too serious with all that dough to spend."

"A scratch, Willie. That's all. I promise. You know I can shoot real good."

Litton smiled and nodded. "Yee-hah!" he yelled. "Then let's go an' cut some throats."

O'Hara pointed the way and the two thugs, whooping and hollering, kicked their horses into a gallop. Then they broke into song, bellowing "Dirty Dolly and Her Mama" at the top of their lungs.

There was no breeze and smoke rose straight as a string from the cabin chimney. The day was shading into evening but inside the lamps remained unlit and the glow of burning logs cast scarlet shadows on the windows.

"Not too sick to light a fire," Horn Tate said, his face sour. "I don't like the look of that."

"I guess McPhee lit the fire," O'Hara said. "Flintlock is so sick he can't get out of his bunk. He lies there hoping for death to take him." He placed a hand on his belly, bent over and made retching sounds. "Flintlock sick as a poisoned pig."

The three men sat their horse within the pines and Tate, always careful and suspicious, studied the cabin.

"I don't see any sign of life," Litton said.

"Me neither," Tate said. "But the smoke still bothers me."

"You can deal with McPhee if he's still on his feet," O'Hara said.

"Damn it. I'll say it again: Are you sure about Flintlock?" Tate said. "Is he really as sick as you say? I don't want to bust in there and find him standing."

"He's a dead man," O'Hara said. "Don't let a dead man put the crawl on you, Tate."

Tate's anger flared and his eyes got ugly. "Nobody, and I mean nobody, puts the crawl on Horn Tate," he said.

He swung out of the saddle and drew his Colt. Litton, his grinning face eager, followed suit.

"Hell, I'm gonna enjoy this," Litton said.

"Yes," O'Hara said. "Enjoy it well."

O'Hara, still mounted, rode after the two men at a discreet distance, a faint smile playing around the corners of his mouth. He watched Tate and Litton step quietly to

173

the door.

As far as O'Hara could tell, they hadn't been seen.

The sky was hung with red, jade and amber bunting and among the pines an early owl hooted and fussed. The thin air smelled of wood smoke and the coming night.

Horn Tate held his Colt at shoulder level, the muzzle pointed upward. He leaned back, raised his booted right foot and kicked in the cabin door. Roaring, he rushed inside and Litton followed.

A second ticked past . . . then another . . .

Boom!

O'Hara smiled. He recognized the emphatic statement of a Hawken. It was a devastating weapon in the close confines of a cabin.

Inside furniture crashed and glass shattered. A man yelled. Then followed the rapid, racketing roar of revolvers. A shriek of pain . . .

And afterward a hollow silence.

A few moments passed and a mist of gray gunsmoke drifted out of the cabin door.

Horn Tate emerged clumsily from the smoke like a man with his legs entangled in a rope. He clutched at his belly and his eyes moved to O'Hara.

"Gut-shot," he said, black blood in his mouth.

Tate dropped to his knees, his face a twisted mask of agony, his eyes still on O'Hara. "You sold us down the river," he said. "You damned, lying half-breed."

"Never trust a part-Pawnee," O'Hara said. "His Indian half will lie to a white man every time."

Tate cursed and tried to raise his Colt but the effort was beyond him. He pitched forward and fell onto his face, all the life that was in him gone.

Sam Flintlock stepped out of the cabin, gun in hand. He saw O'Hara and scowled. "You in on this?" he said. "Say you are and I'll drop you right where you stand."

"I led them here, Flintlock, to open the ball," O'Hara said. "I figured even you could finish it."

"Damn you fer a low-down skunk, O'Hara. You could have gotten me killed," Flintlock said. "Those two boys busted in without a howdy-do hunting for my scalp."

·"Seemed like, when I spoke to them," O'Hara said. "They seemed quite keen to put a bullet into you. Where's the other one?"

"Inside, dead. When I saw his drawn iron

I scattered his brains with the Hawken, then I done for t'other with the Colt."

"Is McPhee hurt?"

"Yeah, he's hurt, hurt that the chessboard got upended when he was winning for a change."

"So that's why you were so quiet," O'Hara said. "Playing checkers while you should have been out scouting around."

"It was chess. Who hired them, O'Hara?"

"I'm tired of saving your skin, Flintlock. I think you should get out of the bodyguard business. I think you might prosper in the hardware business, selling nails and stuff."

"Who hired them?" Flintlock's eyes hardened.

"I can't tell you," O'Hara said. "My treachery toward a paying client only goes so far."

"Who were they?" Flintlock said.

"The one you gut-shot went by the name Horn Tate and —"

"The other is Willie Litton. I've heard of them, a couple of dark alley back shooters. Why does your client want me dead?"

"He don't really give a damn about you, Flintlock. It's McPhee's scalp he wants. You're just in the way, that's all."

"You gonna try and give McPhee to him, O'Hara?" Flintlock said. His Colt was still in his gun hand and he had the kill glitter in his eyes.

"Hell, isn't that just like a white man," O'Hara said. "I've saved your life twice and you're still ready to throw down on me and shoot me down like a dog."

"Like you, I'm protecting my client."

"I wasn't hired to kill McPhee, only to lead Tate and Litton here. I told them you were abed, as sick as a colicky pup. That's why you took them boys so easy."

"It wasn't easy. Tate was good with a gun and he come mighty close."

"So you got mad because he shaded you and shot him in the belly for spite."

"Something like that. Light and set and have a cup of coffee."

"I'll pass. I'm not your enemy, Flintlock, but I'm not your friend."

"Then stay the hell away from me, O'Hara."

The breed smiled. "Yup, that's all the thanks I'm going to get for saving your hide twice."

"The jury is still out on that," Flintlock said. "Just remember this —"

"I eagerly listen for the wise white man's words," O'Hara said.

"After I plant these two I'll have four men buried on this property," Flintlock said.

"But there's always plenty of room for a fifth."

O'Hara's smile was as fragile as it was fleeting. "Know your real enemy, Flintlock," he said. "I think old Barnabas is right."

"About what?"

"That you're an idiot."

O'Hara turned his horse and rode into the shadowed evening.

Flintlock watched him go, his face thoughtful.

CHAPTER TWENTY-TWO

"The trouble with you, McPhee, is that you don't know your real enemy," Sam Flintlock said.

"You mean the man who hired these two," Jamie McPhee said, nodding to the bodies that lay on the ground beside the graves he and Flintlock had almost finished.

"Yeah, that's what I mean. How come he wants you dead so badly?"

"The whole town of Open Sky wants me dead," McPhee said.

"When a man goes to the trouble and expense of hiring two killers, he particularly wants you dead."

"Who could he be?" McPhee said.

"See, you don't know your enemies."

"Do you, Sam?"

Flintlock grinned and shook his head. "Hell, no, I don't," he said. "That is, if you leave out everybody in Open Sky."

A lantern flickered between the open

graves and spread a strange amber light. Night birds pecked at the first stars and heat lightning flashed to the north over distant mountains. The air smelled of burning lamp oil, damp earth and dead men.

After Tate and Litton were in their graves and covered with earth, McPhee said, "Have you anything to say?"

"No. Do you?"

"Well, may they rest in peace," McPhee said.

Flintlock nodded. "And I'm sure sorry for the gut-shot," he said. "I should have aimed higher. Amen."

"That about does it," McPhee said, slapping his hands together. He gathered up the shovels and the lantern.

As Flintlock reached the cabin he stopped. Old Barnabas sat cross-legged at the peak of the roof, juggling three bright red balls.

"Visitors coming in, Sam," he said. "Strange folks."

The old man let the three balls thud into his right hand, and then he was gone.

"What do you see up there, Sam?" McPhee said, glancing at the roof.

"Just looking at the sky. I don't see any sign of rain."

"No rain," McPhee said. "We'd smell it by now."

"We sure would," Flintlock said. Then he tilted his head and listened into the night. "What's that?" he said.

From the distance among the trees, the atmosphere carried a dim clanking, tinkling, chiming, jingling sound and Flintlock's skin crawled.

"What the hell is that?" he said.

"Look!" McPhee said, his voice breathless and urgent.

Two great, green eyes shone in the darkness, bright as stars, and relentlessly approached closer . . . and closer . . .

Flintlock stepped into the cabin and reappeared with his Winchester. He pulled the Colt from his waistband and tossed it to McPhee. "I don't know what that thing is, but if it comes this way just fire in its general direction," he said. "Got it?"

McPhee swallowed hard then nodded. "Maybe it's another infernal machine," he said.

Flintlock heard the thud of his heart in his ears. "Stand fast," he said, realizing how old-timey mountain man that sounded. He wiped his sweaty trigger hand on his pants but his mouth was as dry as mummy dust.

The eyes drew closer . . . brighter . . . and the chiming got louder, like a vibrating stack of cheap tin trays.

"What the hell is that?" McPhee said.

Flintlock made no answer. He didn't know.

Slowly . . . noisily . . . the strange presence closed the distance . . .

Then, as though the darkness had parted like a stage curtain, it appeared in a space between the pines . . . an apparition the like of which Flintlock had never seen.

It was a wagon, vaguely Chinese in appearance, and large, round paper lanterns shimmered with green radiance on either side. The wagon seemed loaded inside and out with pots and pans and other kitchenware that clattered and clanged with every turn of the wheels.

A big gray draft horse, its tufted hooves as large as soup plates, strained mightily in the traces and a small black-and-white dog trotted silently alongside.

Flintlock made out the dark silhouettes of two people up on the seat and he raised the muzzle of his rifle.

"You in the wagon, stop right there and state your purpose!" he yelled into the gloom. "There's a passel of shooting going on around here."

"We're merely passing through," a man's voice answered. "No need for such hostility, old chap."

"Then come on in, real slow," Flintlock said.

"That's the only speed my horse has, I'm afraid," the man said.

"Deuced impertinence if you ask me." This from a woman, the voice young, high and pleasant but obviously irritated.

"Now, now, Ruth," the man said. "The gentleman is within his rights to demand information from traveling strangers. For all he knows we could be desperate brigands."

"He should be horsewhipped," the woman said. "Threatening his betters with violence is unforgivable."

Flintlock's anger, always on a hair trigger, exploded. "Git the hell in here," he yelled. "And keep your hands where I can see them."

"Do as he says, Father," the woman called Ruth said. "We're obviously dealing with a violent ruffian."

"Walk on," the man said to the gray, and the big horse lurched into motion.

Flintlock turned to McPhee. "Get the lantern," he said.

But when the wagon stopped outside the cabin with a reverberating clangor the swaying paper lanterns at the four corners of the dray splashed pools of green-tinted light that lit up the night for yards around.

The little dog planted his feet and barked at Flintlock, not liking what he saw and obviously considering some ankle biting.

But McPhee held his own lantern high, the forgotten Colt hanging loose at his side, and his jaw dropped as he beheld what he would later describe as "a wonder of the age."

CHAPTER TWENTY-THREE

"My name is Sir Arthur Ward and this lovely young lady is my adopted daughter, Ruth," the Englishman said. "I can't tell you how nice it is to meet you, Mr. Flintlock."

"Call me Sam now we're acquainted," Flintlock said. "This feller here with his eyes popping out and his chin hitting his belt buckle is Jamie McPhee."

"How droll," Ruth said, smiling. " 'Chin hitting his belt buckle.' How exquisitely whimsical."

"Very pleased to meet you too," McPhee said, blushing.

His eyes were fixed on Ruth, like a man who'd never met a stunningly beautiful, eighteen-year-old Chinese girl before in his life.

"May we come inside?" Sir Arthur said. "The night grows cool."

Before Flintlock could speak, McPhee said, "Yes, yes, please do."

■ ■ ■ ■

"More tea, Sam," Sir Arthur said, lifting the pot from the table.

Now pushing sixty, the Englishman remained a handsome man with sky blue eyes, thick yellow hair, graying at the temples, and a clipped mustache in the British military fashion. He wore a bright red Chinese robe decorated with blue dragons and a peculiar, at least to Flintlock, round hat with a tassel in the same shade as the robe.

"Yeah, please. It's good," Flintlock said.

"It's Chinese green tea," Ruth said. "Excellent for the health of your heart."

Flintlock smiled. "You don't think me a violent ruffian any longer, Miss Ward, huh?" he said.

The girl had the good grace to blush. "First impressions are often misleading," Ruth said. "I took you for a typical frontier tough. But now I think you have a little more breeding than that."

"I was raised by mountain men," Flintlock said. "They didn't have any breeding, at least none that showed."

"How interesting for you, Sam," Sir Arthur said. "You must have learned a great deal. Those lads were an intrepid, well-traveled bunch, and very brave."

"I learned that a mountain is always farther away than it looks. It's always higher than it looks and it's always harder to climb than it looks."

The Englishman laughed. "Is that all?"

"No, I learned other things, but the man who taught me most of what I know was only slightly less stupid than myself."

Another laugh, then Sir Arthur said, "I'm sure you sell yourself short, Sam. And your teacher."

They sat in the luxurious cabin where the Englishman and his daughter made themselves quite at home after supplying tea, a teapot and tiny porcelain cups that all but vanished in Flintlock's big hand.

"Forgive me for asking this, Sir Arthur, but why are you so oddly dressed?" McPhee said, his face guileless.

The Englishman smiled. "It's quite a boring story, I'm afraid."

"We'd still like to hear it," Flintlock said, shifting in his chair as he glanced at Sir Arthur's gaudy robe.

"Well, let me start by saying that I've always had a keen interest in the culinary arts and when the British army posted me to China at the end of the Second Opium

War I fell madly in love with Oriental cooking," the Englishman said. He poured more tea, then continued, "I was ordered to Kowloon as the adjutant of the 45th of Foot and there, insofar as my duties would allow, continued my studies: rice, soy and noodles mostly, but also herbs and seasonings."

"It was during Sir Arthur's time in Kowloon that he adopted me from the Moonlight Camellia Blossom," Ruth said.

Entranced, McPhee said, "How beautiful. That was the name of the orphanage?"

"No," the girl said. "That was the name of the whorehouse."

"Indeed," Sir Arthur said. "Well, shortly after I adopted Ruth my regiment received orders to ship out for India. Now, though Indian cuisine has its charms, it lacks the delicacy of flavor one finds in the Chinese, so I resigned my commission at once and went on with my exploration of Oriental culinary arts."

The Englishman glanced down at his robe. "This was given to me by the famous Chinese chef Wang Qiang after he sampled my winter melon soup. There was a rumor current in Hong Kong that when Wang realized he could never match my artistry he committed suicide."

"We don't know if that's true or not,"

Ruth said. "Certainly, after he tasted Sir Arthur's soup Wang Qiang was never heard of again."

Jamie McPhee was fascinated. His fixed gaze caressed every delicate feature of Ruth's face and lingered on her beautiful almond eyes.

Sam Flintlock, however, whose culinary taste ran all the way from fried steak to salt pork and beans, was less than enthralled. "So how come you're here . . . um . . ."

"Arthur is just fine, Sam. I inherited my knighthood, you know. And I've done nothing much to deserve it since."

"Not much call for Chinese grub around these parts," Flintlock said.

"Ah, but that's where you're wrong, Mr. Flintlock," Ruth said.

Sir Arthur smiled. "After I thought I'd learned all I could in Cathay, Ruth and I decided to travel to the United States, where people are much more adventurous about food than they are in England."

"Are they?" McPhee said, eager as a boy.

"That has been my experience, dear chap," Sir Arthur said. "I worked as a chef in New York —"

"And did very well, I must say," Ruth said.

"In a modest way, you understand," the Englishman said, nonetheless nodding as

189

though his daughter had more fairly stated the case. "But I never lost my sense of adventure and the lure of the wide-open Western territories beckoned."

"Not the Oklahoma Territory," Flintlock said. "Folks around here don't cotton to Chinese grub."

"But that's where you're wrong, Mr. Flintlock," Ruth said. "As soon as the tracks arrive, Sir Arthur will prosper."

Flintlock's face showed his puzzlement. "I'm not catching your drift, young lady," he said.

"New railroads are being built all over the West, Sam," Sir Arthur said.

"And for the past few years we've followed the tracks," Ruth said.

The Englishman read Flintlock's face and said, "My dear sir, who lays the railroad tracks? Why, the Chinese of course. And the Paddies too, certainly, and believe it or not your typical Irishman has a strong liking for Oriental cuisine."

"I heard a rumor about a railroad being built way out here," Flintlock said. "But it's only a big story. You took a long trip for nothing."

"I can assure you that the Atchison, Topeka and Santa Fe plans to lay tracks in a month, if the Union Pacific doesn't beat them to it," Sir Arthur said.

An alarm bell started ringing at the edge of Flintlock's consciousness.

"Who told you this?" he said.

"My father has shares in both companies and they keep him well informed," the Englishman said. He smiled. "My aged parent does not approve of my lifestyle, so in answer to your question, my younger brother told me. As well he might. He runs the family estate in Kent and fervently desires to keep me well away."

"Through the rather miserable stipend he allows father and me," Ruth said.

"Five hundred pounds a year is nothing to be sneezed at, my dear," Sir Arthur said.

"You should have ten times that, Father," Ruth said. "The estate prospers."

"You will stay in Open Sky until the railroad crews arrive, Sir Arthur?" McPhee said.

"I've heard of that particular town," the Englishman said. "But no. I heartily dislike the confinement of hotel rooms so we'll find a pleasant place to camp and there we will wait."

"Around here?" McPhee said, hope shining in his eyes.

"Yes, if we can find a peaceful place near water," Sir Arthur said.

Flintlock hadn't been listening until that last. Now he laid down his cup, his face solemn.

"Arthur, you've told me what someone else has already told me, and if what you and him say about the railroads is true, and now I got no reason to believe it isn't, there won't be a peaceful place around these parts," he said.

"And why not, for heaven's sake?" the Englishman said.

"Because I believe somebody is trying to start a range war, and we'll be right in the middle of it," Flintlock said.

CHAPTER TWENTY-FOUR

"Nobody knows better than me that we took a big loss when the barn went up, boss," Frisco Maddox said. "But nobody in town blames it on Brendan O'Rourke."

"Of course they don't," Trace McCord said. "Hell, O'Rourke's cook got shot. I've threatened to plug a trail cook plenty of times, but I never actually did it."

"I reckon whoever burned our barn also shot the Circle-O cook," Maddox said.

"Jeez, Frisco, I could never have worked that out by myself," McCord said. "For God's sake, don't state the obvious."

"Sorry, boss. But try as I might, I can't get a handle on who it could be."

"O'Rourke's just mean enough to shoot his own cook," McCord said. "The man burned the biscuits or something."

Maddox smiled. "But you don't really believe that, do you?"

McCord shook his head. "No, I guess I don't."

The rancher stood in the stirrups and studied the land around him.

"The range still looks good on account of the rain we've had. If we don't get a bad drought we'll have calves on the ground."

"Seems like," Maddox said, the corners of his eyes wrinkling as he stared against the glare of the sun into distant shaggy acres where placid Herefords grazed.

Then after a few moments, "You should have brought the boy, boss."

"He's worthless, Frisco. I know it, you know it and he knows it. Sometimes I think I should've drowned him at birth or after he killed his mother with worry and grief."

"Harsh words, boss," Maddox said. "You can't blame Steve for what happened to Martha. She was very sick."

"You've told me that before, Frisco. Don't tell it to me again."

McCord took a silver cheroot case from his shirt pocket, selected one and then passed the case to his foreman.

The two men smoked in silence for a spell, then Maddox said, "I got an idea, boss."

"About what?"

"About Steve."

"I thought we'd done talking about him."

"Just one more thing."

"Then say it. I'll half listen."

"I got kinfolk who have a ranch down on the Rio Grande near Laredo way. It's a fair-size spread, about a hundred thousand acres with good summer grazing and some broken land for winter pasture."

"How many cattle?"

"In a good year, a cow and calf to five acres."

McCord nodded, approving. Then, "So what's all this got to do with Steve?"

"Cousin Judd Rawlings hires only vaqueros coming across the border from Mexico. They're good cattlemen, fast with the gun and blade, as rough as cobs and as tough as they come."

"I'm still not catching your drift, Frisco."

"Boss, we send young Steve down to Webb County and cousin Judd puts him to work with his vaqueros. They'll make a man of him quicker than . . . well, in no time. Depend on it. Steve will be a better hand with cattle and an hombre with bark on him when he rides back to Oklahoma after say, three, four years out on the range."

"Like finishing school, huh?"

"You could say that. But with no book learning and a sight tougher teachers."

"He's had enough book learnin' already,"

McCord said.

The big rancher was silent for a while, turned in on himself, and Maddox said, "It was only an idea."

"No, it's a plan," McCord said. "I've been around vaqueros once or twice and they don't take any damned sass or back talk."

"That has also been my experience," Maddox said.

"How do we play it?"

"It's easy, boss. I write Steve a letter of introduction to cousin Judd, put the boy on a good hoss and point him south. Texas is hard to miss."

Trace McCord kneed his mount into motion.

"Then write your letter, Frisco. He'll leave tomorrow at first light and I'll be rid of him."

Steve McCord let his Winchester's sights drift away from Frisco Maddox's chest.

It would be a sure shot all right, and Maddox was a broad target, but the young man hesitated to pull the trigger. Frisco had always been kind to him and had even encouraged his poetry. The big foreman often acted as a barrier between himself and his father when Pa went off on a rant and threatened to have him horsewhipped for some perceived offense or other.

It would be a real pity to kill Frisco, even though it could start the range war he needed.

But there were other considerations.

A narrow trail led up the crest of the rise where he lay, and if Pa let Frisco lie on the trail and followed the smoke drift he could get to the top of the ridge in a couple of minutes.

Steve shook his head. Too close. He wouldn't shoot today. It was too risky.

He let the sights slide back to Frisco. It was a good feeling to have a man's life, all he was and all he was planning to be, right in the palm of his fist.

All he had to do was squeeze . . . the trigger, that is . . . and poor Frisco would soon be making his excuses to Saint Peter at the gate. That last made Steve smile. He was highly amused, and such a fine feeling it was . . . the power over life and death.

His pa kicked his horse into motion and Steve laid the sights on him. But only for a moment.

"You have to wait your turn, Trace," he whispered. "The time isn't right."

He and Lucian Tweddle hadn't yet worked out the details of his takeover of the McCord ranch, but he knew how it would end.

After Pa realized he'd lost everything, Steve would put a bullet into his guts then piss on him as he lay screaming on the ground.

The youngster flopped onto his back and watched clouds, baby clouds, he imagined, chase one another across the flat, blue expanse of the sky.

He picked a pimple on his chin until it bled and slowly came to a decision.

It was time to talk to Lucian again. He needed his advice . . .

On who lived and who died.

CHAPTER TWENTY-FIVE

"You have to admit, Sam, what Sir Arthur did with some scrag ends of beef and a few herbs and peppers was almost miraculous," Jamie McPhee said. He shook his head in wonder. "What an elegant meal! Fit for an emperor."

"It was all right, I guess," Sam Flintlock said. "Now turn the salt pork before it burns and cut them green parts off."

The morning sun bladed into the cabin and made dust motes dance, and outside the shadow of a hunting hawk flashed across the open ground like an obsidian arrow-head.

McPhee flipped over the slices of pork, then talking through a smile said, "Of course, the presence of beautiful Ruth added immensely to the dining experience."

Flintlock, more than a little hungover and sour, grunted, "Be glad the subject of Polly Mallory never came up."

McPhee frowned. "Sam, I'm sure Ruth would have listened and then told me she was certain of my innocence."

"Maybe," Flintlock said. He stood behind McPhee. "Now remove the salt pork and cut out them green spots like I already told you then crack six eggs into the fat."

"How come you never cook?" McPhee said.

"Because bad cooks have delayed human development long enough and I got no desire to add to it."

McPhee, his voice heavy with a sigh, said, "How do you want your eggs?"

"Done," Flintlock said.

After breakfast Sam Flintlock took his coffee outside and sat in the sun, the thunderbird tattoo across his throat vivid in the morning light.

From the warehouse barn he heard the rat-tat-tat of a small hammer as McPhee tried to get the infernal machine's steam engine working. The young man had said at breakfast that steam engines would one day power hansom cabs and the like, replacing horses. Recalling that idiot remark, Flintlock grumpily shook his head as he built a cigarette.

As though anything would or could ever

replace horses. They'd still be dropping turds by the ton on our city streets a hundred years from now. Flintlock drew deep on the cigarette and leaned his throbbing head against the cabin wall. He closed his eyes and let himself drift.

The rap of McPhee's hammer receded . . . the burned-out cigarette dropped from Flintlock's fingers . . . jays quarreled in the trees . . . a deer nosed through the pines, lifted its head then turned and bounded away . . . lazy flies droned . . .

And Sam Flintlock dreamed of running with horses.

Horses!

Flintlock woke with a start and grabbed the rifle he'd propped beside his chair.

A dogcart drawn by a lathered gray skirted the tree line and jolted over rocky, broken ground, coming toward him at a smart canter. The small, slight figure of Frank Constable was up in the seat, cracking a whip over the gray's back. The man looked grim.

After he drew rein, the lawyer looked down at Flintlock. "Trouble," he said.

"Light and set," Flintlock said. "I've got coffee on the bile."

"No time," Constable said. "Get your horse. Don't dillydally now."

But Flintlock was not a man to be rushed. "Explain yourself," he said.

The lawyer clicked his tongue in irritation. "Clifton Wraith has been shot," he said. "He's asking for you."

"Where is he?"

"Open Sky of course. At the hotel."

"He hurt bad?"

"How bad is a bullet in the belly, Mr. Flintlock? Now saddle up. There's no time to be lost. The man's at death's door and suffering terribly."

"I'll get my horse," Flintlock said.

As he passed the open door of the building that housed the infernal machine, he yelled, "McPhee! Get out here!"

The young man ran after him, shouting questions.

Flintlock answered only one.

"Cliff Wraith has been gut-shot."

"Oh God, no," McPhee said.

"Oh God, yes. Help me saddle my hoss."

A couple of minutes later Flintlock and McPhee stopped at Constable's wagon.

"Mr. Constable, can it be true?" the young man said, his face pale.

"Think," the lawyer said. "Would I drive all the way out here to tell you a thing that wasn't true? Use your head, boy."

"Rifle," Flintlock said.

McPhee passed the Winchester to Flintlock, who slid it into the boot under his knee.

"What is to become of me?" McPhee said. "Mr. Wraith was the only hope I had of clearing my name. I'm in terrible trouble."

"Don't build houses on a bridge you haven't crossed yet, Mr. McPhee," Constable said. "You must go to ground while we're gone. Come now, Mr. Flintlock. Let us cast the die."

CHAPTER TWENTY-SIX

The sun was at its highest point in the sky and the day was already hot when Sam Flintlock followed the dogcart into Open Sky. He hadn't mentioned the burned body in the barn, figuring to hold that for later.

"You go on into the hotel, Mr. Flintlock," Frank Constable said. "Room 12. I'll follow shortly."

Flintlock had expected open hostility from the citizens of Open Sky, but it seemed that every woman and able-bodied man in town had crowded into the Rocking Horse saloon. Judging from the press of people at the door, inside was standing room only.

Flintlock nodded in the direction of the saloon.

"Is that about Cliff?"

"Hell no," Constable said, his face bitter. "It's about Beau Hunt. The fools are watching him partake of lunch, as they did his breakfast."

He looked at Flintlock with lusterless eyes. "A Texas draw fighter attracts an adoring crowd while a better man than he lies dying alone and in pain," he said.

Flintlock swung out of the saddle. "It's always the way of it," he said. "Even a cold-blooded killer like Wild Bill Longley drew a crowd of admirers everywhere he went."

But Flintlock had talked into the wind.

Constable had already wheeled his cart around . . . and cut off a brewer's dray to the belligerent curses of its red-faced Teutonic driver.

After he stepped into the hotel lobby Flintlock stood for a few moments to let his eyes grow accustomed to the gloom. He was still nearly half blind when the clerk said, "What can I do for you?"

"Room 12," Flintlock said.

"Upstairs, last door on the left. But you can't go in there. Marshal Lithgow is interviewing the wounded man."

Flintlock nodded and began to climb the stairs.

"I said you can't go in there," the clerk said.

When Flintlock turned, his Colt was in his hand at eye level. "Are you going to give me trouble?"

The clerk, scowling and officious until

then, went rag-doll limp. "You have no trouble with me," he said.

"Glad to hear it," Flintlock said.

Behind the door of Room 12 Clifton Wraith lay on the brass bed, his teeth gritted against pain that was beyond pain and well nigh impossible to bear.

Marshal Tom Lithgow sat in a chair beside the bed, his face drawn as he watched a man dying hard. The room smelled of blood and a man's guts.

When Sam Flintlock stepped inside, Lithgow's gaze went to the Colt in the other man's waistband and then to eyes turned to stone. "He's been asking for you," the marshal said. "He's had morphine but it don't do a whole lot for a gut-shot man."

Flintlock nodded. "Who did it?" he said.

"I don't know."

Flintlock sat on the bed. It squealed under his weight. Across the road at the saloon a woman laughed.

"I'm here, Cliff," he said. Then, "It's Sam Flintlock."

Wraith raised his right hand. It had no fingernails. "Sam . . ."

"I'm listening, Cliff."

"They hurt me real bad, Sam."

Flintlock glanced at Wraith's bloody hand.

206

"I know they did," he said.

"Who done this to you?" Lithgow said. "Give me names, by God. I'll gut shoot every last mother's son of them."

"Sam . . . listen . . ."

"Go ahead, Cliff."

"The boy . . . Jamie . . . innocent . . ." Blood filled Wraith's mouth.

"Easy, Cliff, easy," Flintlock said. "Say it slow."

"Guilty . . . big man . . ."

Wraith's back arched as a wave of pain hit him.

"Oh, merciful God," he whispered. "Sweet Jesus, let this cup pass from me."

Flintlock held Wraith's hand. "I know McPhee is innocent. Now pass on, Cliff," he said. "Just let yourself go."

"Get . . . big . . . man . . ."

"Who is he?" Flintlock said.

"O Jesu!" Wraith shrieked, his eyes wide.

And then his soul rushed from him.

Flintlock raised cold eyes to the marshal. "Don't say a word, Lithgow. Not a word. Not yet. Not if you value your life."

The lawman turned away from the bed, stepped to the window and opened it wide.

"For Clifton Wraith's spirit to pass," he said.

After several minutes ticked away, Flintlock rose from the bed and pulled the bloody sheet over Wraith's face.

He spoke to Lithgow. "You heard him."

"About McPhee. Yes."

"Do you believe him?"

"I guess a dying man will tell the truth," the marshal said.

"A dying Pinkerton will tell the truth."

Lithgow said nothing.

"What does 'guilty big man' mean?" Flintlock said.

"I don't know. This town has plenty of big men, most of them guilty of something."

"Was Cliff tortured and killed in town? They pulled out his fingernails."

"No, not in Open Sky. A couple of drovers found him on the trail a mile west of here and brought him in," the marshal said.

Flintlock's face hardened. "Who do they work for, Tom?"

"Nobody. Just a couple of scrawny young punchers riding the grub line."

"I'll talk to them anyhow," Flintlock said. "Maybe —"

Someone tapped on the door. Flintlock answered it.

A man of medium height, grossly obese, stood sweating in the doorway. He was dressed in fashionable gray; a red cravat pinned in place with a diamond added a splash of gaudy color.

"My name is —"

"Come in, Mr. Tweddle," Lithgow said.

When Flintlock stepped aside, Tweddle waddled into the room, trailing an odor of sweat and cologne behind him like the track of a snail.

"Sam, this is Mr. Lucian Tweddle, the town's banker," Lithgow said.

Flintlock took an instant dislike to the man, his porcine face and crafty little eyes, but he managed a polite nod and a "Howdy."

"I know who you are, Flintlock," the banker said, looking the other man up and down with obvious disapproval and dislike. "I've heard the name before."

"What brings you here, Mr. Tweddle?" Lithgow said.

The fat man was an important and wealthy member of Open Sky society, so the marshal's tone had been suitably respectful.

"I just heard about poor Mr. Wraith's murder and I was told you were investigating, Marshal. Naturally I came over right away. In recent weeks Clifton and I had become friends."

Tweddle's eyes moved to the bed where Wraith lay as still as a marble effigy on top of a tomb. "Is that he?" Tweddle's face was anguished. "Oh, say that it's not Clifton."

He stepped to the bed and quickly twitched the sheet from the dead man's hollow, shadowed face.

That action surprised Flintlock. In his experience when someone, especially a friend, uncovers a dead man's face, he does it slowly, tentatively, with reverence, as though a little afraid of what he's about to see. Tweddle had no such reservations. He flicked the sheet from Wraith without a second thought, surely the action of a hard, unfeeling man and not the grieving friend he pretended to be?

"Yes, it's Clifton and cruelly done to death," Tweddle said.

He replaced the sheet with the same quick motion and looked at Lithgow. "We need a quick arrest on this, Tom," he said.

The marshal nodded. "I'll find the killer, Mr. Tweddle. You can count on it."

"His identity is patently obvious, is it not?" the banker said.

Lithgow and Flintlock exchanged puzzled glances, a thing Tweddle noticed.

"Come now, Tom," he said. "Everyone in Open Sky knows that Beau Hunt rode into town yesterday and immediately afterward Wraith was murdered. Hunt is a hired killer well known to the law in Texas so the connection is plain to see."

No *Clifton* this time, Flintlock noted. Just the coldly spoken *Wraith.*

"I'll talk to him, Mr. Tweddle," Lithgow said.

The lawman didn't lack sand but he seemed ill at ease. As Flintlock did, Lithgow knew the Beau was a man to be reckoned with.

"Talk be damned," Tweddle said, anger in his pouched, piggy eyes. "Arrest him on a suspicion of murder, Tom. Root him out of the saloon where he holds court, at gunpoint if need be. And then make him tell you who hired him. Hunt's kind will always spill the beans to save their own necks."

"I figured the killer was Jamie McPhee," the marshal said.

"Not this time. My bank clerks don't have the money to hire Texas draw fighters," Tweddle said. He hooked his thumbs in the armholes of his vest and looked pompous. "Someone else in this town has an agenda, the one who had Wraith murdered." The fat man gestured impatiently. "Arrest Hunt and force him to tell you who hired him. Do your duty, Marshal."

Flintlock realized Tweddle was railroading Lithgow into bracing Beau Hunt. He didn't know why this should be, but he decided to put a stop to it.

"I'll talk to him," he said.

The banker's eyes spat hate. "This is the marshal's business and none of yours, Flintlock," he said.

"Hunt and me go back a ways," Flintlock said.

"It's still none of your business."

"He'll listen to me."

"Bring in McPhee to face the hangman, Flintlock," the banker said. "That's all this town wants from you."

"Try to arrest the Beau and he'll kill you, Lithgow," Flintlock said.

"It is a mighty big coincidence," Lithgow said. "I mean Hunt being in town an' all."

"Beau Hunt wouldn't tear out a man's fingernails then gut-shoot him," Flintlock said.

"He's a hired killer," Tweddle said. His face was vicious. "Such men are capable of any atrocity."

Flintlock said, "He'd never take on a job that demands he shoot a middle-aged Pinkerton. Not his style, Tweddle."

"Mr. Tweddle to you."

"I'll be sure to remember that, Tweddle."

The banker turned to Lithgow, furious. "Marshal, do your duty," he said. "Arrest

Hunt now."

"Flintlock?" Lithgow said. "Will he lie down?"

"He'll kill you. He won't be arrested."

"Then what will I do?"

"Nothing right now. As I said, I'll talk to him."

Tweddle's face was so red it looked as though it might burst. Beside himself with rage, he said, "Marshal, arrest this man for obstructing justice."

"I won't be arrested either," Flintlock said.

"Uh-huh," Lithgow said. "Figured that."

Flintlock turned eyes as friendly as shotgun muzzles to Tweddle.

"Why do you want the marshal dead?"

"I want him to do his duty."

"You want Hunt to kill Lithgow. Why do you want the law out of the way so all-fired badly, Tweddle?"

"I won't be insulted."

"You didn't answer me."

"I don't bandy words with a two-bit outlaw."

"Then get the hell out of here."

Tweddle was angry enough to spit. He stepped to the door, then turned. "Flintlock, I'll see you and McPhee hung."

"Any time you want to come for us, come."

"Count on it. I will."

The banker stared hard at the flustered Lithgow, who shifted his weight from one foot to the other. "I want Beau Hunt dead or in jail, Marshal."

Tweddle stepped out of the door but the rank odor of his sweat and cologne lingered.

"Why does he want you out of the way, Lithgow?" Flintlock said.

"He doesn't."

"And birds don't fly."

"I don't know what he wants." The big marshal sighed. "Any way you size it up, I'm jiggered anyhow," he said. "On my best day I can't shade Beau Hunt."

"I'll talk to him," Flintlock said. "Hear what he has to say."

"I'll join you."

"No point in both of us getting killed."

"I'd feel cowardly and low down."

"You'd be alive." Flintlock smiled. "If Beau guns me, then lay for him in an alley and cut him in half with a scattergun, Lithgow."

"I sure will," the marshal said. He looked relieved.

"In the back, mind. That way you'll have an even chance."

Chapter Twenty-Seven

The sun had lowered a little and Sam Flintlock's shadow walked in step beside him like a black dwarf as they crossed the street. Heat lay on Open Sky like an anvil. The matrons would not come out to shop until early evening, the sporting crowd a couple of hours later. The boardwalks were deserted and the air smelled of dust and horse manure.

Flintlock, to appear less threatening, had left his Winchester in his room and carried only the Colt tucked into his waistband, the walnut handle high and handy. Paying a social call on Beau Hunt always called for a measure of caution.

The doors of the Rocking Horse were pinned open in the forlorn hope of catching an errant breeze and Nancy Pocket stood outside nursing a beer and a black eye.

Flintlock touched his hat and said, "Ma'am," as he stepped through the door

215

and Nancy said, "You went to West Point, huh?"

Smiling at the woman's jibe, Flintlock stepped into the saloon.

The crowd had thinned some, but there were still a couple of dozen men and a few women in the saloon. They watched Beau Hunt or watched one another watching Beau Hunt.

"Well, Sam Flintlock as ever was."

The man's voice came from a far corner to Flintlock's right.

"Howdy, Beau," he said.

The draw fighter sat with his back to the corner as was his habit, a hand of solitaire spread out in front of him on the table.

"Still on the buttermilk, I see," Flintlock said.

Hunt picked up the milk jug — with his left hand, Flintlock noted — and said, "Care for some?"

"Never touch the stuff."

Hunt, immaculately dressed, his chin shaven close and his magnificent mustache trimmed, ran a critical eye over Flintlock, from his battered hat to scuffed boots then lingered for a moment on his Colt. "Sam, you really must do something about your tailor," he said.

"Hell, I bought these pants new a year

ago," Flintlock said. "Or maybe it was two."

"Very commendable of you, Sam. A step in the right direction."

Hunt smiled and turned the silver gambler's signet on the little finger of his left hand.

"But the buckskin shirt really must go and I won't even mention the hat and your choice of footwear. As for your cologne, well, you aren't wearing any, are you?"

"I'm not here to discuss my wardrobe and how I smell, Beau."

"Oh, how disappointing. And I thought this was a social call."

"It's more serious than that."

"Oh dear."

Hunt pushed a chair forward with a polished, elastic-sided boot.

"Then you'd better take a seat, Sam."

Beau Hunt always carried an air of danger with him, as palpable as the expensive cologne he wore. At the moment his eyes were smiling, but they could change to ice in a moment. He carried a short-barreled Colt in a shoulder holster and he was almighty sudden with it.

Flintlock sat and Hunt said, "Drink?"

"Anything but buttermilk."

"A beer then?"

"Sounds good."

After Flintlock was served his beer and had a cigarette lit, Hunt said, "Will we talk about business or pleasure?"

"A bit of both, Beau."

"Very mysterious, Sam. Talk away."

Hunt had hazel eyes and now they looked very green, like the shallows of an icebound ocean. He never seemed to blink.

"A friend of mine was murdered yesterday, gut-shot, a Pinkerton by the name of —"

"Clifton Wraith."

"You heard already?"

"It's the talk of the town, Sam. Where have you been?"

Flintlock lifted his beer glass, with his left hand, and his eyes met Hunt's over the rim.

"Did you kill him, Beau?"

That last was loud in the hushed saloon and now people craned forward, listening. Most expected a gunfight and a few already looked toward the door, planning their stampede when the lead started to fly.

"You don't think much of me, Sam, do you?" Hunt said.

"We're in the same kind of business."

Hunt smiled. "Doesn't really answer my question though, does it?"

"No, I don't think you killed him. It's not your style. Cliff's fingernails were pulled out before he was gut-shot."

"Then there's your answer. I didn't kill him."

"Do you know who did?"

"Sam, I just got into town."

"Of course."

Hunt tasted his milk. "It's sour," he said. "Do you think you soured my buttermilk, Sam?"

Flintlock smiled. "Probably. I have a habit of doing that to folks."

"Then don't ever do it again." Beau Hunt's voice sounded like a death knell.

"What? Sour your buttermilk?"

"No. I mean accuse me of murdering a man."

Flintlock rose to his feet, his smile firmly in place. "Thank you for your time, Beau. I just wanted to clear that matter up."

"We're not enemies," Hunt said. "At least, up until now."

"No, we're not enemies."

"Then don't make me draw down on you, Sam. In other words, don't push me too hard."

"I wouldn't like that."

"If I have to, Sam, I will."

"Why are you here, Beau? Can't you tell me for old times' sake?"

"We don't have any old times' sake, Sam."

"I reckon not. In the past we've always

219

stepped wide of each other."

"Then let's keep it that way."

Flintlock turned to walk away, but Hunt's voice stopped him.

"Sam, the game's afoot so let it play out to the end. Don't take a hand."

"Clifton Wraith was a friend of mine, Beau. I'm not playing a game."

"Then step careful, Sam."

Flintlock nodded. He was no longer smiling.

"And you too, Beau. You too."

Sam Flintlock recrossed the street to the hotel. Marshal Tom Lithgow waited for him in the lobby. "Well?" he said.

"Well, what?"

"Did you brace Beau Hunt?"

"I spoke to him. He bought me a beer."

"What did he say?"

"He said he didn't kill Cliff Wraith."

"Do you believe him?"

"Yeah, I believe him."

"What did he say about me?"

"Nothing. I never mentioned your name."

"What do I do now, Flintlock?"

"Stay the hell away from him."

"What do I tell Mr. Tweddle?"

"Tell him his plan to have you killed didn't work."

Flintlock stared into the lawman's concerned eyes. "Lithgow, deep down you've got sand. You've proved that in the past."

"I don't go on the brag about it."

"But you don't have enough sense to spit downwind."

"I'm not catching your drift, Flintlock." Lithgow looked peeved.

"Why did Tweddle want you to arrest Beau Hunt?"

"You know why. Because of Wraith's murder."

"No. He wants you out of the way. He knew Hunt would kill you."

"Maybe Mr. Tweddle has more confidence in my draw than you."

Flintlock didn't hear that. Or pretended not to.

"I'm still trying to figure out Tweddle's angle and I plan to study on it some. In the meantime, as I said already, stay the hell away from Beau Hunt. You're way out of your class."

CHAPTER TWENTY-EIGHT

When Steve McCord reckoned he was a good twenty miles south of the ranch house, among the western foothills of Blue Mountain, he drew rein and pondered his situation.

Not that he had much to ponder. The stark fact was that he'd been thrown off his inheritance and forced like scarred Cain to wander the earth.

And Cain went out from the presence of the
   Lord, and settled
in the land of Nod, east of Eden.

Steve McCord's smile was bitter. No, he wasn't bound for the land of Nod, but Laredo, Texas . . . six hundred miles away and east of nowhere.

His father hadn't even come to see him off. Frisco Maddox had done the dirty work.

■ ■ ■ ■

"Cousin Judd will see you all right, Steve. Make a man of you."

"Suppose I don't want to go?"

"Your pa wants you off the ranch, boy. You got no choice."

"I didn't think he hated me that much."

"He doesn't hate you, Steve. You're just a disappointment to him."

"And when I come back?"

"We'll see. Things may be better then."

"He wants to get married, have another son."

"I don't know about that. Keep my letter of introduction safe, Steve. Cousin Judd will see you all right."

"You told me that already."

"Then there's nothing else to be said. Ride easy, pardner."

Frisco Maddox had slapped the rump of his horse . . . and that had been that.

And you will be a fugitive and wanderer on the earth.

Steve McCord stared at the blue sky through the canopy of the pines, smiling.

He wasn't about to wander anywhere. This far and no farther.

223

All at once he was hungry for breakfast. His pa had wanted him off his land so badly that Maddox had stuffed a stale biscuit into his mouth, given him a wallet with two hundred dollars, then shoved him toward his horse.

Three, maybe four years of exile, the big foreman had said.

But Steve knew his pa meant forever.

He rode deeper into the pines, leading a mouse-colored packhorse, and up a gradual rise where dark green ferns grew in abundance. As Steve followed a wisp of game trail the land leveled again, forested with a mix of pine and oak, and noisy birds flew in and out of the branches. Deer and bear signs lay everywhere and once he caught a glimpse of a cougar as it glided through the trees like an amber flame.

A break in the trees promised a camping spot and the young man had seen a rock pool just a short ways back where birds came to drink.

He swung out of the saddle and searched through the pack, where he found a slab of bacon, a loaf of sourdough bread, coffee and a small sack of sugar. In addition there was a coffeepot and frying pan.

There was plenty of dry wood around and

when he had a fire going Steve took the coffeepot and headed back to the rock pool. The surface of the water was streaked with strands of green algae. Those he brushed aside with the back of his hand before he filled the pot.

When he returned a man kneeled by his fire, slicing bacon into the frying pan. A skinny yellow mustang with a blanket thrown over its ridged backbone grazed nearby.

When the man saw Steve McCord he rose to his feet, grinned with bad teeth and said, "Howdy."

"You're making mighty free with my grub," Steve said.

"Figured your camp was abandoned, young feller."

"You figured wrong."

The man by the fire was a dusty, uncurried brute with greasy yellow hair that lay thick and tangled on his shoulders. His beard fell over his chest and his black eyes were alert and cunning. He was dressed in stained buckskins and cavalry boots and a worn Smith & Wesson Schofield in a cross-draw holster lay handy on the front of his left hip.

"Well, see, sonny, you abandoned your camp and I'm taking it over, like," the man said. "No hard feelings, huh? Fair is fair."

Steve McCord had a Colt with a pearl handle on his hip, as was his preference. Frisco Maddox had done his best to teach him the draw and shoot with the revolver but up until then he didn't know if he'd learned anything.

"Get on your horse and ride out of here," Steve said.

"Hell, I'm a grown man, sonny, and you're a boy. Boys don't give orders to grown men."

"You're trash and a thief. Now ride out."

Suddenly the man in buckskins looked like a tourist seeing one of the Seven Wonders of the World for the first time. He was so taken astonished he couldn't speak for a moment.

When he could, he said, "Why, you young whelp, I ought to take a stick to you." But he said it grinning.

Steve McCord was not amused nor would not be intimidated.

"Take my bacon off the fire and get the hell out of here," he said. "I won't tell you again."

"How old are you, kid?"

"Twenty."

"Damn it, boy, you're just a younker but you've got sand."

"Take the bacon off the fire."

"Sure, sure. Then we can share it and I'll be on my way."

The man kneeled again, grabbed the handle of the fry pan and jerked his hand away. "Jeez, it's hot, hot, hot!" he yelled, shaking the fingers of his right hand.

It was a fatal mistake.

Steve McCord drew and fired.

The bullet crashed into the man's side two inches under his left armpit and knocked him onto his side. He staggered to his feet and stood bent over, feeling for the wound.

Steve's second round clipped off the man's middle finger and plowed into his chest. He fell over and this time made no attempt to get up.

"Yee-hah!" Steve hollered, his boots pounding the ground in an odd little jig. "I done you for sure."

Grinning, he hopped and danced his way to the fire, his face split in a wild grin.

He moved the pan off the fire with the toe of his boot and holstered his Colt. With the point of his Barlow knife he speared a strip of bacon and shoved it into his mouth.

Talking around a mouthful of hot grease, he nudged the prone man with his boot and said, "You dead yet?"

To Steve's surprise the man had life enough left in him to raise his head. "You had no call to shoot me," he said. "I was only hungry and I meant you no harm."

"Mmm, good bacon," Steve said. Then, "You would've shot me."

"Sonny, I never shot at another human being in my life."

"Then why do you carry a gunfighting revolver, huh?" He kicked the man's shattered ribs a few times. "Huh? Huh?"

"I . . . stole . . . it."

"Well, don't that beat all," Steve said. "Me mistaking you for a gun and you just a grub line tramp."

The man said nothing as he battled pain.

"Well, I got to eat breakfast and then be on my way," Steve said. "Busy, busy you know."

He drew his revolver and smiled. "Slow in the belly or fast in the head? Call it."

Grimacing, hurting bad, the man said nothing.

"Ah, I see. Well, now you're boring me," Steve said, his smile gone. He shot the man in the temple.

As he ate a bacon-and-bread sandwich and enjoyed the tree-shaded sunlight, Steve McCord contemplated the stillness of the

228

dead man. He didn't twitch or make a sound, just lay there all crumpled up like a puppet that just had its strings cut.

Steve lay back on his elbows then reached out and toed the dead man's bloody chest.

Nothing. Only . . . deadness.

The young man sighed and lay on his back, his clasped hands under his head. It was, he considered, amazing what a couple of ounces of well-aimed lead could do to a man.

And it was a thing to remember.

Fringed by tree branches, the sky was blue but Steve much preferred a thunder sky, especially during the mad days of March when the wind drove off the Great Plains with the sound of locomotives and gray and black thunderheads towered upward like titanic boulders.

Ah, such a noble sky, one where the demon gods disported themselves. Steve smiled, well satisfied with himself. Indeed he had the soul of a true artist, but now he was much more. He was a warrior poet! A battle bard! A troubadour!

Jumping to his feet, he pumped a fist at the sky.

He'd finally proven himself a man, a status his father had long denied him. The evidence lay soundless and still at Steve's feet.

The man had been armed and he'd out-drawn and killed him.

He wanted to shout to the world that Steve McCord was a man to be reckoned with, a draw fighter like Hardin, Longley and even the great Hickok himself.

Ah, but it was a fine feeling to be young and tough with fast hands and hellfire in the belly. Another couple of kills and no man would dare try to cut him down to size.

Hell, his father would welcome home his famous son with open arms.

And that would be his big mistake . . . because the next time they met Steve Mc-Cord would have a gun in his hand.

Chapter Twenty-Nine

It was the custom of mountain men like old Barnabas to hold a riotous wake for their dead that could last for days or even weeks.

But Sam Flintlock could give Clifton Wraith no such send-off.

He pinned the Pinkerton's badge on his chest and buried him that evening. The only mourners were himself, Marshal Tom Lithgow, the preacher and a couple of blanket Indian gravediggers. Frank Constable should have been there but wasn't.

Under a purple sky that flickered with heat lightning, the preacher said the words and Flintlock threw a shovelful of dirt onto the pine coffin that lay at the bottom of the dank, root-ragged hole.

When the prayers were done, the clergyman left. Lithgow put a hand on Flintlock's shoulder, gave him a wan, sympathetic smile, then he too headed back to town.

The Indians, both middle-aged Tonkawa,

stared at Flintlock in silence. Waiting. Flintlock nodded and they chanted their death song.

Oh Sun, you go on forever but we must die.
Oh Earth, you go on forever but we must die.
The dark of endless night draws closer.

When the song was done Flintlock gave the men each two dollars and walked away. He didn't look back.

Sam Flintlock spent the night at the hotel and at first light saddled up and headed back to the cabin at Bobcat Ridge. He'd not spoken to Frank Constable because it seemed the little man had vanished. Flintlock thought that strange but didn't dwell on it. The lawyer was a strange one and could be anywhere, up to anything.

There was no sign of Jamie McPhee when Flintlock rode in, and he fancied that the young man was still abed. Then, as he rode past the large building on his way to the barn, disaster struck.

A thunderous, clanking roar preceded the outward flattening of the structure's doors by a mere second. Spooked, Flintlock's buckskin reared, threw him off and then ran, its stirrups bouncing.

Flintlock, stunned for a moment, looked up from the ground and saw two massive, steel-rimmed yellow wheels churning straight at him. His yelp of sheer terror was lost in the greater bellow of the infernal machine.

Rolling frantically to his right, eyes big as porcelain saucers, Flintlock avoided the crushing wheels by scant inches. He glanced up, sunlight flashing in his eyes, and saw the fire-breathing dragons trundle past, then the boiler and then the cabin.

McPhee was in the driver's seat, wearing goggles that made him look like a crazed owl.

"Damn you, McPhee!" Flintlock yelled. "You nearly killed me."

"I got it started, Sam!"

The machine clanked past, belching steam and wood smoke.

"Then stop it!" Flintlock hollered.

"I don't know how!" McPhee yelled. "I can't find the brave lever." Then, "Help! I can't steer it either!"

The truth of that statement was confirmed when the infernal machine turned on a dime and headed in Flintlock's direction again. Aghast, he scrambled to his feet and dived into the prickly cover of a thorn bush.

The machine roared past as McPhee frantically yanked at levers, his mouth an O of alarm.

Again the machine made a turn and Flintlock crawled out of the thorns, his face and hands crisscrossed with scratches. "Damn you, McPhee!" he yelled, jamming his hat back on his head.

At the best of times Sam Flintlock's temper was a finger looking for a trigger and now he was mad enough to chomp a chunk out of an ax head.

He drew his Colt and sprinted after the runaway machine.

But then horror piled on horror, disaster on disaster.

"Not the barn!" he yelled.

He saw McPhee desperately trying to steer. A hellish behemoth designed to destroy life and property, the infernal machine remorselessly stayed on a course for the barn.

Flintlock raised his revolver and fired. Fired again. Aiming for the boiler. But the infernal machine was a weapon of war and the thick steel boilerplate shrugged off both bullets.

Flintlock ran after the runaway again. When he was almost parallel with the driver's cab he hollered, "Turn it, McPhee."

"I can't!"

The young man's face was a white mask of fright as he batted at the controls.

Flintlock glanced ahead of him. *Oh my God!* Fifty yards to the barn across flat, open ground. The infernal machine clanged, clanked and roared forward.

"I can't stop her!" McPhee shrieked. "Where's the brake?"

Forty yards . . .

"I'm going to jump!" McPhee yelled.

"Damn you, McPhee, stay where you're at," Flintlock hollered. "Stop that thing or turn it."

Thirty yards . . .

"She's out of control!" McPhee cried. "She's a runaway!"

"Stay with it! Turn!" Flintlock shouted.

Twenty yards . . .

McPhee's horse, terrified by the approaching clamor, bolted from the barn like a cork out of a bottle, hay in its mouth.

Ten yards . . .

McPhee rose from the seat, opened the cabin door and jumped.

"Damn you, McPhee!" Flintlock roared. "I told you to stay with it."

The infernal machine broadsided the barn, crashing, splintering, cracking through thin, brittle timber. Shattered, the barn wall caved in and immediately afterward the entire roof collapsed with a grinding *craaash*!

Flintlock stared openmouthed as a few errant spars clattered onto the debris then one more, shaped like an L, *dinked* on top of the others. A cloud of yellow dust rose from wreckage and hid the calamity from view.

The infernal machine tried to lurch forward, but finally defeated, it groaned and hissed for a few moments like a dying dragon then lapsed into a ticking silence.

Flintlock, appalled, looked around him at the devastation that Jamie McPhee had wrought.

The doors to the large building lay flat and broken on the ground and would never again shield the secrets of the infernal machine. The barn, once lofty and proud, was now a pile of kindling and the lordly tin rooster from its roof that once pointed the way of the wind had been reduced by the machine's wheels to a corkscrew of mangled metal.

And then, when Flintlock figured the worst was over, the heap of smashed lumber that had been the barn began to burn. As smoke and flames rose higher, McPhee stepped beside him.

"Oh dear, what will Mr. Constable say?" he whispered.

CHAPTER THIRTY

Night riders. A tip-top idea.

But where to recruit them?

Lucian Tweddle pondered that question as he lay beside Nancy Pocket and lazed in the relaxed aftermath of sex. The banker lay on his back like a white, hairless slug and stared at the slanted, scrap lumber and tar-paper roof of Nancy's shack.

Surely there were enough ruffians in Open Sky to mount a raiding party of say, half a dozen men? Using Beau Hunt for this job was out of the question. Named draw fighters didn't make good night riders.

But he already had Pike Reid, Lithgow's vicious deputy, in his employ and the man had dealt efficiently enough with the meddling Pinkerton.

Call it five then.

Tweddle elbowed the woman who lay beside him naked and sleek as a seal.

"Hey, how many badmen do you know in

238

this town?"

Tendrils of damp hair curled over Nancy Pocket's sweaty forehead. Lucian Tweddle's massive weight made for a stifling load.

"None," she said.

Tweddle smiled and hit the side of the woman's head with the heel of his hand. It was intended to be a playful blow, but it hurt and she yelped.

"Think. How many?"

"One or two," Nancy said.

In truth she knew none. But she didn't want to be hit again.

"I need more than that."

"Why?"

Another heel of the hand. Harder this time.

"None of your damned business."

Tweddle sighed. "Why the hell am I asking you? You're only good for one thing."

The whore smiled and tried to be provocative. "That's why you love your Nancykins, huh?"

"I don't love you, you're a whore. I use you, that's all."

Tweddle stared at the roof again. He was a man destined for great things, but he was surrounded by idiots like Nancy Pocket and that slowed his progress. Damn, but it was

239

unfair how underlings treated men of promise.

But then the woman surprised him.

"There's always Hank Stannic, if you can find him," she said.

"Stannic, yeah. I quite forgot about him. He worked for me that time I had trouble with the McGuiness clan. Took care of all of them squatters, grandparents, parents, brats . . . and an aunt and uncle as I recall."

Nancy stayed silent, but she remembered well the McGuiness Massacre as it came to be called. Fourteen men, women and children were killed that day.

Tweddle had made sure the blame fell on a young farm laborer named Abe Dell who'd had been sparking one of the McGuiness daughters.

Dell had been tried, found guilty and hanged in less than a week.

Nancy remembered Tweddle and Hank Stannic laughing over that as they drank at the Gentleman's Retreat brothel on the day of the hanging.

"Abe was a rube who never had a lick of sense and the son of a bitch owed me money," the banker had said. "He's no great loss."

Now it seemed Stannic's services would be called on again. But for what reason,

Nancy Pocket could not guess.

"Where can I find him?" Tweddle said.

"The Gentleman's Retreat is a good place to start, Lucian," Nancy said. "Josette will know where he is."

"What was Stannic's latest?"

"Bank job down El Paso way. I heard he killed the manager and a teller."

"I told Stannic before that I don't approve of bank robberies."

"It was a small bank, Lucian."

"So is mine."

Tweddle thought for a moment, then said, "Get the hell up. Go find Pike Reid and bring him here."

Thin as a cadaver, his alligator eyes darting to Nancy Pocket, Deputy Marshal Pike Reid stood hat in hand close to the bed where Lucian Tweddle lay, his belly forming a massive mound under the sheet.

Nancy, with an experienced whore's disdain for modesty, had stripped to the waist and used a sponge to bathe her breasts and shoulders.

"You can have her later, Pike," Tweddle said, following Reid's eyes. "First we need to talk business."

The stench of the fat man's sweat was rancid in the stifling heat of the tiny cabin.

241

Sunlight slanted through the cabin's only window and puddled around Reid's feet.

"Boss, I couldn't make him tell me what he knew," the man said.

"Are you talking about the Pinkerton?" Tweddle said.

"Yeah. He was tough."

"No matter, you got rid of him and made him pay for the inconvenience he caused me. I don't want to talk about the damned Pinkerton."

Reid waited and turned his hat in his hand.

The man's eyebrows met in a thick V over the bridge of his nose and gave him a sly, ferrety look. He looked like a man born for the noose.

"Pike, you'll head out to the Gentleman's Retreat —"

The man grinned. "Now you're talking, boss."

The interruption irritated Tweddle. "This is business, not pleasure."

"Sorry, boss."

"You'll talk to Josette and ask about the whereabouts of Hank Stannic and then you'll find him."

Reid looked uneasy. "Hank ain't right in the head," he said.

"I know. That's why I need him."

"And all his boys are crazy. Herm Holloway does his killing with an ax and Slick
Trent is a cutter who can't be left alone
around women."

"The character flaws of Stannic's men
don't interest me in the least. Just bring him
here to Open Sky."

"Can I talk money to him right away,
like?"

"I'll discuss that when I see him."

"Suppose he don't want to come?"

"We've done business in the past. He'll
come."

"What about Lithgow?"

"Lithgow is nothing, but he won't know,
will he? You'll bring Hank Stannic to my
home under cover of darkness."

"What's the job, boss?"

"You'll be present when I tell Stannic
what I need done."

Tweddle adjusted the pillow behind him
and his enormous bulk seethed sweat.
Nancy bathed her shapely legs with the
sponge.

"Well?" Tweddle said. "Why are you still
here?"

"When should I ride out, boss?"

"Now, of course."

"But my duties . . ."

"Don't matter a damn. You never performed your duties anyway."

"I'll be going then," Reid said. He seemed confused.

"Yes, do that, Pike," Tweddle said. "Don't let me stand in your way."

Before Reid closed the door behind him, he heard Tweddle say, "Idiot."

And Nancy's vulgar laugh cut through him like a knife.

CHAPTER THIRTY-ONE

Frank Constable had an excellent view of the street from his office window. A man who slept little, he'd already been behind his desk when Sam Flintlock rode out early that morning.

He'd not gone to Clifton Wraith's burial, preferring to remain home with his Bible and his thoughts. But Marshal Tom Lithgow had told him about the funeral and the Pinkerton's last words.

Guilty big man . . .

Those three words had haunted him.

Why had the Pinkerton refused more of Dr. Thorne's morphine, choosing to die in agony only to utter such a meaningless clue?

Guilty big man . . .

Constable had just read Isaiah 9:2 when the meaning of the words dawned on him.

The people who walk in darkness
will see a great light;

Those who live in a dark land,
the light will shine on them.

And Frank Constable, attorney-at-law,
had seen the light.

Guilty big man . . .

Lithgow had flippantly told Sam Flintlock
that Open Sky had any number of big men,
most of them guilty of something. And as
an attorney, Constable knew that was true.

But Wraith had desperately endured his
pain long enough to tell Flintlock that Jamie
McPhee was innocent of the murder of
Polly Mallory and that a big man was the
real killer.

Big man . . .

Clifton Wraith meant a *notably* big man.
A large man . . . huge . . . immense . . .
hulking . . . vast . . . colossal . . .

There were muscular males in town, but
none of those proportions. But there was
one who did measure up . . . a man who
was the mother lode of bigness . . .

The grossly obese Lucian Tweddle!

Now, with the patience of the aged, Frank
Constable kept a close eye on the street. He
had no specific reason for doing so, only a
hope that something might transpire that
could lead him in the right direction.

He needed proof of Tweddle's guilt, evidence that would stand up in court. The rambling words of a dying man were not enough for a murder conviction.

Then, on what was to be the last day of his long life, Constable caught a break.

He saw Pike Reid, that venomous piece of filth, ride out of an alley and swing into the street. Fifteen minutes later Lucian Tweddle left the same alley, stepped laboriously onto the boardwalk and headed in the direction of the bank, beaming, touching his hat to the ladies he passed, hand extended in a warm handshake to their menfolk.

He looked what he wasn't . . . a respectable, prosperous businessman on his sunny way to his office.

Frank Constable pondered that. He decided that Reid and Tweddle using the same alley was too much of a coincidence. Back there, behind the main drag, there was nothing but a scattering of shabby shacks, storage buildings and cactus.

The lawyer smiled. And Nancy Pocket.

The young whore was the attraction. He was sure of it. Though Reid and Tweddle made for strange bedfellows. Too strange for Constable not to be intrigued.

Did Nancy know anything about Polly Mallory's murder?

A man will sometimes confide in a whore with all the fervor of a repenting sinner. Had Lucian Tweddle?

It was a long shot, and the lawyer knew it. But it was better than sitting in his office twiddling his thumbs while he waited for others to make a move.

Constable rose to his feet, put on his hat and grabbed his dragon cane. He carefully locked the office door behind him and stepped onto the boardwalk.

The morning was hot and a haze of yellow dust hovered over the street. A dray trundled past followed by another drawn by an ox team, and a steady clang-clang-clang of a hammer came from the blacksmith's forge. Over at the general store the proprietor had hung red, white and blue bunting to attract attention to the sign in his window that declared:

SILK PARASOLS $2.
All boots and shoes at cost.

The new day smelled of dust and the heavy odor of ancient manure drifting from the cattle pens. Heat lay on everything and everyone, dense and draining, and legions of fat blue flies buzzed lazily behind the store windows.

Constable crossed the street, his cane raised like a weapon, his thunderous eyes ready to intimidate any teamster who might take it into his head to drive too close to him.

He safely made it to the alley and a few moments later tapped the silver dragon on Nancy Pocket's door.

"Come in, Mr. Constable," Nancy Pocket said.

And when the lawyer stepped into the cabin she smiled and said, "What can I do for you today?"

"Information, dear lady," Constable said. "Come now, I'm too old for anything else."

The woman looked disappointed. "What kind of information?"

"The kind that deals with murder."

"I don't know nothing about murders."

"A double negative. What a pity," Constable said. Then, "I'm here to talk about the death of Polly Mallory."

"I told Marshal Lithgow all I know. She was pregnant."

"Who was the father?"

"How should I know?"

"Was it Lucian Tweddle?"

Nancy looked like a wounded bird staring at a snake.

"Well, speak up, woman," Constable demanded.

"I don't know what you're talking about," Nancy said.

"Did Lucian Tweddle murder Polly Mallory when she told him she was pregnant? The truth now. Be frank. Be brief. Above all be honest."

"Get out of here," Nancy said. A pulse throbbed in her slender throat. "Now!"

"I can read the truth in your face."

"Get out!"

The woman made a dive for the door but Constable stepped in her way. "If you're covering up a murder, I'll see you hang with Tweddle," he said.

Nancy's shoulders sagged. Tears sprang into her eyes. "I don't want to hang. All right, I'll tell you all I know," she said.

"I thought you might," Constable said. "And afterward we'll talk with Marshal Lithgow."

The lampblack that darkened Nancy's lashes mingled with her tears and gave her panda eyes. She dashed the mess away with the base of her thumb and said, "I must get a handkerchief."

"Please do, and try not to distress yourself so much," Constable said, with all the warmth of a prosecutor addressing a witness for the defense.

"I'm so sorry," the woman said.

"No need to apologize for a display of female emotion," the lawyer said. "Distressing as it is."

Nancy stepped to her tiny dresser, opened the top drawer and when she turned she pumped two .41 bullets into Frank Constable's thin chest.

The rounds tore great holes through the lawyer's frail body and he fell back against the door, his face almost dreamlike, like a man who'd just taken his first step into a nightmare.

Tendrils of smoke rose from the barrels of Nancy's derringer and she stared at Constable in horror. "I'm . . . I'm sorry," she whispered.

But Frank Constable didn't hear.

He was already dead.

CHAPTER THIRTY-TWO

When Pike Reid stepped through the doors of the Gentleman's Retreat he almost collided with a drunken reveler, both his arms around a giggling girl, one of them holding a fizzing bottle of champagne. But before the laughing, singing towhead lurched away Reid thought he recognized him. He looked like young Steve McCord.

A moment later he dismissed the thought from his mind.

Trace McCord would never allow his son to visit a cathouse, and besides, the word around town was that Steve mooned around writing sappy poems and his inclinations did not run toward ladies.

Reid shook his head. It sure looked like him, though.

His attention was distracted by the large and imposing figure of Madame Josette, who stepped toward him in some kind of flowing, flapping robe that made her look a frigate under full sail.

"Monsieur Reid!" Josette cried, still at a distance. *"Quel plaisir de vous revoir!"*

Reid had time to say, "Huh?" before Josette's massive arms enfolded him and hugged him to her huge breasts.

A moment later, six inches taller and two hundred pounds heavier than the scrawny, gasping deputy, she held him at arm's length and smiled.

"I said, 'How nice to see you again.' "

"Yeah, you too, Josette," Reid said. "Here, did I catch sight of young Steve McCord when I came in?"

The woman put a finger to her lips. "Some gentlemen wish to remain anonymous at Josette's place."

She hugged Reid again, not as close this time. "I've been keeping a sweet girl just for you. She's come all the way from France by way of Tangiers." Josette's hands fluttered like released white doves. "Her name is Lulu Le Mer and she's as pure as milk . . . 'ow you say . . . in a bucket."

"Josette, I'm here on business," Reid said.

The woman scowled and shoved the deputy away from her. "Then why are you wasting my time?"

"I'm here on Lucian Tweddle's business."

Josette sighed and blinked. "Oh, *mon Dieu,*

the fat man is not threatening to foreclose on me again."

"No, not this time."

"Then what is your business?"

"I'm looking for Hank Stannic." Then, for insurance, "On Mr. Tweddle's account."

"He's not here," Josette said.

"Then where is he?"

"Je ne sais pas."

"What does that mean?"

"It means I don't know."

"Mr. Tweddle won't be happy."

"Come with me," Josette said.

She led Reid to a large, comfortable room furnished with overstuffed chairs, sofas and small tables. A bar had been set up opposite the door where a small, neat man with pomaded hair and scarlet arm garters stood polishing a glass.

The young puncher Reid had seen earlier sprawled on a velvet sofa, nuzzling his girls. He laughed too loudly and seemed half drunk.

Before the deputy could take a good look, Josette propelled him to the bar.

"Drink?" she said.

"Whiskey," Reid said.

The tidy bartender filled a shot glass and placed it in front of Reid.

"Charlie, this fellow is looking for Hank

Stannic," Josette said.

Charlie hesitated and the woman rolled her eyes. "Lucian Tweddle," she said.

The young man on the sofa leaned forward, suddenly alert. But nobody noticed.

The bartender nodded, his face empty. "A couple of months ago Stannic was managing a stage stop for the Butterfield Overland Mail up by Bandy Creek. He's living there with an Osage woman and has three, four kids by her."

Reid drained his glass then grinned. "A stage robber working for Butterfield. That's rich."

"Maybe he got religion," Charlie said. "A dollar for the drink."

"It's all right, Charlie," Josette said. *"C'est sur la maison."*

"Whatever you say, ma'am," Charlie said, looking displeased.

"Hey, did I hear somebody mention Lucian Tweddle?"

The youth had gotten off the couch and now stood, legs apart, in the middle of the floor.

Pike Reid didn't like what he saw.

The kid was a poseur. His hand hovered close to his holstered Colt and his expression was both arrogant and belligerent. Reid figured Steve McCord, now he could see that it was indeed he, had once read a dime novel about a famous shootist and decided, *Gee, I could do that.*

But it didn't make the young man any less dangerous. The kid was on the prod, anxious to add to his score, if he had one.

Josette drained the tension out of the air. "All of us here are friends of Mr. Tweddle," she said.

"How about him, Josette?" McCord nodded at Reid, besides himself the only man present who carried a gun.

"I'm a friend of Mr. Tweddle," the deputy said.

"I asked the lady," McCord said.

Reid twigged it then. Urged on by alcohol, the kid was hunting trouble and he wanted it real bad. He needed to kill a man so folks would look up to him and say as he passed, "There goes Steve the Kid, the famous pistolero."

"Deputy Reid and Mr. Tweddle are very good friends," Josette said.

That gave the young man pause. The last thing he wanted right now was to upset the banker. He needed Tweddle . . . at least for a while.

"That's just as well for you, mister," he said to Reid.

Reid fought when he had to and killed

256

only when the money was right. He'd gunned five white men and had nothing to prove.

"No hard feelings, huh, kid?" he said.

"Don't call me kid," McCord said.

"Then it's Steve. That set all right with you?"

"How do you know my name?"

Reid knew he was about to score a hit. "Everybody knows your name, Mr. Mc-Cord."

That did it. Steve smiled and said, "Buy you a drink . . . ah . . . ?"

"Pike. That's my handle as ever was. But I'll have to refuse the drink."

He watched a scowl about to be reborn on the young man's face and said quickly, "Mr. Tweddle wants me to bring in Hank Stannic."

"The outlaw?" Steve said. He searched his memory. "Ran with John Wesley Hardin for a spell?"

"That's him, though I've just been told he's going straight."

The young man's eyes flicked to the bartender then back to Reid.

"He's a gun?"

One of the young women pulled on Steve's arm and whined, "Come back to the sofa, honey." He pushed her roughly away. "I

257

said, is he a gun? How does he stack up?"

Reid smiled inwardly. It was obvious that McCord was eager to measure himself against a gunman of reputation who once rode with Wes Hardin.

"He's good," he said.

"How good?"

"I'd say at least a dozen men are pushing up daisies who found out the hard way just how good Hank Stannic is with a gun."

"I want to meet him. I'll ride with you."

"Sure thing," Reid said. "But ain't your pa expecting you back at the ranch?"

"He can go to hell," Steve McCord said.

Pike Reid was surprised at the bitter hate the kid conveyed in just five words.

That was a thing Mr. Tweddle should know.

CHAPTER THIRTY-THREE

The barn was destroyed, the infernal machine burned beyond saving and Sam Flintlock felt glum.

Jamie McPhee, trying to help, said, "Don't worry, Sam. I'll explain all this to Mr. Constable."

Flintlock gave him a look that would have withered a sunflower at ten paces and McPhee decided to keep his mouth shut. The young man picked up a piece of charred wood, studied it closely, sighed and threw it back onto the pile.

"Why did you start the damned thing when you knew you couldn't stop it?" Flintlock said.

"Figured I'd learn by doing," McPhee said. "A lot of men do that, learn by doing."

"I should've shot you right out of that cabin, you know," Flintlock said.

"Why didn't you?"

"My aim was off."

"Rider coming in, Sam," McPhee said.

Flintlock followed the younger man's eyes. O'Hara came through the blue twilight at a walk. Like all Pawnee, he rode with a poker-backed posture that gave him the look of a Prussian Uhlan. But every now and then he leaned from the saddle and swatted the heads off wildflowers with the stick he carried.

Flintlock adjusted the angle of the Colt in his waistband then he and McPhee walked as far as the cabin.

O'Hara drew rein a few moments later. Without a word he held the stick upright then tossed it to Flintlock.

"This is Frank Constable's cane," Flintlock said.

The breed nodded.

"Where is he?" Flintlock said.

"Nowhere. He's dead," O'Hara said.

Beside him Flintlock heard McPhee's strangled gasp. "How did it happen?" the young man said.

"And why did it happen?" Flintlock said.

O'Hara lifted his head and stared at the pink sky. A few purple clouds drifted westward, as stately as adrift galleons. "I'm a man who's partial to coffee," he said finally. "A visiting man should always be offered coffee. It's considered polite, even among the Pawnee."

"Light and set and come inside, O'Hara," Flintlock said. He stared at the cane's silver dragon, then at the breed. "Tell me this wasn't you," he said.

"I don't kill old white men," O'Hara said. He returned Flintlock's stare. "Only young ones."

O'Hara poised his cup halfway to his mouth. "Why did you burn the barn?" he said.

"It was an accident," McPhee said.

The breed absorbed that, then said, "Dead men don't cast blame." He glanced at Flintlock. "Except Barnabas. That's because they can't keep him in hell."

When a man wants an Indian to tell him a thing, it's best not to push it. Let him say it in his own time. "I saw Barnabas after Frank Constable was killed," O'Hara said. "He sat at the top of the church spire and wore a black pointed hat."

Flintlock said nothing. Waited. McPhee bit his lip with anxiety.

"Barnabas said he got the hat from a . . . *stoo* . . . a witch woman in the white man's tongue."

"What did he say?" McPhee asked, breaking his silence.

"He said he planned to cast a spell to

make his grandson less of an idiot." O'Hara shrugged. "Flintlock, I don't know if he told me that before or after you burned down the barn."

Now irritated, Flintlock pushed it. "Forget the damned barn, what happened to Frank Constable?" he said, in a tone that was less than friendly.

"Good coffee," O'Hara said. Then, smiling at Flintlock's anger, "He was shot twice in the back as he left the shack of the whore Nancy Pocket."

"Oh my God," McPhee whispered. "First Mr. Wraith and now Mr. Constable." He shook his head. "Sam, what does it mean?"

Flintlock didn't answer. "Constable was too old for whores," he said.

"Who decided that? You or him?" O'Hara said.

"Who did it?" Flintlock said.

"I don't know. No one knows."

"What about Nancy Pocket? What did she say?"

"Marshal Lithgow says that as Constable stepped out the door of her shack she heard two shots. The old lawyer fell back inside and died on the floor."

Flintlock thought for a while. Finally he said, "Cliff Wraith was getting too close to something and had to be gotten rid of. And the same goes with Constable." He studied the dragon-topped cane. "I wish this thing could talk."

"Mr. Wraith talked to you, Sam," McPhee said. "He said a big man was guilty of Polly Mallory's murder."

"And Frank Constable discovered who the big man is?" Flintlock asked.

"Seems likely," McPhee said. "I have no other answer." He bent his head and stared into the inky depths of his coffee cup. "Sam, now with both Mr. Wraith and Mr. Constable gone, you have no call to guard me any longer," he said.

"Don't even think like that," Flintlock said. "I took on the job and I'll see it through."

"We're dealing with a man who has a lot more power than we have," McPhee said. "I don't think I want to prolong the agony."

"What does that mean?" Flintlock said.

"I think I should ride out of the territory and never come back."

"That was Constable's plan in the first place, remember?" Flintlock said.

"I know. But I was too bullheaded to see his logic."

"Hell, all you wanted to do was clear your name," Flintlock said. "I can't fault a man for that."

"I'll ride out today," McPhee said.

"We'll need to find your hoss first," Flintlock said. "It's probably halfway back to Open Sky by this time."

"I'll search for your horse, McPhee," O'Hara said.

"Thank you kindly," the young man said.

"Except you're not going anywhere on it, McPhee," Flintlock said.

Both O'Hara and McPhee stared at him in surprise.

"When Cliff Wraith was murdered, this became personal," Flintlock said. "I aim to find the man who did it and kill him."

"How will you do that?" O'Hara said. "The men who could have told you are both dead."

"I don't know. Not yet, I don't."

Flintlock poured coffee into his cup with a rock-steady hand. "I'm still not angry enough to raise a hundred different kinds of hell," he said. "But by God I'm working on it."

Chapter Thirty-Four

"It's strictly a business proposition, Hank," Pike Reid said.

"What does Tweddle want?" Stannic said.

"He wouldn't tell me."

"A Tweddle business proposition usually means a killing."

"I don't know," Reid said.

"It must be something else. Mr. Tweddle knows I can do his killing for him," Steve McCord said.

"You're Trace McCord's son, huh?" Stannic said.

"I was. I've disowned him."

"Or he disowned you," Stannic said.

Steve tensed. It was a deliberate move, aimed at getting the point across that he was a revolver fighter and a man to be reckoned with.

But Stannic, a man who'd seen the kid's like many times, ignored him.

"I got a wife and young 'uns, Reid," he

265

said. "Look around and you'll see how it is with me. We ain't exactly living high on the hog here."

Stannic's three black-haired children clung to the skirts of their Osage mother's skirts, wary of strangers. The woman was tall and stately, and when she looked at Reid her eyes burned with resentment. The cabin was untidy and somewhat dirty, more akin to a poor white laborer's abode than the home of a famous outlaw.

Stannic was a bull-necked, bearded brute of a man, his head shaven but for a scalp lock at the crown, no doubt his wife's influence. But his brown eyes revealed a quick intelligence and the creases at the corners a willingness to smile.

"Big money, Hank," Reid said. "Just one quick job."

"Sounds like a go to me," McCord said.

Stannic ignored that and said to his wife, "We need the money, Misae."

The Osage said, "I need my husband and my children need their father."

"One quick job," Stannic said.

"Maybe one job too many," the woman said.

"Aw, don't listen to the Indian, Hank," Steve McCord said, grinning.

"Misae is my wife," Stannic said, whisper

266

quiet, but edged with menace.

Reid read the warning sign and said, "The kid's just joshing, Hank." Then, "At least come back with me and talk with Mr. Tweddle."

McCord wouldn't let it go. "I don't josh," he said. "I don't like Indians."

"Steve, shut your damned trap," Reid said. "You got nothing to prove in a man's home."

Stannic said, "Kid, you're on the prod. Best you calm down a little. No one will hurt you while you're under my roof."

McCord didn't want to back up in front of Reid and Stannic's woman, but then, from under the table he heard a triple click and something hard pushed into his groin.

"What do you say, huh?" Stannic said.

Reid's smile was sick and forced. "You always were such a joker, Hank," he said.

Steve McCord felt the gun muzzle push harder.

"What do you say?" Stannic said.

This wasn't the glamorous world of the draw fighter as the young man had imagined it. This was down and dirty and without honor. An outlaw's trick. But he knew if he talked sass to Stannic the man would, without a moment's hesitation, blow his balls off.

"I say I'm just excited about meeting you, Hank, is all."

"See, we're all perfect friends here," Reid said.

The pressure left Steve's groin and Stannic placed his revolver on the table. It was a scarred blue Colt with a worn rubber handle, a working gun. The outlaw rose to his feet then shoved the Colt into the pocket of his frayed canvas coat.

"I will talk with Tweddle," he said. His big Mexican spurs ringing, Stannic opened the cabin door and yelled, "Herm! Slick!"

"Yeah, boss?" a man's voice answered.

"We're riding. Saddle my horse."

Pike Reid sat his horse beside a sullen Steve McCord. Behind them, probably by design, Herm Holloway and Slick Trent watched Stannic's wife step out of the cabin door, her young children clinging to her.

Holloway was a tall angular man, a steel Cheyenne war ax stuck into his belt. He also wore a Colt and had a Winchester under his right knee. Slick Trent was much younger, a towhead with crazy eyes and a constant grin. He wore two guns high on his waist and he stared at Steve McCord in open amusement. Trent had killed six men and was fast and accurate on the draw and shoot. He was also a savage and determined rapist and not to be trusted around women.

Hank Stannic swung into the saddle.

In silence, he and his wife gazed at each other for long moments, then Stannic nodded and swung his horse away.

CHAPTER THIRTY-FIVE

Sam Flintlock carefully locked the door of Frank Constable's cabin then mounted his horse. After a last look around at the devastation he and Jamie McPhee had wrought, he said, "Let's go."

As McPhee kicked his horse into motion, he said, "Sam, do you think the folks in Open Sky have forgotten about me?"

O'Hara answered the question.

"If it wasn't for Flintlock's gun, they'd string you up quicker'n scat."

McPhee turned his head and glared at Flintlock. "Sam, I don't think this is such a good idea," he said.

"It ain't," Flintlock said. "We're riding into the lion's den."

"Why?"

"Because it sure as hell beats hanging out here twiddling our thumbs and burning stuff."

O'Hara said, "Whoever killed the Pinkerton and Frank Constable will come after you, Flintlock. You're the last link to McPhee."

"I'm counting on that. My being in Open Sky will bring the killer out into the open."

"You like to live dangerously, Flintlock."

"And you, O'Hara, whose side are you on, huh?"

"My own."

"A man can't say fairer than that, I guess." Flintlock noticed a slight change in the gait of his buckskin. "Damn, he's cast a shoe," he said.

"There's a blacksmith close by," O'Hara said. "Or you can wait until you reach town."

"I better do it now," Flintlock said. "When I get to Open Sky I might need the hoss in a hurry." He threw a puzzled look at O'Hara. "What's a blacksmith doing in this wilderness?"

"He's set up at a settlement to the west of Buzzard Gap, if you can call a general store that doubles as a saloon and a pole corral a settlement."

"What do they call it?"

"They don't call it anything."

"I call it right handy," Flintlock said.

The blacksmith, a taciturn blond Swede

with a surly attitude, hammered at some red-hot iron thing as Sam Flintlock led the buckskin into the forge.

"He's lost a shoe," he said.

"Leave the horse, wait your turn," the Swede said. He plunged the scarlet, hissing iron into a water tank.

"How long?" Flintlock said.

"Depends," the smith said.

"On what?"

"On how long you stand there pestering me with damned fool questions."

O'Hara left without saying where he was going, and Flintlock and Jamie McPhee figured to visit the saloon in search of coffee and maybe some grub. Flintlock left his Winchester on the saddle, but took the Hawken.

Three horses stood in the corral next to the two-story building and above the door a weathered wooden sign proclaimed: FINEST WINES & SPIRITS.

The proprietor, a gray-haired man, stepped from behind the store part of the building, wiping off his hands on a white apron. "What can I do for you gents?" he said.

"Coffee," Flintlock said.

"Pot's on top of the stove over there. Cups on the hooks."

"Grub?" Flintlock said.

"Beans in the pot beside the coffee. Plates on the shelf."

"We'll stick to coffee," Flintlock said.

"Suit yourself. Cost you two bits."

"Expensive."

"It's the going rate."

"Ain't too many real sociable folks around here, huh?" Flintlock said.

"If you lived here, mister, would you be sociable?"

The gray-haired man stepped away and went back behind the store counter.

Flintlock and McPhee poured coffee and McPhee said, "Watch out for that, Sam." He nodded to a black puddle on the floor that had leaked from a molasses barrel.

"Sticky that," Flintlock said.

"Hey you, mountain man."

Flintlock earlier noticed the two young men who sat at a table eating crackers and blue-veined cheese. A bottle of whiskey stood between them.

He'd seen their like before, all duded up like dance-hall cowboys but too lazy for that kind of work. Or any kind of work. But they were hunting trouble, eager to stack up against a buckskinned man who carried an ancient rifle that might explode when he fired it and an unarmed ranny who had the

273

meek, bullied look of a counting-house clerk.

"What can I do for you boys?" Flintlock said. He stood with his back to the rough timber bar and carefully placed the unloaded Hawken upright beside him.

"You too good to eat beans?" one of the men said. He had insolent blue eyes and a week's growth of beard. Flintlock thought he looked a little like Billy Bonney, but without Billy's dazzling smile and significant presence.

"I don't see you eating them," he said.

"That's sass, Ben," the other man said. "I'd sure call that sass."

"I know it is, Lou." The man called Ben smiled. "Question is, what am I gonna do about it?"

"Nothing," Flintlock said. "You're not going to do anything about it because I don't need any more trouble than I already have."

"I reckon Ben will decide that," Lou said.

The man looked mean, on the prod, and he should have been old enough to know better.

But the proprietor recognized exactly what Flintlock was and the sudden danger he represented. "Let the man drink his coffee in peace, boys," he said.

"You shut your trap, Slaton," Ben said.

Flintlock drained his cup. "Good coffee," he said to Slaton. "I reckon I'll see if the smith has started on my hoss yet."

"Hey, you don't think you're just walking out of here after the way you back-talked Ben," Lou said around a smirk.

"Yeah," Flintlock said. "That's what I'm going to do, walk on out of here."

"Sam . . ." McPhee said.

"I see him."

Lou was on his feet, smiling, his hand close to the Colt on his hip.

"Boy, are you really so anxious to get another notch on the handle of that hog-leg?" Flintlock said. He glanced at the revolver. "Seems to me you already got enough."

Lou grinned. "Enough is never enough."

"Cutting a notch on your gun for every man you killed is a tinhorn trick and low-down," Flintlock said. "How many do you have?"

"Six and pretty soon seven."

"Hell, are you sure I can't talk you out of this? I mean, it just ain't civilized."

"Nope. I'm primed up to kill me a big ol' mountain man."

"You tell him, Lou," Ben said.

"You want to do the honors, Ben?" Lou

said, his amused eyes never leaving Flintlock.

"Nah. You can take him. I'll watch."

Then Flintlock got good and angry and,
as was his habit, moved quickly from mad
to damned mad. "You lowdown scum," he
said, "pickin' on a peaceful man who just
drank his coffee." His hands hung by his
sides. "All right, shuck your iron, Lou. Open
the ball."

For a moment a glimmer of doubt showed
in Lou's eyes. Flintlock looked too confident, like he'd been there before. But he
drew.

In a life full of mistakes and wrong
choices, pulling his Colt was Lou's worst.
He realized that a half second before Flintlock's bullet crashed into his chest, splintered breastbone and tore through his heart.

Flintlock took a step to his left and swung
his gun on Ben. For a moment he thought
he'd be too late on the shoot. But he was
wrong.

"Noooo!" Ben yelled. "For God sakes,
no."

He tossed his gun away from him and it
clattered into a corner.

"Damn you!" Flintlock roared, his rage
consuming him like a red flame. "Pick up

the iron you piece of filth and get to your work."

Ben, his face frightened, shook his head.

"Pick it up, damn you!" Flintlock yelled.

"Sam! No! It's over!" McPhee said. "He's out of it."

Like a man falling from a great height, it took Flintlock a while before he hit the flat. He shoved his Colt back into his waistband and in a calm voice said, "Yeah, it's over. Almost."

Slaton looked up from where he kneeled beside Lou.

"He's dead," he said.

Flintlock nodded. Then, "Slaton, that there spilled molasses is a mess. Sticky, you know what I mean?"

"I'll mop it up," Slaton said. "Right now I've got other things on my mind, mister."

"It shouldn't go to waste," Flintlock said. "Molasses is expensive."

He stared hard at Ben. The man read Flintlock's eyes and said, "I ain't gonna mop it up."

"Yeah, that's right, you're not. You're going to lick it up like the mangy dog you are."

"The hell I will," Ben said.

Flintlock pulled his gun. His words iced over. "Get on your hands and knees, make like a cur and lick it up, or I'll drop you right where you stand."

"Here, that won't do," Slaton said.

"It does for me," Flintlock said.

Ben's eyes darted to the corner where he'd tossed his gun. Too far. He'd never make it.

"Lick it up," Flintlock said.

"Go to hell," Ben said.

Flintlock fired.

At a distance of just twelve feet, his aim was true. The big .45 bullet hit the base of Ben's right thumb and left him with a bloody stump.

The man screamed, held up his hand and stared at the horror that had just befallen him.

"You picked on a poor mountain man for no other reason than you thought he would be easy to kill," Flintlock said. "It seems you were wrong."

"You shot off my thumb, you son of a bitch!" Ben shrieked.

"That I am," Flintlock said. Then, "McPhee, pick up Ben's gun and stick it in your pants. He's got no further need for it." He nodded in the direction of the dead man. "Slaton, I'm sure he's got money in his pocket enough to bury him. Maybe Ben will help you dig the hole."

"Who the hell are you, mister?" Slaton said.

"Name's Sam Flintlock."

"You're a hard, unforgiving man, Mr. Flintlock," Slaton said.

"I won't be bullied or railroaded," Flintlock said. "They should have known that and extended me some common courtesy." He glared at Ben. "Never pick on a stranger who carries a gun, boy, often as not you're going to let loose a hundred different kinds of hell."

"Well, I guess he knows that now," Slaton said.

"Cost him a thumb, but the lesson was worth the price. Let's get my hoss, McPhee," Flintlock said.

A man wearing a plug hat stuck his head inside and summed up what had happened in a single glance. His face gray, he vanished again.

Ben glared and grimaced and held up his right arm with his left. "Damn you," he said. "You've crippled me."

"You right handed, boy?" Flintlock said.

"The hell with you. What do you think?"

"Ah well, too bad. Get that mitt bandaged and practice with your left and in a few years you'll be just fine," Flintlock said as he walked to the door, McPhee ahead of him.

McPhee opened the door and stepped into a bullet.

CHAPTER THIRTY-SIX

"War, Mr. Stannic, that's the name of the game," Lucian Tweddle said, reclining in an easy chair, a brandy snifter in one chubby hand, a cigar in the other.

"And you want me to start it?" Hank Stannic said.

"In a word: Yes." Tweddle shrugged. "The death toll doesn't need to be too high, a few here, a few there, that's all."

"You can count on me, Mr. Tweddle," Steve McCord said, his young face eager.

"I know I can. But right now my business is with Mr. Stannic."

"Masked?" Stannic said.

"No. Brendan O'Rourke or one of his hands must see and later identify young Mr. McCord here."

"What about the old man himself? Does he get a bullet?"

"Not yet. He must live to retaliate."

Stannic nodded in a tall man's direction.

"What about him?"

"Mr. Hunt won't join the raid. I want him here with me. The same thing goes for Deputy Reid."

"You object to that, Hank?" Beau Hunt said.

Stannic shook his head, a quick, spare movement. "No objections, Beau. Ain't your style to ride with ruffians, is it?"

Hunt smiled. "I don't mind." His eyes flicked to Holloway and Trent. "If they take a bath once in a while."

Holloway glared and fingered the head of his ax. Slick Trent grinned.

"Nancy, fill the gentlemen's glasses and pass around the cigars," Tweddle said. "We must take care of our guests."

The woman's yellow silk gown rustled as she passed him, and Trent's hot eyes followed her every movement.

"Poor Miss Pocket recently had a most unsettling experience," Tweddle said. "A man was shot and killed on her very doorstep. I've taken her into my home and under my wing until she's quite recovered from the shock."

"Handy, ain't it?" Trent said, his permanent grin in place.

Tweddle ignored that and said, "Mr. Stannic, all I'm asking you to do is ride in, shoot up the place, then ride out."

He smiled and squeezed his cigar. "Now if in the confusion dear Mrs. O'Rourke was mortally wounded by a stray shot, that would be a most fortunate happenstance."

"That's easy," Steve McCord said. "Hell, I'll put a bullet into the fat old cow."

"Very commendable of you, Mr. Mc-Cord," Tweddle said. He looked across the parlor at Stannic. "Will you take on the job, Mr. Stannic?"

"Maybe. If the money is right."

"You'll be on a retainer initially," Tweddle said. "Five thousand now, a further five thousand when the task is completed. In addition, six hundred dollars a kill, if such kill is in the line of . . . ah . . . duty."

Stannic mulled that, then said, "How many on the raid?"

"You and your two colleagues and our young Mr. McCord," Tweddle said. The brandy had given him dyspepsia and he let a series of little burps escape his pursed lips.

"Thin numbers," Stannic said.

"O'Rourke's men are a bunch of stove-up old punchers who've probably never fired a revolver in anger in their lives," Tweddle said. "You'll have no trouble."

"Sounds easy," Stannic said. "I don't like riding into situations that sound easy. Look what happened to the James boys at Northfield. They thought that raid would be easy but it sure as hell didn't turn out that way."

"The Circle-O isn't Northfield, Mr. Stannic."

"You won't be there."

"No, I won't. But I've been there many times in the past."

Steve McCord grinned. "Hell, that's hard to believe."

Tweddle lifted an eyebrow. "Are you calling me a liar, young man?"

McCord quickly plowed around that stump. "Not at all, Mr. Tweddle," he said, blinking. "I mean, I —"

Stannic considered any conversation with Steve McCord a waste of time and effort.

"I'll take on the job, Mr. Tweddle," he said, cutting across anything further McCord had to say.

"Excellent, excellent, Mr. Stannic," Tweddle said. "Now the success of this venture is assured."

"When?" Stannic said.

"Stay in Open Sky tonight and enjoy the whiskey and whores," Tweddle said. "Nancy will point you in the right direction for both."

"I'm married and I don't drink," Stannic

said. "But I feel like bucking the tiger."

"There you go, Mr. Stannic," Tweddle said. "Each to his own I always say. Then relax this evening. The raid will take place tomorrow night at an hour of your choosing."

Stannic got to his feet. "I guess our talking is done for now."

"Indeed it is," Tweddle said, smiling. He looked like a smug Humpty Dumpty before the fall. "Come to the bank tomorrow morning and I'll pay you the first part of the retainer," he said.

Tweddle made no attempt to leave his chair.

"Now, gentlemen, I'll bid you good night," he said. "I grow weary from the business of the day." He waved a hand. "You stay, Mr. Hunt. I need a quick word."

After Stannic and the others filed out, Tweddle said, "Mr. McCord, have you heard of Captain William T. Anderson?"

Steve McCord stopped and grinned. "Bloody Bill? Sure I have. He killed plenty."

"I had the honor to ride at his side," Tweddle said.

McCord stood silent, uncertain of what to say.

Beau Hunt helped him through that particular doorway. "Stay close to Stannic tonight," he said. "You may learn something."

After the youth left, Tweddle said, "Mr. Hunt, I have no intention of paying Stannic all that money. You may have to get rid of him."

"That's what you pay me for," Hunt said.

"You don't seem shocked."

"Stannic is in a hard business. He knows the risks."

"Jamie McPhee and that Flintlock person are still thorns in my side," Tweddle said. "I want them out of the way."

"I'll see what I can do," Hunt said.

"The Pinkerton who was on McPhee's side and the lawyer who hired him are both dead, the latter thanks to pretty Nancy here. Isn't that so, my dear?"

"He gave me no choice," Nancy Pocket said.

"No, none at all," Tweddle said. "You did us all a service."

"Lucian, was Frank Constable right?" Nancy said.

"About what?"

"Did you murder Polly Mallory because she was pregnant with your child?"

"No, dear girl, I didn't. I murdered Polly Mallory because she was pregnant with

286

someone else's child."

Beau Hunt and Nancy exchanged a glance that Tweddle intercepted. "What will you do, turn me over to the law?" he said.

"I killed a man to save you from the rope, Lucian," Nancy said. "I won't turn you in and play traitor."

"And I won't forget it. And you, Mr. Hunt, what about you?" Tweddle said. "Under all that fine linen are you a Judas at heart?"

"I'm loyal to the man who pays my wages," Hunt said. "I don't examine my conscience any closer than that."

"A gentleman's answer and the one I expected," Tweddle said. He looked around him and then smiled broadly. "My, my, aren't we a fine trio of rogues?" he said.

CHAPTER THIRTY-SEVEN

Jamie McPhee stumbled backward and Sam Flintlock eased him to the floor, then gun in hand charged into the street.

Under a dazzling sun that cast no shadows, events piled one atop the other very quickly.

A rifleman in a plug stood behind an abandoned fruit and vegetable stand that stood tipped over on one wheel opposite the saloon. The man threw a Winchester to his shoulder and fired at Flintlock.

He hurried the shot and Flintlock heard the round split the air close to his right ear.

Flintlock fired and his bullet hit the wood frame of the stand with a venomous smack. It was close enough that Plug Hat broke and ran.

Flintlock went after him. The man ran for about twenty yards, then stopped and turned. He shouldered the rifle and fired, levered another round into the chamber and fired again.

The first bullet tugged at the sleeve of Flintlock's shirt and the second zinged through his hat and came mighty close to braining him.

"Damn you!" he yelled. "Stand your ground and fight like a white man."

The man in the plug hat, a little fellow with yellow hair and heavy eyebrows, ignored that and cranked the Winchester again.

Flintlock took his time. Now was the moment for a grandstand play. He two-handed the Colt to eye level, sighted carefully and fired.

He and the rifleman shot at the same time.

This time Flintlock took a hit, a sledgehammer blow to his right thigh. But his bullet scored. The man in the plug hat shrieked and fell, blood all over his shattered mouth.

Stunned by the impact of the bullet that hit him, Flintlock watched the downed man writhe for a while, the heels of his boots gouging dirt, then lie still.

Flintlock removed his hat, stared at the sky for a moment then wiped sweat from his forehead with the back of his gun hand. He felt blood trickle down onto his boot.

"You killed him! You killed my brother Tom!"

289

The man called Ben stood outside the saloon door, his raised right arm glistening crimson blood from his knuckles to his elbow.

Suddenly Flintlock felt very tired and sick to his stomach. He ignored Ben and stepped to the body. It had been an aimed shot but a lucky one.

The .45 had crashed into the man's open mouth, splintering teeth, and had passed through his head and exploded out the back of his skull, scattering blood, bone and brains.

It was a fearsome, horrific wound.

"No man should die like that," Flintlock said, aloud, but only to himself.

Ben still stood in front of the saloon, burning hatred in the eyes he pinned on Flintlock. But Flintlock brushed past him and stepped into the saloon.

Slaton kneeled beside the groaning McPhee. "Shoulder," the man said. "The ball is still in there." He looked up at Flintlock. "Another dead man?"

"Yeah. I should've remembered there were three horses in the corral."

"Get your friend away from here."

"Can you take out the bullet?"

"No."

"How about the blacksmith?"

"He can't either."

"I'll take him to Open Sky, find a doctor."

"There's a cathouse closer."

"He needs a doctor, not a whore."

"Madame Josette runs the house and she's good with wounds. God knows, she's seen plenty."

"Where is this place?"

"A mile north of Buzzard Gap. You can't miss it."

Flintlock nodded. "I'm beholden to you."

"I just want you the hell out of here. And him."

Flintlock raised McPhee to his feet, then said, "Can you ride?"

The young man shook his head. "No I can't."

"Hurting?" Flintlock said.

"Yes I am."

"Good, that means you ain't dead and you can still ride."

Flintlock helped McPhee outside. Behind them they left two thin trails of blood.

The sky was an endless blue and overhead a single buzzard rode the air currents. A gusting wind lifted skeins of dust around Flintlock's feet.

Then a shot and a noise like an angry hornet close to Flintlock's ear.

Ben, his face twisted in fury, stood over

291

his brother. The dead man's smoking Winchester was propped up on his bloody right arm and he worked the lever awkwardly with his left.

"My name's Ben Ross!" he yelled. "And I'm gonna kill you for what you done to my brothers."

McPhee's horse had pulled away from the hitching rail and stood at a distance, its head lowered, tail to the wind-blown sand.

"Let's go," Flintlock said.

Ben Ross fired and dust kicked up under between McPhee's feet. "Sam, he'll kill us," he yelled.

"No, he won't. There's already been enough killing."

"Tell *him* that," McPhee said.

Now Ross staggered forward, shortening the distance. His face was stony, determined.

"I'll get you to your hoss," Flintlock said.

Ross walked toward them, firing as he came.

"Sam!" McPhee yelled.

As though he hadn't heard, Flintlock continued toward the horse.

The blacksmith yelled something, but the rising wind took the words away. A dog trotted into sight and started to bark.

Flintlock took a second hit. The thick bicep of his arm opened up and seeped blood as a bullet grazed him.

McPhee, the entire front of his shirt red, yelped in frustration. "Damn you, Sam!"

Then he did the unexpected.

The move took Sam Flintlock by surprise. McPhee wrenched away from his supporting arm, did a half turn and his hand reached out and snaked the Colt from Flintlock's waistband.

Flintlock yelled and stretched to grab the young man. But his entire weight landed clumsily on his wounded leg and it gave way, tumbling him into the street.

"Damn you, McPhee!" he cried out.

But the young man paid no heed. He walked toward Ross, the Colt at waist level.

"Leave us alone!" McPhee yelled. "You go back inside now."

Ross frantically tried to work the Winchester lever, panic glinting in his eyes. McPhee was now only five paces away and the hammer of his revolver was thumbed back.

The two young men eyed each other. Both looked as though they'd been splashed by buckets of scarlet paint. The Swedish blacksmith stood in front of his forge and yelled something that nobody heeded.

Four paces . . . three . . . spitting distance.

Both McPhee and Ben fired at the same time.

The Winchester's forestock slipped on Ben Ross's blood-slick forearm as he pulled the trigger. A clean miss.

McPhee shoved the muzzle of the Colt into the other man's belly. He fired. A gut-shot.

Ross screamed, knowing he'd just got his death wound, and staggered back a step.

McPhee fired again. A hit. Fired again. A hit.

He triggered the Colt but the hammer clicked, clicked, clicked on the empty chamber and then spent cartridges.

"He's done," Flintlock said.

He wrenched the Colt from McPhee's hand. "For God's sake, how many times do you have to kill a man?"

Jamie McPhee stared at Flintlock, his eyes unbelieving. "I killed him, Sam," he said.

"Yeah. I know."

"What do I do now?"

"You live with it."

McPhee stared at the dead man. "I was crazy mad," he said. "For a moment or two I went insane."

"We all go crazy at one time or another in our lives. That's what helps us keep our sanity."

"Look at him, Sam. He was young once, just like me, and now . . . and now he's just nothing."

"That's what death does to a man."

"Sam, I swear, as long as I live I'll never pick up a gun again."

"Guns don't go crazy and kill folks. Only people do that. Let's get you to your hoss."

"Look at us, we're all shot to pieces, Sam," McPhee said.

"Seems like," Flintlock said.

CHAPTER THIRTY-EIGHT

When Flintlock and McPhee reached the Gentleman's Retreat the morning had given way to afternoon and rain clouds piled above the Sans Bois Mountains like meringue on a pie. The wind had risen and talked in the trees and the tattered French tricolor on the building's roof looked as though it had been ironed flat against the graying sky. Somewhere close by chickens cackled.

Cathouse doors, unless at times of civil unrest or natural disaster, are never locked and Sam Flintlock, aware that he and McPhee looked like victims of a train wreck, stepped into the cool, perfumed hall of the main building. A very large woman stood at a doorway and berated a half-naked girl who'd apparently referred to a paying customer as a "dickless john."

"A guest is a gentleman and always a gentleman, no matter the size of his *equipe-*

ment do you understand, *mon chère*?"

The girl, her face full of dumb insolence, nodded.

"Good. Now don't let it happen again or I'll use . . . 'ow do you say . . . your guts for garters."

The girl looked over the big woman's shoulder and her face took on a horrified expression and the madam followed her stricken stare.

"Mon Dieu! Qu'est-ce-que c'est?" Josette shrieked.

Flintlock and McPhee ticked blood spots onto the polished wood floor. "Wounded men who need your help," Flintlock said.

Josette's eyes summed up the two intruders and didn't like what she saw. The thunderbird on Flintlock's throat gave her a frowning pause for a moment.

"We can pay," Flintlock said, reading the madam's face.

She turned to the insolent girl, a shapely little brunette with wide brown eyes who had some fine lines of experience around her mouth. "Ruby, whiskey for the gentlemen and tell Charlie Park I want to see him right away," Josette said.

She indicated a stone bench in the foyer. "Sit there. I don't want you bleeding all over my furniture."

The woman waited until Flintlock and McPhee were seated, then stepped gingerly toward them with all the caution of a cargo ship drawing alongside a dock. She cast an eye over the men's wounds, smiled and said, *"Soyez petits soldats courageux."*

Seeing their baffled look, Josette said, "Be brave little soldiers." She turned her head as footsteps sounded behind her. "Ah, here is Charlie at last."

The neat little bartender took in the situation at a glance. He examined McPhee's shoulder wound first, then Flintlock's leg. "The bullets must come out," he said. He nodded to McPhee, who was ashen and in a lot of pain. "Him first."

His face expressing his doubt, Flintlock said, "Can you do that, Charlie?"

"Yes. I was a doctor once."

"How come you ain't one now?"

"Sick people. Medicine is a fine profession, but sick people spoil it for everybody. Seems like every damned ailment they get is either horrible or catching and sometimes both. Who wants to even touch them?"

Charlie had intelligent black eyes and a mouth too thin and hard to ever smile.

"Back in '78 I took one look at a necrotizing fasciitis patient and quit that very day," he said.

"Necro . . . necrotiz . . . what the hell is that?" Flintlock said.

"It's a flesh-eating disease. You don't want to know any more than that."

Charlie turned to Ruby. "Bring my bag from my room, girl. And put some clothes on. You'll be my nurse."

Ruby hesitated and Josette said, "Do as you're told."

The girl frowned and flounced away and Josette said, "I don't know what to do with that *fille.*"

"She's young," Charlie said. "She'll learn. I'll operate right here."

"On a stone bench?" Flintlock said.

"Would you rather lie in a whore's bed?" Charlie said.

"Well, come to think of it. I —"

"Right here," Charlie said. "Take off your shirt and pants."

"I don't know if you noticed, but I'm shot in the leg, Doc. And there are ladies present."

"Hell, man, this is a brothel. You've got nothing they haven't seen before, bigger and better. I'll give you a shot of morphine to ease the pain." He nodded to the miserable, groaning McPhee. "And him."

After Flintlock stripped off his buckskin and pants, Charlie stared at him in amazement. "Dear God in heaven, man, how many times have you been shot and cut?" he said. He examined Flintlock's chest and back. "I count three old bullet wounds and . . . one, two, three, four . . . five knife wounds," he said.

Flintlock smiled. "Like medicine, bounty hunting would be a fine profession if folks didn't shoot at you and stick you with a blade."

"I think you maybe should try another line of work," Charlie said.

He stripped off McPhee's blood-soaked shirt. The bullet wound in the young man's shoulder looked raw, red and angry. "It's deep," Charlie said.

He swabbed off McPhee's upper arm then plunged a syringe of morphine into him.

"This won't hurt a bit," Charlie Park, MD, said.

Jamie McPhee was unconscious for most of the digging and cutting and after he extracted the bullet, Charlie proclaimed the operation a success. Or at least as far as he could tell.

Flintlock, fearing the needle more than the knife, passed on the morphine and gritted it out. Luckily the bullet had missed bone and Charlie was able to remove the lead without too much difficulty. Only the fact that Ruby held his hand to her breast prevented Flintlock from crying out in pain during the surgery, and afterward she called him, "True blue and a right brave gentleman."

But Flintlock knew better. If it hadn't been for the girl's presence he'd have squealed like a baby pig caught under a gate.

McPhee wasn't fit to ride, and Flintlock was in no shape to brace the hostility of Open Sky either. He paid for two nights of room and board, in advance, as Josette demanded, and the grateful madam told him he could occupy the George Washington Suite while McPhee was given lesser quarters.

The suite turned out to be a narrow, closet-sized room with an iron cot and a collection of mops, pails and brooms in one corner. Judging by the dust and cobwebs no one had used it in some time. But Flintlock was pretty much used up. He pulled off his boots and lay back on the protesting cot, his wounded leg punishing him. In the distance he heard a rumble of thunder but so far the evening that closed around the Gentleman's Retreat was quiet . . .

The lull before the storm.

Flintlock closed his eyes and descended into pain-streaked sleep.

CHAPTER THIRTY-NINE

Lucian Tweddle stared at Hank Stannic's face then turned away, waiting for an answer. Beau Hunt sat at ease in a chair and watched both men.

"I'm game," Stannic said.

"Then it's tonight," Tweddle said. He looked relieved.

"The Circle-O won't know what hit them," Stannic said.

"But make sure Steve McCord's face is seen."

"If O'Rourke can see him that clearly, the kid will probably take a bullet."

"Do you care?" Tweddle said.

"Me? Hell no. I don't give a damn."

Stannic turned to Hunt. "The O'Rourke outfit have any that are slick with the iron?"

"Not that I know of," Hunt said. "Mr. Tweddle?"

The banker shook his sleek head. "I heard they have a puncher called Matthews or

Maitland or a name like that. They say he killed a rustler over on the Canadian one time."

Hunt smiled. "That scare you, Hank?"

Stannic snorted a laugh and said nothing.

"Remember what I said about Mrs. O'Rourke," Tweddle said. "Plug her so old man O'Rourke gets good and mad."

"Mad at who?" Stannic said.

"At whom? Why, at Trace McCord, of course," Tweddle said.

"You plan to start a range war," Stannic said.

"Very perceptive of you, Mr. Stannic. Yes, a range war, and when it's over and done I plan to pick up the pieces."

"Make you a big man in these parts," Stannic said.

"I already am a big man in these parts, but I want to be bigger, a whole lot bigger."

"Big results require big ambitions," Hunt said.

"Precisely, Mr. Hunt," Tweddle said.

"You can count on me," Stannic said. He rose to his feet. "I'll go round up Steve McCord and my boys."

"Guns blazing tonight, Mr. Stannic," Tweddle said. "But don't kill too many. O'Rourke will need a few left to fight with."

Stannic nodded and left Tweddle's office.

Hunt got up from his chair.

"It's time I breakfasted," he said. "My admirers will be gathering."

Tweddle's smile was slightly envious. "It must be fun to be so famous, huh?" he said.

"They're afraid of me." Hunt shrugged. "People like to be scared."

"Good. There will be scares aplenty ahead of them."

"We got a long day ahead of us, McPhee," Sam Flintlock said. "Can you ride?"

"No, the poor boy can't ride," Josette said. "He must rest."

"What do you say, McPhee?" Flintlock asked again.

"I don't know, Sam," the young man said. "I honestly don't know."

"Then get up out of bed and find out," Flintlock said.

Irritation niggled at him. To his chagrin, McPhee lay in a brass bed in a room three times the size of his own, a girl's room, judging by the female froufrou lying around.

"How's your leg, Sam?" McPhee said.

"It hurts like hell, I can barely walk and the pain kept me awake most of the night on a mattress that was stuffed with rocks," Flintlock said. "I was stuck in a broom closet with a growly rat, but you don't hear me complain."

"I'll try it," McPhee said. "I'll try to walk."

"Damn right you will. Spoken like a white man," Flintlock said.

"You could kill this boy on the trail today," Josette said.

"Yes, he could. Poor Jamie."

This from a plain-faced girl Flintlock hadn't seen before. She stabbed him with her eyes. "What's your all-fired hurry, mister?" she said. "Are you on the scout?"

"No. We have important business in Open Sky," Flintlock said.

"Shady business, I'll be bound," the girl said.

"I'll get up," McPhee said. "I feel better."

"Good. I'll saddle your hoss," Flintlock said.

A good-sized barn lay behind the house and when Flintlock stepped inside he saw wicked old Barnabas straddling a partition between a couple of stalls, a cup-and-ball toy in his hand.

The old mountain man tried to get the ball into the cup but missed by inches.

"Dang, I just can't get the hang of this," he said. "I'll try it again."

He did, but with the same lack of success.

"You-know-who gave me this," Barnabas

said. "It's just another devilish way to torment poor sinners."

"What do you want, Barnabas?" Flintlock said. "I'm kind of busy this morning."

"See you're favoring your right leg. Get shot, did ye?"

"I'd guess you already know I did."

"You're in deep, boy. Too deep. Dark forces gathering agin you."

"You're telling me something I already know, Barnabas."

"When you find yourself in a hole, stop diggin', boy."

"I'll remember that, Barnabas," Flintlock said.

But he was talking to empty space.

CHAPTER FORTY

Night had fallen and a bright moon hung like a silver dollar in the sky when Sam Flintlock and Jamie McPhee rode into town. The buildings cast angled cobalt blue shadows but lamps were lit everywhere and glowed in a hundred windows like fireflies.

McPhee was in bad shape. Barely hanging on to consciousness, when Flintlock laid his hand on the young man's forehead it felt burning hot to the touch.

"You got a fever, McPhee," he said. "I'm taking you to the doctor."

McPhee, wrapped in the cocoon of his own misery, said nothing.

A piano played in the Rocking Horse saloon and loud sounds of mirth drifted into the street. A woman laughed and the sporting crowd gents roared. Something funny had happened, Flintlock reckoned. He wished he was in on the joke.

Flintlock drew rein outside the hotel,

checked on McPhee, who sat hunched in the saddle, then stepped inside.

"I need a doctor," he said to the startled desk clerk.

"You came back?" the man said.

"Yeah. I'm back."

"Is Jamie McPhee with you?"

Flintlock ignored that. "Where can I find the doctor?" he said.

"Down the street. When it runs out, swing left. Doc Thorne's is the yellow house on the hill. Is McPhee with you?"

Flintlock turned away, and the clerk called after him, "The doc is retired but he still sees patients now and again."

"God save us from retired doctors," Flintlock muttered.

A plump, middle-aged woman with curling pins in her hair opened the door to Flintlock's knock. She carried a single candlestick and a concerned expression.

"I have a sick man here," Flintlock said. "He's burning up with fever."

The woman had a kindly face. "Bring him inside," she said. "I'll lead the way."

Candlelight bobbed along the hallway as Flintlock, supporting McPhee, followed the woman.

"Who is it, Mrs. Grange?" A man's voice,

accented, coming from a side room with an ajar door.

"A patient, Dr. Thorne."

"Good Lord, at this time of night?"

"He has a fever."

"Then bring him into the parlor."

The house smelled of roast beef, fruit pie, cake, bread and fried chicken and reminded Flintlock that he hadn't had a decent meal in days. He carried McPhee into the room with the open door, where a short, plump man with a florid face and bright blue eyes awaited him.

"I am Dr. Thorne," he said.

Then, after running an experienced eye over McPhee, he said, "Lay him on the sofa. I don't have a surgery. Retired, y'know. Oh yes, enjoying the leisurely life."

Flintlock did as he was told, and the doctor unbuttoned McPhee's shirt, a homespun castoff that Josette had found for him. "Bullet wound," he said.

Flintlock nodded. "Happened yesterday."

"Who treated him?"

"A retired doctor."

"He does excellent work," Thorne said. "The suturing is excellent. I could have used a chap like him in India. Oh dear, yes. Once it comes time for slaughter, there are never enough doctors."

"If this is excellent work then why does he have a fever?" Flintlock said.

"It's not unusual after a gunshot wound, old fellow," Thorne said. "The wound itself is clean and I detect no odor of gas gangrene. I think with rest he'll be fine but he'll stay here tonight as a precaution."

Thorne looked directly into Flintlock's eyes. "He's young Jamie McPhee, if I'm not mistaken and I know I'm not."

"Yeah, it's McPhee all right."

"And you must be Sam Flintlock, the violent desperado Frank Constable hired to guard him."

"Right on all counts, Doc," Flintlock said.

"You don't seem very well yourself, Mr. Flintlock. A bit pale, perhaps."

"I got shot in the right thigh."

"Pants down. Let me take a look. Mrs. Grange, can we have some sustenance for Mr. Flintlock. I declare that he's as thin as a fiddle string."

"Yes, Doctor, he's looking a bit gaunt, the poor dear." the woman said.

She said to Flintlock, "Some roast beef sandwiches and a nice cup of tea will set you up a treat."

"Just so, Mrs. Grange," Thorne said. "Carry on."

After the woman left, the doctor examined

Flintlock's thigh. "First-rate work, I must say, really tip-top," he said. "Where did you meet this surgical paragon, Mr. Flintlock?"

"He's the bartender at the Gentleman's Retreat cathouse," Flintlock said. "He was a doctor once, but quit the profession."

"A great loss, I'm bound to tell you," Thorne said. "In the past I've treated patrons of that particular den of iniquity. An hour with Venus, a lifetime with Mercury, alas."

"How's my leg, Doc?"

"Coming along quite nicely. I'll clean and rebandage the wound." Thorne smiled. "Men of your stripe always heal quickly, Mr. Flintlock. The coarse, violent life they lead toughens them up like Sheffield steel. Ah, here's Mrs. Grange at last."

The woman laid a platter of sandwiches in front of Flintlock and a pot of steaming tea.

"Do you care for anything, Doctor?" she said.

"No, not even a morsel of beef or a crumb of bread. I rather fancy that I partook of dinner a trifle too enthusiastically."

"Very well then, I'll leave you to your patients," Mrs. Grange said.

Panic flitted across the physician's rubicund features and he said hastily, "But, on reflection, perhaps I could force myself to a few slices of roast beef and a wedge of boysenberry pie. When there are patients on hand, a physician must keep up his strength."

For his part, Flintlock ate with gusto and the sandwiches quickly disappeared from his plate, as did the tea in the pot.

Mrs. Grange returned with reinforcements, and together he and Thorne cleaned every bite.

McPhee, temporarily ignored by the two trenchermen, slept soundly on the couch and the doctor did pause once to assure Flintlock that the patient was doing fine.

After they'd finished eating, Thorne lit his pipe and Flintlock built a cigarette.

"I'm glad to see you smoke, Mr. Flintlock," the doctor said. "All the medical associations concur that it's very good for the lungs and for those with a delicate heart. More tea?"

After Thorne poured, Flintlock said, "Doc, did you talk with Frank Constable before he was murdered?"

The physician seemed a little surprised by the question. "My dear chap, why do you ask?"

"Because Frank knew the identity of the man who strangled Polly Mallory."

"He learned this from the Pinkerton he'd hired?"

"Clifton Wraith was getting close to the truth. That's why he was killed."

"Mr. Constable questioned me about poor Polly's death."

"What did he say?"

"He said that Jamie McPhee was not the killer."

"Did he say who he was?"

"No. He told me he'd keep his own counsel for a while longer. The poor fellow was killed the next day. Two bullets to the back at close range, in my estimation." Flintlock made no answer and Thorne said, "Mr. Flintlock, the lawyer told me something I already knew."

"You know McPhee is innocent?"

"I examined Polly Mallory's body."

"She was pregnant."

"Yes, probably three months."

Again Flintlock said nothing and waited.

"Polly's trachea was crushed by a man who was able to exert enormous pressure with his hands. He was strong. Very strong."

Thorne rose to his feet and stepped beside the unconscious McPhee. He grabbed the young man's right hand and held it up where Flintlock could see it. "Look at that hand," the doctor said. "It's never done a hard day's work in its life. It's the hand of a clerk, Flintlock, a pen pusher."

"Now I study on it, it looks like a woman's hand."

"Certainly not strong enough to crush a healthy young girl's throat."

Thorne gently laid McPhee's hand back on his chest. He sat again and said, "It's takes a certain kind of murderer to strangle a woman. The whole time the victim is dying he must look into her eyes and not be moved by the terror and pleading he sees in their depths."

Thorne tamped down the tobacco in his pipe with a stubby forefinger. "What kind of man kills like that?" he said. He talked into Flintlock's silence. "Cruel, heartless, ruthless, determined and on the day of the murder perhaps desperate. But I would say a man who has killed with his hands before and enjoys it."

"Who is he, Doc?" Flintlock said.

Thorne shook his head. "I don't know. I only wish I did."

CHAPTER FORTY-ONE

The Circle-O ranch was bathed in moonlight and sleep, a tranquil oasis of moonlight, stars, and blue shadow in the middle of a rugged and often cruel land.

Hank Stannic and the three riders with him were in the hills now, sitting their horses on the rise where Steve McCord had lain when he assassinated the ranch cook.

There was no need for words. Every man present had already been briefed by Stannic, a simple order to "Stampede the horses and then kill every damned human that moves."

The gunman noted that the windows of the house were dark, silvered by the moon. Asleep. Unseeing. Finally Stannic grunted, kicked his horse forward and descended into shadow and mist-filled hollows. The others followed.

When he was less than twenty yards from the corral, Stannic drew rein and pulled his

Colt. "Ready?" he whispered.

Steve McCord looked eager, his eyes glittering. Holloway and Trent had been there before and had adopted an air of professional detachment.

"Then let's get it done."

Stannic shrieked a rebel yell and set spurs to his horse.

"Jesus, Mary and Joseph and all the saints in heaven, what is that, Brendan?" Audrey O'Rourke said, sitting bolt upright in bed.

"Night riders!" her husband yelled. He threw the blanket off his hairy legs and sprang to his feet. "Stay there, Audrey," he said. "Don't move."

O'Rourke, thin, wiry and tough as hickory, grabbed his hat and gun belt from a rack beside the door. As guns banged outside the old man buckled his Colt over his long nightshirt and hurried outside.

A chaotic, flame-streaked scene greeted him.

Terrified horses galloped past the ranch house door, followed by a shadowy rider who yelled and fired his revolver into the air. O'Rourke took a shot at the man, then beat a hasty retreat back inside as bullets splintered wood and shattered glass around him.

"Brendan, are you hurt?" his wife said. Like her husband she still wore her nightdress, but she had a Winchester in her hands. Years before she and Brendan had fought off Comanches together and the old ways died hard.

"Stay inside, woman, or I'll be taking a stick to you," O'Rourke said. He replaced the round he'd fired and filled the empty chamber that had been under the hammer.

"Indeed I will not, Brendan O'Rourke," the woman said. "Our home is under attack and my place is by your side."

"Stay here, wife!" O'Rourke said.

He rushed into the roaring, blazing night.

Steve McCord dropped a man who ran out of the bunkhouse and he winged another right behind him. Hit hard, the puncher dived back through the door.

Young McCord grinned and looked around him. God, he was good! Maybe the best there ever was!

Stannic's horse reared as he drew rein alongside. "Slick is down," he yelled. "I think old man O'Rourke shot him."

What Stannic didn't anticipate was that three or four punchers had spread their blankets outside, taking advantage of the fine weather away from the smelly, stifling confines of the bunkhouse. He'd downed one but the others had steadied and were getting their work in and now bullets zinged close.

Stannic thumbed off a couple of shots then swung his horse away. "Let's get the hell out of here!" he said.

But Steve McCord ignored him. Just ten yards ahead of him was the plump form of old lady O'Rourke, her white nightdress standing out like a beacon in the darkness. She carried a rifle, but clutched it to her chest. In the gloom and noise of the gun battle she flustered around like a mother hen, seemingly uncertain of what to do next or in what direction to move.

McCord grinned and viciously spur-raked his horse.

The pained animal jumped forward and McCord saw the pale, startled blur of Audrey O'Rourke's face. From somewhere in the dark, a man yelled, "No!"

McCord fired. The bullet crashed into the old woman's chest and she collapsed against the doorframe and blood bloomed on her breast like a ghastly corsage.

Audrey O'Rourke stared at the young man, her face full of wonderment. "Steve . . ." she whispered. "How could you . . . how . . ."

Now belted, angry men ran toward Mc-Cord, shooting. The young killer turned his mount on a dime and galloped away, bullets chasing him. In the darkness the Circle-O punchers scored no hits.

Steve McCord was highly amused. He'd killed the old biddy, he was sure of that, and the hands had gotten a good look at his face. When he heard the happy news, Mr. Tweddle would be so pleased.

CHAPTER FORTY-TWO

"You're the only damned gun for hire around, that's why," the puncher named Rick Walsh said, his face angry. "And my arms are getting tired."

"Just keep them up there until I say you can put 'em down," Sam Flintlock said. His cocked Colt was pointing at the young puncher's belly. "All this happened last night, huh?"

"Yeah. Night riders attacked the ranch. Mrs. O'Rourke is in bed, like to die, and we got two men killed and another wounded. One of the night riders is dead."

"And you say Trace McCord's son led the raiders and shot the old woman?"

"That's what I say because that's what I know."

"Who is the dead raider?"

"I don't know. I never seen him before." Walsh worked his cramping, blood-drained fingers. "Why are you such a mean, nasty son of a bitch, Flintlock?"

"I guess because I was raised by one o' them. All right, you can take down your mitts now."

Flintlock lowered the hammer on the Colt and laid it on the table beside him.

"How did you hear about me?" he said.

Walsh rubbed his numbed hands together. "Everybody knows you're the gun hired to protect Jamie McPhee when decent Christian folks planned to hang him," he said.

"Is that what they are, huh?"

"I reckon."

"Who sent you?"

"I told you. Mr. O'Rourke himself."

"Why doesn't he do his own shooting?"

"Because the Circle-O can't go up against Trace McCord and his hired guns. Not if we want to keep breathing, we can't."

"You ride for the brand, Walsh. You fight its wars."

"I'm no gunman. None of us are gunmen."

"How many hands does O'Rourke have left?"

"Counting me and the old man — and before you say anything, I aim to stick — we got seven. Eight if Rube Elliot is still kicking."

"How many riders does McCord count?"

"More'n twenty. McCord's foreman, Frisco Maddox, is the best of them with the iron."

"I've heard of him," Flintlock said. "He got the name Frisco because he worked as a police officer in San Francisco's Barbary Coast red-light district for a spell. He killed nine badmen in the line of duty, or so they say."

"Well, you can see what we're up against," Walsh said.

"You ever come across an English feller by the name of Sir Arthur Ward? He's a white man but wears them heathen Chinese robes."

"Can't say as I have."

"He's got a real pretty daughter, so if you ever met him you'd remember."

Walsh consulted a watch he took from his shirt pocket. "Where are we headed with this, Flintlock?" he said.

"I want your boss to meet Ward before he goes off half-cocked and attacks the McCord ranch."

"Damn it, man, he's already half-cocked. If Ma O'Rourke dies he'll kill the McCords, father and son, or die in the attempt. We're talking war here."

"A war is what I'm trying to prevent," Flintlock said.

"You're a gun for hire. Why do you care who fights and who dies? You'll still get your wages."

"I've got reasons of my own."

"Then you'll sign on with Mr. O'Rourke?"

"On one condition."

"Name it."

"O'Rourke listens to what Sir Arthur Ward has to say before he makes a move against Trace McCord. He won't believe it coming from me, but maybe he'll heed the Englishman."

"O'Rourke is Irish. He doesn't like the English. One time he told me that."

"He must listen or he'll be destroyed. It's a simple yes-or-no choice."

"Where is this Sir What's-his-name?"

"His wagon is probably on your range somewhere. Find him."

"I'll tell Mr. O'Rourke what you said. But if his wife dies, all bets are off."

"Then say a prayer, Walsh," Flintlock said. "If you don't know how ask Brendan O'Rourke to teach you."

"A beefsteak with you, Mr. Flintlock, and perhaps you'd care to make a trial of Mrs. Grange's curried kidneys?" Dr. Isaac Thorne said.

"Only coffee, thanks," Flintlock said.

Dr. Thorne looked disappointed.

"How are you feeling, McPhee?" Flintlock studied the young man across the breakfast table. McPhee was pale, but the fever flush had left his cheekbones and his eyes were clear.

"I'll live," he said.

Flintlock thanked Mrs. Grange after she filled his coffee cup, then said, "I need you to ride with me."

"Hell, Sam, we just got here."

"I know, but circumstances have changed."

Flintlock told him about the visit of the Circle-O puncher and the raid on the ranch house. "Two dead and Mrs. O'Rourke likely to join them," he said.

"How do you plan to play this, Sam?"

"We go talk with Brendan O'Rourke and try to stop a range war."

"I don't think Mr. McPhee is fit for travel," Doctor Thorne said. He used his napkin to dab curry sauce from his chin. "An excellent dish. Ah, it takes me right back to Mangalore and my days with the old 51st of Foot."

"Are you fit to ride?" Flintlock said.

"I don't . . . I mean, I think so," McPhee said.

"If my plan works out, Sir Arthur Ward

325

will be at the Circle-O with his daughter," Flintlock said.

McPhee looked across the table at Thorne. "I reckon I can ride," he said.

"On your own head be it, young man," the doctor said. "I can't guarantee your recovery. You need rest and lots of it."

"Sam, I'll ride with you," McPhee said.

Flintlock smiled. "I thought a mention of Ruth Ward might do the trick."

McPhee shook his head. "It's not because of Ruth," he said. "It's because I won't leave you to face this fight alone."

Dr. Thorne slammed a hand on the table so hard the crockery jumped.

" 'Pon my soul, young man!" he exclaimed. "That's damned British of you. Well said."

Flintlock drained his cup then rose to his feet. "Your hoss is outside, McPhee," he said. Then to Thorne, "Doc, where does the woman live who last saw Frank Constable alive?"

"Nancy Pocket? Why, she conducts business out of a shack behind the Rocking Horse saloon."

Flintlock nodded and the physician said, "You may be treading on dangerous ground, Mr. Flintlock."

"I reckon I'm doing that already," Flint-lock said.

CHAPTER FORTY-THREE

"You won't find her there."

Sam Flintlock turned away from the shack door and said to the old woman who'd just spoken, "Where is she?"

"Wouldn't you like to know," the woman said.

She was a skinny old hag with a thin bird's beak of a nose and muddy brown eyes.

"Has she left town, ma'am?" Jamie McPhee asked.

"And wouldn't you like an answer to that?"

Flintlock reached into his pocket and found a five. He held it up where the woman could see it. "This loosen your tongue?"

The woman's skinny arm flicked out like a snake's tongue and she grabbed the bill.

"Mr. High-and-Mighty took Nancy into his house."

"Who is he?"

The old woman stepped closer, then whispered, "Lucian Tweddle, the banker." Her breath smelled of gin.

"I used to do for her, you know, clean up this place," she said. "No longer."

"What's your name, ma'am?" Flintlock said.

"Mrs. Drabble as ever was. Mr. Drabble, God rest his drinking soul, has been in the grave this past twenty year."

"Mrs. Drabble, who killed Frank Constable?" Flintlock said.

The crone smiled, revealing few teeth and those bad. "He killed himself, the lawyer did."

"How do you figure that?"

"Like you, he asked too many questions."

"Did Nancy Pocket kill him?"

The woman swung a skinny fist, as though trying to punch Flintlock in the chest.

"Open your eyes and look around you, fool. He was shot twice in the back and didn't see it coming, huh?" The woman turned away, muttering to herself. She stopped and called over her shoulder, "You're an even bigger idiot than the town marshal."

But Flintlock understood the woman perfectly.

Garbage and empty whiskey bottles lit-tered the area around the shack and there was at least thirty yards of open ground between it and the next tar-paper hovel where Mrs. Drabble stood fumbling with a key.

It was hard to believe that Frank Constable did not hear or see the approach of his killer.

He'd been shot at close range, Doc Thorne reckoned. And he didn't see it coming? Mrs. Drabble had said, scorn in her voice. Flintlock looked at McPhee. "What do you think?"

"I think Mr. Constable was shot in Nancy Pocket's cabin and staggered outside," the young man said.

"Then who shot him?"

"Nancy, obviously."

"Or someone who was with her that day."

"Why would banker Tweddle take her under his wing?" McPhee said.

Flintlock smiled. "A nice way of putting it. You mean under his belly."

"Maybe he knows Nancy killed Mr. Constable and wishes to protect her," McPhee said.

"Or he did it and taking her into his home is his way of making sure she stays quiet."

"But why would Nancy murder Mr. Constable in the first place?"

"Because she was trying to protect somebody."

"Tweddle?"

"Maybe. But I'm starting to smell a mighty big rat," Flintlock said.

Trouble showed when Flintlock and the ailing McPhee rode back into the main street, busy now with pedestrian and wagon traffic as the morning progressed. Dust churned up by steel-rimmed wheels hung like a yellow mist and drifted onto the boardwalk, clinging to the hems of women's dresses and the cuffs of men's pants.

Marshal Tom Lithgow, the scowling Pike Reid beside him, stood on the corner of the boardwalk as the two riders left the alley.

"Hold up there, Flintlock," Lithgow said. "We have business to be settled."

Flintlock drew rein. "What's on your mind, Lithgow?" he said.

"I'm in a mind to arrest yon Jamie McPhee."

"On what charge?" Flintlock said.

"For the murders of Clifton Wraith, Pinkerton, and lawyer Frank Constable."

Flintlock shook his head. "That's ridiculous, and you know it. Who's paying you to do this, Lithgow? Lucian Tweddle maybe?"

That hit the lawman hard and it showed

in his stiff face. "Nobody pays me, Flintlock. Now, McPhee, get off that horse. You're under arrest."

Now people had stopped to watch, sensing trouble. Most recognized McPhee and their muttered conversations took on a dark, angry edge.

"We won't be arrested today, Lithgow," Flintlock said. "Now step back and give us the road."

It might have ended right there and then in a Mexican standoff, but Pike Reid, seeing an advantage for Tweddle, decided to push it.

"McPhee, git off that hoss or I'll shoot you off it," he said.

"Pike, I wouldn't do that if I was you," Flintlock said.

"You stay out of this, Flintlock. This is between me and McPhee."

"Let it go, Pike," Lithgow said. "There are too many innocent people in the street."

But as intent on his prey as a cobra, Reid didn't listen. He badly wanted a kill, especially in front of the whole town, and the hated and reviled McPhee was a made-to-order target. Hell, after the smoke cleared he'd be a gold-medal hero.

Flintlock tried to end it. "Pike, don't do this," he said. "McPhee is wounded and he isn't going anywhere."

The crowd was hushed now. Scarcely breathing. Eyes big. Waiting.

Pike Reid shucked iron.

Drawing from the waistband, Flintlock was faster, the split second difference that separated the professional from the amateur. Hit twice in the chest, Pike Reid's thin body shuddered under the impact. Like a groggy prizefighter his legs turned to jelly and he staggered back a few steps then fell . . . at the polished toes of Beau Hunt's elastic-sided boots.

"Lithgow, don't try it!" Flintlock yelled. He was on edge, aware of Hunt.

The marshal let his gun hand fall to his side. "I ain't that ambitious, Flintlock," he said.

"We're riding out of here," Flintlock said. "Me and Jamie McPhee."

"I'm not stopping you," Lithgow said. "Not today."

Beau Hunt stepped from the saloon doorway to the edge of the boardwalk. He smiled.

"You got your work in real fine, Sam," he said. "Fast on the draw and shoot."

Then, resplendent in gray broadcloth, snowy linen and bright brocade, he looked down at Pike Reid and shrugged. "But then, he wasn't much, was he?"

"You taking a hand, Beau?" Flintlock said.

"As the good marshal said: No, not today."

Flintlock nodded, then kneed his horse forward. McPhee, ashen and frail, followed.

The crowd gawking gathered around the body of Pike Reid. None made any move in the direction of Flintlock and his charge.

"Fine day, Marshal," Hunt said, lighting a long cheroot.

"For some maybe," Lithgow said. "Not for me."

CHAPTER FORTY-FOUR

Brendan O'Rourke, a dark, brooding figure, sat in the gloom of the ranch house parlor like an ancient Celtic king grieving for a battle lost.

When Isa Mae, the young black servant girl, attempted to light a lamp, O'Rourke warned her away with a growl.

"I will wait one hour longer and no more," he said. "Then if you are lying to me I will hang you and attack the lands of Trace McCord with fire and sword."

"All you need to do is listen to Sir Arthur Ward," Flintlock said. "He'll speak the truth."

He didn't take the old rancher's threat lightly.

"When did the English ever speak the truth to the Irish?" O'Rourke said. Then, his face like thunder, "Where is he?"

"Your men will bring him in, Mr. O'Rourke," Jamie McPhee said.

"You'd better hope they do and pray I hear truth in his words."

Two Circle-O punchers sat on a sofa by the parlor window, silent, dark silhouettes in the scarlet-tinted murk of the early evening. Their blurred faces turned to Isa Mae when the girl stepped back into the room.

"How is she?" O'Rourke said.

The maid's fingers tangled and untangled in front of her white apron. "Still the same, sir. No better, no worse."

"I will go to her again," O'Rourke said, getting to his feet. He waved a hand in the direction of Flintlock and McPhee. "Feed them, girl. I will not hang hungry men," he said.

Flintlock squinted at the grandfather clock against the far wall. As far as he could make out the time was six fifteen . . . and each relentless tick of the clock moved him closer to his death.

He and McPhee had been disarmed and the shotguns across the laps of the two punchers reminded Flintlock of that fact with quiet authority.

Ten minutes passed then Isa Mae brought beef sandwiches and coffee. McPhee had no appetite, but Flintlock was hungry and ate heartily.

From out of the gloom one of the punch-ers said, "I'd rather feed you for a day than a week, Flintlock."

"The threat of being hung gives a man a hunger," Flintlock said.

"Where's your Chinaman?" the same voice said.

"He'll be here. That is, if Circle-O hands can find two people and a wagon in open country."

"If he's out there, they'll find him."

"The question is when?" the second puncher said.

"Yeah, that's the question on my mind," Flintlock said. "Your maid makes lousy cof-fee."

"She ain't our maid."

"And our cook got shot."

"But he made lousy coffee as well."

"Well, that's too bad," Flintlock said.

"What's that noise?" McPhee said, sitting forward in his chair. Flintlock listened into the night. He heard the distant and familiar clanking clamor of Ward's wagon.

One of the punchers was already on his feet, staring out the window. "Hell, some-thing's coming," he said. "It's all lit up like Friday night at the whorehouse."

"It's Sir Arthur Ward's wagon," Flintlock said, relief flooding through him.

"Your Chinaman?" the puncher said.

"None other."

"Knows how to make an entrance, don't he?"

"Yeah. The Chinaman's got style," Flintlock said.

"It may be your style to kidnap honest people and drag them across the prairie at gunpoint, but it's certainly not mine," Sir Arthur Ward said.

"This is an outrage," Ruth said. "And one that will not go unpunished, Mr. O'Rourke, depend on it."

"I reckon it's better than the alternative," the rancher said.

"And what is that, pray?" the girl said.

"If you hadn't showed up when you did, I would've hung these two," O'Rourke said, waving to Flintlock and McPhee.

"Thuggish behavior and thuggish threats, sir," Ruth said. "You should be ashamed to call yourself a gentleman."

"Ruth dear, that will be quite enough," Ward said. "We are under Mr. O'Rourke's roof, remember." Then, to the rancher, "Come now, sir, speak up. What is your reason for bringing us here? And why do you sit in darkness like melancholy Achilles in his tent?"

338

"In darkness, because my wife lies dying in the next room," O'Rourke said. "As for my reason for bringing you here, best you ask Flintlock."

As Ward's eyes grew accustomed to the gloom, the shattered panes in the windows and walls pockmarked by bullets became apparent. "What happened here?" he said.

Using as few words as possible and sensing O'Rourke's growing impatience, Flintlock told him.

The Englishman was horrified. "My dear sir, you surely don't think that I —"

"The raid was led by the son of a rancher by the name of Trace McCord, a man who has long envied my winter grazing," O'Rourke said. "I believe he now plans to take it by force. It was his son who shot my wife."

"Abominable," Sir Arthur said, his handsome face frozen in shock. "Dastardly behavior."

"Father and son, damn them, will hang from the same tree," O'Rourke said.

For a moment there was a minor distraction. Isa Mae shyly touched the shoulder of Ruth's vibrant green Chinese robe and said, "Pretty." And Ruth smiled at the girl.

Flintlock said, "Sir Arthur, tell O'Rourke about the railroad."

The man seemed puzzled.

"That's why you're here," Flintlock said.

Ward stared into the baffled face of the old rancher. "Mr. O'Rourke, a railroad, probably the Atchison, Topeka and Santa Fe, plans a depot in Open Sky. The most direct route for the track is across your land and Trace McCord's. The company will pay big money for the right-of-way as you'll no doubt learn soon."

"And McCord wants it all," O'Rourke said.

"I don't know about that, sir," Sir Arthur said.

"Why are you here, Chinaman?" O'Rourke said.

"I'm British actually. Railroad crews need fed and I will feed them."

"Sir Arthur is a famous chef," McPhee said, looking to Ruth for approval. Then he winced, this time hunting sympathy. He got neither.

"O'Rourke, somebody wants it all, but I don't think it's McCord," Flintlock said.

"So why did he send his son to raid my ranch last night?" O'Rourke said.

"Because if Trace McCord was behind it he would have come himself with all his riders and wiped you out," Flintlock said. "He isn't the kind to send a boy to do a man's job."

He tried to meet the rancher's eyes in the growing darkness but failed.

"I've no doubt McCord wants your range and is planning to take it," Flintlock said. "But I don't think you can lay the blame for last night at his feet."

"What the hell are you telling me, Flintlock? To fall over and play dead?" O'Rourke said. "You want me to go to McCord and say, 'Your son shot my wife, but all is forgiven.' No sir. I bear a noble name and it's not in me to grovel at the feet of any man."

"O'Rourke, there's a third party who wants a war between you and McCord and he tried to start it last night. After the shooting is over, he aims to move in, take both ranches and become rich on railroad money." Then, in a sudden moment of inspiration, "That's why Beau Hunt is in Open Sky, to take care of any opposition that might be still standing."

One of the punchers snorted a laugh. "Beau Hunt wouldn't be caught dead in a hick town like Open Sky."

"I've spoken to him and big money lured him," Flintlock said. "He was hired by Lucian Tweddle."

341

"You're saying the banker is behind all this trouble?" O'Rourke said.

"That's my belief," Flintlock said.

"Was the damned sodomite Beau Hunt the one who shot my cook?"

Flintlock shook his head. "No. Hunt doesn't shoot ranch cooks."

O'Rourke lapsed into silence. Then, "Flintlock, I've listened to you and the Chinaman —"

"British, old chap, actually," Ward said.

"And I think there's truth in what you say about the railroad and maybe Lucian Tweddle. But Steve McCord shot my wife last night and I aim to find him and hang him." He rose to his feet. "Abe, go rouse Cole and Dick. You and them saddle up," he said. "Roy, you stay here and guard the prisoners."

"I am not your prisoner, sir!" Sir Arthur said.

"You're my prisoner until I say you ain't," O'Rourke said.

"Where are you headed?" Flintlock said.

"The McCord ranch. If Trace is hiding that murdering son of his, I'll know it."

"I'll come with you," Flintlock said.

"Why?"

"Another way of proving my bona fides."

O'Rourke thought that through, then said,

"All right, you can ride along. Roy, give him that old Hawken of his. It's the only gun you get until I feel I can trust you, Flintlock, an' that may be never."

CHAPTER FORTY-FIVE

The evening was drawing in and Lucian Tweddle was once again at home entertaining in his lamp-lit parlor. The room smelled of cigar smoke and good whiskey and a faint reminder of Nancy Pocket's perfume lingered in the air.

"So you shot the old O'Rourke lady, young Mr. McCord?" he said.

"Put two bullets into her." Steve grinned. "What made it more fun was that she recognized me, stupid old —"

"McCord, circumstances force us to breathe the same air," Beau Hunt said. "But I will not listen to you make sport of an old woman's death."

Hunt was angry, a stark contrast to his usual cool, professional demeanor, and Tweddle read the warning sign.

"Of course, let us be done with that sorry subject," he said. "Mr. Stannic, we lost one of our own?"

"Yeah, Slick Trent is no longer with us."

"And that Flintlock creature gunned down Pike Reid this morning," Tweddle said. He looked as though he had a bad taste in his mouth.

"I saw it," Hunt said. He smiled. "Flintlock's good. Real good."

"Slick and Pike will be greatly missed," Tweddle said with a straight face.

Stannic shrugged as though the matter was not worthy of further discussion.

"How long before O'Rourke retaliates against Trace McCord?" Tweddle said.

"Maybe he's retaliated already," Stannic said. "We could be sitting here talking about dead men."

"My pa ain't dead until I put a couple of bullets into him," Steve said, grinning.

"Mr. Hunt, what's your take on the matter?" Tweddle said.

"I go with Stannic. Both ranchers are hotheads and I reckon the ball has already opened."

"I need to know for sure," Tweddle said. "Have they destroyed themselves? I want an answer."

Nancy stepped into the room, smiled at the men present and her silk dress whispered as she walked to Tweddle, kissed one fat jowl, then stood behind him.

The banker sat in thought for a while, pudgy hands folded over the great swell of his belly. Nancy played with a thin strand of his hair.

"I've made up my mind. Mr. Hunt, you will accompany Mr. McCord and scout both ranches. Any survivors you see, especially Trace McCord and O'Rourke, you will kill immediately." Tweddle smiled. "Is that clear?"

"Now I start earning my money, huh?" Hunt said.

"Yes. And when you bring this affair to a successful conclusion you will find me more than generous."

"We'll move out at first light," Hunt said.

"Wouldn't it be most unfair if it's not all over by now?" Tweddle said. "I mean, tiresome."

"One way or another it will be over," Hunt said.

"And I get dibs on Daddy," McCord said.

His face was alight and it was then Beau Hunt realized that Lucian Tweddle had created a monster.

"Mr. Stannic, you and Mr. Holloway will remain in town," the banker said. "Depending on what Mr. Hunt tells me on his return, I may have further needs of your services."

Tweddle smiled. "Keep your ax sharp, Mr. Holloway."

"It's sharp enough. I buried it in a drover's skull at the O'Rourke place."

"Crackerjack!" Tweddle exclaimed. "Is that not crackerjack, Nancy?"

The woman nodded and smiled. "It is indeed," she said faintly.

"Good. Now serve another round of drinks, woman. I've got thirsty men here. Cold buttermilk for Mr. Hunt, of course."

CHAPTER FORTY-SIX

Midnight moonlight bleached out the land around the McCord ranch house.

The house was in darkness but for a lamp that glowed yellow behind a single-hung window to the right of the door. The charred wreckage of the burned barn had been cleared away but the rising wind sounded like the whinny of dead horses.

Sam Flintlock sat his buckskin to the left of Brendan O'Rourke, the three other riders formed up to his right.

For long moments the old rancher sat in silence and stared at the house, like a dark knight wary of entering the cave of the Holy Grail. Finally he threw back his head and yelled.

"Trace McCord! Be a man worthy of his name and show yourself!"

Insects chirped in amethyst shadows and among the tall grass small things scurried and squeaked. A minute passed . . . then two . . .

The lamp in the house was extinguished, then the front door opened silently on oiled hinges.

From the bunkhouse the silhouettes of belted men stepped through the night, two score strong, and confident of their strength.

"Who wakes a man at this time of the night?"

Trace McCord stood outside his doorway, a rifle in his hands.

He wore a dull red smoking jacket, eyeglasses pushed high on his forehead. He blinked away the printed pages of Sir Walter Scott and concentrated on the angry men who faced him.

"It is I, McCord, Brendan O'Rourke, whose sleep your riders disturbed last night with fire and sword."

McCord took a step forward. "What the hell are you talking about, O'Rourke?"

Flintlock saw McCord's hands deploy in a skirmish line. He reckoned the tall, significant figure directing them must be Frisco Maddox.

"Last night," O'Rourke said, "your son led night riders to my home. They killed two of my men and your son shot down my wife on her very doorstep."

"That's a damned lie," McCord said. "Steve is by now halfway to Texas to live with kin."

"Who are you to call me a liar, McCord? My ancestors were great lords when yours scraped plows across their mean acres in Tyrone and Armagh. Your son was seen and by others beside my wife."

Then, after a moment, "It is you who is the damnable liar, Trace McCord."

The fuse was in place and needed only a match to light it.

Flintlock, a named fast gun, armed with a Hawken that lacked powder and ball, knew he would be the first target. Twenty against five, one of them unarmed, were not odds to his liking.

The atmosphere around Flintlock was tense, stretched tight like a rubber band ready to snap.

Frisco Maddox, aware that he sat on a powder keg, remained perfectly still, his hand away from his gun, and called out to O'Rourke, "Is Audrey dead?"

"No, but she lies at death's door."

"I'm moving, O'Rourke," Maddox said. "No guns."

"Then move and be damned to ye," the old rancher said. "We will not shoot."

Maddox stepped beside McCord. "Steve

didn't go," he said.

"That's nonsense," McCord said. "Of course he went. He knew there was no longer a home for him here."

"Audrey O'Rourke saw him. She wouldn't make that kind of mistake."

"In the dark?"

"Steve had to get close, make his shot count."

"Shots, damn you," O'Rourke said. "He shot my wife twice, once when she was already falling. What kind of a man does that? Where is the honor in that?"

McCord said, "I told you, he's . . ." His voice faltered, grew weaker. "Bound for Texas."

"Steve didn't go, boss," Maddox said again. "He turned back."

"Trace McCord, is the murderer of my wife in your home?" O'Rourke said.

Suddenly McCord seemed years older. "No, he's not." He waved a hand. "Search the place if you want."

"Your word is enough," O'Rourke said. The old rancher's saddle creaked as he leaned forward, his eyes on McCord's face. "When did you hear about the railroad?" he said.

McCord didn't hesitate. "What railroad?"

"Flintlock," O'Rourke said.

"The Atchison, Topeka and Santa Fe plans to lay rails to Open Sky," Flintlock said.

"Across my land?" McCord said.

"Yours and O'Rourke's. There will be big money involved in contracts for the right-of-way."

"I didn't know any of this," McCord said.

"Maybe your son does," Flintlock said.

Frisco Maddox spoke. "What's your drift, Flintlock?"

"If your boss and O'Rourke fight a war, Lucian Tweddle is ready to step over the dead and take over both ranges. He'll make a fortune from the railroad contract and he's got Beau Hunt on the payroll to make sure things go smoothly."

"Where is Beau Hunt?" Maddox said. "He's a weapon of war." The big foreman seemed alarmed.

"He's in Open Sky, biding his time. When Steve inherits your ranch, Tweddle will use him for a spell and then order Hunt to get rid of him. O'Rourke's spread is even easier. A banker can forge papers to say he's foreclosing on a delinquent loan."

"Lucian Tweddle, the banker? I find that hard to believe," McCord said.

Flintlock's smile was far from friendly. "You make a habit of calling folks a liar,

McCord?"

"I believe Flintlock," O'Rourke said. "And I heard about the rails from another source. I think Tweddle tried to start trouble between us when he burned your barn, McCord. But it didn't work that time."

The old rancher sat back in the saddle, his talking done.

"Is it war between us, O'Rourke?" McCord said.

"Find your son, turn him over to me," O'Rourke said. "And there will be no war."

"If my son shot down your wife, I'll hang him myself."

"No. A man should not kill his own blood."

"Flintlock, can you prove what you say about Lucian Tweddle?" Maddox said.

"Not a word of it."

"Then find proof."

"Clifton Wraith the Pinkerton found proof, and look what happened to him. And then Frank Constable was killed. I think he found proof just like Wraith did."

"All that was to do with the murderer Jamie McPhee and you know it, Flintlock," McCord said.

"Lucian Tweddle discovered Polly Mallory was pregnant and murdered her," Flintlock said.

"Can you prove it?" McCord said.

"Nope."

"Then you're blowing empty words."

To O'Rourke, McCord said, "I disowned my son. He was no good, a weakling. I sent Steve to Texas and hoped he'd never come back. Now I plan to wed again and have a son I can be proud of." His face looked like a carved rock in the moonlight. "So yes, O'Rourke, find him. Find him and hang him and from this night on there will be peace between us."

"There is blood on the moon and none of this bodes well," O'Rourke said. "Neither of us will enjoy peace, Trace McCord. I see death for both of us and it is a stark, cold vision."

"Then so be it," McCord said. "Let the cards fall where they may."

CHAPTER FORTY-SEVEN

A weapon of war.

It was an odd statement to make about a man, but Beau Hunt fit the bill. Frank Constable would have pegged him a flesh-and-blood infernal machine, even deadlier than his original.

As Flintlock rode back to the Circle-O he considered the man.

Hunt's sexuality had always been in question. He liked women and women liked him, yet there was no account of him ever dallying with a member of the fairer sex. Even Maisie May, the delectable songstress at the Rocking Horse saloon, had failed to attract his attention.

Was that why he'd turned himself into a war gun? To compensate for what others viewed as a lack of manliness? Flintlock shrugged off the question.

Whatever his motives, Beau Hunt was a dangerous man and a deadly killer, the fastest man with Sammy Colt's gun that had ever lived or would ever live. But no matter the peril, Flintlock realized he could not toss his gun away and kneel and kiss the ground in front of such a man.

Those who beat their swords into plows will plow for those who didn't. When the time came, and it would, he'd need to handle Beau Hunt.

As to how, Flintlock had not a clue.

Brendan O'Rourke returned to a house ablaze with lamplight. Incensed, he swung out of the saddle and barged inside. "Who did this?" he roared. "Damn you, Roy, was it you?"

The puncher nodded in the direction of Sir Arthur Ward.

"Ask the Chinaman."

"I'm British actually," Ward said.

"What do you mean by this?" O'Rourke said. His angry gaze locked on Isa Mae, now wearing Ruth's beautiful green robe she'd admired. "You've turned my house of sorrow into an Oriental brothel."

"There should be no sorrow in this house, Mr. O'Rourke," Sir Arthur said. "Your wife will not die."

"What have you done with Audrey?" the old rancher said.

He brushed past Ward and rushed into the bedroom. The Englishman followed, his silk robe rustling. Audrey was asleep, but a little color had returned to her cheeks and she breathed easier.

"We are fortunate indeed, Mr. O'Rourke, that both bullets were fired at close range and passed through her body," Sir Arthur said. "Otherwise she would be in a serious state."

"What did you do to her, Chinaman?"

"I treated her as any doctor would do, with herbs and potions to lower her fever and restore her health."

"You're a doctor? I sent a rider into town for Dr. Thorne, but where the hell is he?"

"As to your first question, no, I am not a doctor. But I made a small study of the medical arts in China." Anticipating the rancher's next question, Ward said, "When one was in an outpost of empire five thousand miles from London, army doctors were few and far between. We officers were expected to treat sick and wounded soldiers as best we could. 'Make do or do without,' we were told. No wonder then that we considered local Chinese physicians a godsend."

Sir Arthur took the woman's pulse and after a while he said, "Much stronger and

357

regular."

Grudgingly, O'Rourke said, "She looks better."

"It will take time," Ward said. "Look, I think she's opening her eyes."

Audrey's eyelids did indeed flutter open. The first sight she saw was Sir Arthur in his celestial robe. "Am . . . am I in heaven?" she said.

O'Rourke took his wife's hand and smiled. "No, dear. It's only a visiting Chinaman."

"I'm British through and through, actually, Mrs. O'Rourke," Ward said.

But the woman had fallen into a deep sleep again.

"We'll let her rest now," he said.

O'Rourke nodded. "Mister, you may be only a heathen Chinaman, but if my wife pulls through I owe you."

"She'll be just fine," Sir Arthur said. "Time heals all, as some wise man once said."

He'd decided to give up on establishing his national identity. If O'Rourke thought he was Chinese, then so be it.

"I'm glad to hear your wife is doing better, O'Rourke," Sam Flintlock said.

"Thanks to the Chinaman," the rancher said.

"Sir Arthur is a man of many talents," Jamie McPhee said.

As was his recent habit, he sought Ruth's approval and this time she smiled at him.

O'Rourke said, "Roy, tell the hands to get a couple of hours' sleep. We'll ride at first light."

"We'll find him, boss," the man called Roy said.

"Yes, we will. And as God is my witness he'll hang," O'Rourke said. "Flintlock, will you ride with us?"

"Yeah, I'll ride with you. But don't be in such a hurry to hang McCord. We need him to implicate Lucian Tweddle and in the presence of Marshal Lithgow."

O'Rourke considered that. Then, "Roy, we'll take him alive and hang him after he talks to Lithgow."

"Suppose McCord makes a fight of it, boss?" Roy said.

"We'll still take him alive," Flintlock said. "Let me handle him."

"Roy, you heard the manhunter," O'Rourke said. "Now go get some shut-eye."

"You've gotten cooperative all of a sudden, O'Rourke," Flintlock said.

"Maybe. But if Tweddle is behind all this, he'll hang with Steve McCord."

The rancher's mouth tightened. "And so will Beau Hunt."

CHAPTER FORTY-EIGHT

Beau Hunt rode through thin dawn light in the forested hill country south of the budding settlement of Red Oak, a post office, stage stop and sawmill with little else in its favor.

"You look tense, Beau," Steve McCord said. "Does leaving town and heading into the high lonesome bother you?"

The kid didn't smile like a man. He affected an impertinent smirk that scraped Hunt raw.

"I sense something," Hunt said. "Riders in the hills."

"Probably what's left of the McCord and O'Rourke punchers," Steve said. "If we run across any, I'll gun them for you."

"I do my own gunning," Hunt said. His gambler's finery set aside, he wore canvas pants held up by suspenders over a faded blue army shirt and scuffed, down-at-heel boots. The gun in his holster was a Colt

Cavalry model with a worn, walnut handle, a working revolver that matched the utility of his duds.

Hunt drew rein, a frown gathering between his eyes. "There are riders behind us," he said.

"I can't hear anything," McCord said. He smirked. "You afraid of boogermen, Hunt?"

Hunt ignored that and said, "I can't hear them. But I feel them."

"So you are getting spooked, huh?"

"Yeah. I sure am."

"Maybe you should head back to town where it's safe, Beau," McCord said, his smirk in place.

Hunt studied the terrain then swung his horse around and said, "We've got a hundred yards of open ground. We'll wait for them here."

"Here?"

"Yes. Right here."

"Hell, you're scared of your damned shadow," McCord said.

Now a niggling little thought burrowed like a vile worm into the young man's brain. Once out of a town where he could cut a dash, Hunt wasn't so much. In fact he was damned yellow. Then it dawned on him. A reputation as the West's most feared gun was within his reach. He could become famous as the man who killed Beau Hunt. Hell, the name Steve McCord would be in all the newspapers and they'd write stories about him in the dime novels as the new Wes Hardin.

"Hunt, you got a couple of minutes more to stare into trees and the pretty squirrels, then we're riding for the O'Rourke place," he said.

Yet again, the man ignored him, as though he were a faceless nobody who didn't deserve an answer.

But McCord didn't mind in the least. All he had to do now was bide his time. He was on the edge of greatness.

Two men rode into the clearing where the ground among the stately red oaks was dappled by the morning sun. Steve recognized them immediately as McCord punchers.

One was a short, stocky man called Stump Wilson, the other a tall drink of water who went by the name Slim Stockton. Both were steady hands, had a used a gun before and were game.

Steve McCord smiled and raised a hand in greeting. "Stump, Slim, what brings you here?"

The punchers exchanged glances, then the

man called Wilson said, "We got to take you in, Steve. This is none of our doing, but we got orders from your pa."

"So my dear father sent you?"

"Yeah, he did, us and others," Wilson said. "He says he's gonna hang you, Steve, on account of how you kilt old lady O'Rourke."

"He's real serious, Steve," Stockton said, his long face tailor-made for a funeral. "The boss don't make threats without he backs them up. You know that." His uncertain eyes flicked to Beau Hunt. "You the Beau?" he said.

Hunt nodded. "That would be me. Real nice to meet you gentlemen."

"You better stand aside, then. We're taking young Steve to his pa."

"No, you're not," Hunt said. "It's not convenient at this time."

Steve McCord's mind worked overtime. If his pa planned to hang him for gunning the old O'Rourke lady, it meant there was no war. And no war meant a serious blow to his and Lucian Tweddle's plans. He decided to bring this current unpleasantness to a close.

He went for his gun. Then played his hand. As Steve knew he must, Hunt drew and fired.

But McCord immediately rammed the

muzzle of his gun into the draw fighter's side and pulled the trigger. Stunned, Beau Hunt turned in the saddle, a disbelieving look on his handsome face.

Steve McCord yelped his triumph and pumped two fast shots into the man's chest. At a range of just a couple of feet, he couldn't miss.

Hunt's horse, stung by a bullet fired by one of the punchers, reared and threw his rider from the saddle.

McCord didn't wait to see the man fall. He turned to the drovers, his gun up and ready. Slim Stockton was on the ground on his hands and knees, coughing blood.

Stump Wilson, his gun drawn but unfired, seemed stunned by what had transpired in the time it takes a man to blink. He looked like a man frozen in place, unable to move.

"Drop the iron, Stump, or I'll kill ya," Steve yelled.

The young puncher hesitated.

"Drop it!" McCord ordered.

Unnerved, Wilson let his gun drop to the ground, a shocked, demoralized look to him. On the ground next to him, Slim Stockton gave a shuddering groan and lay still.

McCord swung out of the saddle and stepped around his horse to Hunt. The famous pistol fighter lay on his back, his last breaths coming in pained, heaving gasps. Frothy blood bubbled scarlet in his mouth, the terrible reaction of a lung-shot man.

Beau Hunt looked into McCord's face and said, "You're a sorry piece of trash."

"Yeah, yeah, yeah," Steve said, grinning. "I've heard all that before. But you're the one that's dead."

He aimed carefully and shot Hunt between the eyes.

The young man was amazed. The most famed, feared and respected draw fighter in the annals of the West now lay at his feet . . . a lifeless lump of nothing.

"Yee-hah!" he shrieked. "I'm the man who killed the great Beau Hunt." Steve McCord advanced on Stump Wilson, whose face bore an expression close to terror. "Did you hear me, Stump? I killed Beau Hunt."

The puncher's eyes flicked to Hunt's lifeless body then nodded. "You surely did, kid," he said. Then, as though he couldn't believe what he was saying, "You killed Beau Hunt."

"Tell them! Tell them all! Tell my pa! Tell him his son Steve done for Beau Hunt!"

McCord's face was wild, alight with elation and a dazzling vision of his future.

Alarmed, Wilson said, "I'll tell them, Steve. By God, I'll tell everybody."

"Call me Mr. McCord. You know what I am, Stump?"

"What are you . . . Mr. McCord?"

"I'm a gunfighter. You ever heard that word before?"

The puncher shook his head. "No, I never did."

"Well, you've heard it now. Tell everybody that Steve McCord is a gunfighter."

Wilson nodded, swung his horse and headed into the trees.

"You hear me, Stump?" Steve McCord called after him. "I'm a gunfighter! The best that ever was."

Chapter Forty-Nine

The sound of distant shots made Brendan O'Rourke draw rein. He turned a questioning face to Sam Flintlock.

"I'd say a couple of miles to the east of us," Flintlock said. "It's hard to tell among these hills."

"Steve McCord?" O'Rourke said.

"Maybe somebody took pots at him," Flintlock said. "But since you and your punchers are right here it's more likely to be a deer hunter."

"Unless Trace McCord's boys caught up with him," O'Rourke said.

Flintlock said nothing. He and the rancher could speculate away the whole morning and get nowhere.

O'Rourke thought about it and stared at the blue sky fringed by the tree canopy. Finally he said, "We're not doing much good here. We'll cut out of these hills, join up with the wagon road and head east in the direction of the shots. It could be Steve McCord or as you said a deer hunter. But it's worth a scout."

"Seems like," Flintlock said. He nodded to the old coonhound that stood beside O'Rourke's horse. "She got a good nose?"

"Not what it was, but Sally can still pick up a scent," the rancher said.

"Then it's up to you to find McCord, Sally," Flintlock said.

The hound sat on her haunches and scratched behind an ear. She seemed unimpressed by Flintlock's confidence in her.

"Roy, give Flintlock his gun back," O'Rourke said. "He might need it."

The puncher took the Colt from his waistband. "Careful," he said. "Don't drop it."

"Roy, your sense of humor might get you dropped one day," Flintlock said.

The Circle-O punchers laughed and in the end Flintlock laughed with them.

Sam Flintlock and the Circle-O riders rode south, crossed a shallow creek where Sally flushed a cougar, and joined the wagon road near the steep rampart of First Mountain.

An hour later the hound lifted her head and read the wind.

"She's onto something," O'Rourke said.

"Good girl, Sally."

"Maybe a coon," Flintlock said.

They were south of the natural amphitheater of Second Mountain when the dog left the road and trotted to the southeast, leading the riders again into treed hill country. The climbing sun had faded the sky to the color of much-washed dungarees and the light that filtered through the trees had the heat and radiance of molten steel. Flintlock sweated and black stains appeared on his buckskin shirt. The heat hammered O'Rourke and his four riders and the men had grown silent, all their talk dried up by the sun. Only the dog seemed cool, and Flintlock, slightly envious, wondered how that could be.

A few minutes later Sally took off running, and Flintlock and the others followed her coonhound bark, loud enough some say to waken the sleeping dead.

Feeling a strange sense of loss, Flintlock gazed down on Beau Hunt's body. "Yeah, it's him all right," he said, answering O'Rourke's question. "It's Beau Hunt."

"T'other one is Slim Stockton, boss," a puncher said. "He was a top hand for Trace McCord."

O'Rourke shook his gray head. "Hard to

believe, ain't it, Flintlock? I mean, Beau Hunt killed in a gunfight with a puncher."

Flintlock kneeled by the body. "Two bullets to the chest, one between the eyes. But the one that puzzles me is in his right side. Look at his shirt."

O'Rourke reached into his vest pocket, took out a pair of spectacles and joined Flintlock on the ground.

"See the charring there? Beau's shirt was set on fire," Flintlock said. "Somebody shoved the muzzle of a gun into his side and pulled the trigger."

"How come he let a man get that close to him?" O'Rourke said.

"The killer was somebody he trusted or at least knew."

Flintlock rose to his feet and stepped to Slim Stockton's body. He picked up the dead man's Colt and inspected the loads. "Slim got off one shot," he said. "Beau was hit four times. "O'Rourke, take a look at this," he said.

When the old rancher drew close, Flintlock pointed to the dead man's chest. "Two shots that you could cover with a playing card," he said.

"Hunt got his work in?" O'Rourke said.

"That how I read it. And while Beau was busy with Slim, somebody shot him in the

371

side, then pumped two more bullets into him as he fell. Then he finished him off while he lay on the ground."

Flintlock looked into O'Rourke's eyes. "Beau Hunt didn't die in a fair fight. I can say with certainty he was murdered."

"Well, he was a known sodomite and my sworn enemy," the rancher said. "But I'd wish that end on no man."

"Yeah. He deserved better," Flintlock said. "Hell, any man deserves better."

O'Rourke's knees creaked as he got to his feet. "Flintlock, who was the murderer?" he said.

"My guess is Steve McCord or someone else in the employ of Lucian Tweddle. But I know this: The man who killed Beau Hunt will wish to boast of it. And when he does, I'll kill him."

CHAPTER FIFTY

Brendan O'Rourke lived by the reckoning, the precept of an eye for an eye, but he was not a vindictive man. He insisted that they take Slim Stockton's body back to the McCord ranch.

"I'll bury Beau Hunt on my own property, unless you know of any kin, Flintlock," he said.

Sam Flintlock shook his head. "No, I never heard of any kinfolk. It's almost like the Beau sprung out of the earth full-grown. And for all I know, maybe he did."

"Then let's get it done," O'Rourke said. "I should be getting back to my wife."

"Lead the way," Flintlock said. He felt hollowed out, strangely grieving for a man he barely knew. Or maybe he grieved over how he died. He didn't know which.

When O'Rourke led the living and the dead into the McCord ranch the place seemed deserted, the corral empty, its gate open. But within moments a puncher stepped from behind the house, a Winchester slanted across his chest. The man, young and stocky, had a holstered Colt at his waist.

He said nothing, waiting for O'Rourke to speak, but his eyes were careful and missed nothing.

"I brought Slim Stockton home," the old rancher said.

The hand nodded. "Yup, I can see that. It's ol' Slim as ever was."

"Where do you want him?"

The cowboy thought for a moment. Then he said, "We'll put him in the bunkhouse for now. That's where he lived and that's where he should rest."

O'Rourke turned in the saddle. "Boys, do as the man says."

The puncher watched as the dead man was untied from the saddle and lowered gently to the ground. "This way, boys," he said. "Carry him easy now."

He led the way to the bunkhouse and when he and the Circle-O hands returned, he said to O'Rourke, "He's in his bunk. ¹ ⌐oks like ol' Slim is asleep, but he ain't."

⌐his was no doing of mine," O'Rourke
ᵛⁱe found your man and Beau Hunt
ⁱe trail."

"I know," the puncher said. "Name's Stump Wilson, Mr. O'Rourke, and I was there when they were killed."

Sam Flintlock tensed. "Explain yourself, mister," he said. "Today I got a short fuse so get the words out in a hurry."

"Hell, look around you," Wilson said. "Everybody's out looking for young Steve. Well, me and Slim found him."

"What happened?" O'Rourke said.

"We told Steve we were taking him back here to the ranch."

"And?" O'Rourke said.

"And? The only *and* is that Steve McCord drew down on us, first him and then Hunt. Hunt shot Slim and Steve shot Hunt. End of story."

Wilson shook his head. "No, that's not the end of the story. Steve told me to spread the word that he's the man who killed Beau Hunt. He says he wants to be known as a gunfighter."

"I don't know where he come up with that handle, but I've got another name for him — a damned murderer," Flintlock said.

Wilson nodded. "He didn't give Hunt an even break, that's for sure."

Flintlock caught a glimpse of old Barnabas. The wicked old rogue sat on the V of the ranch house roof, wearing a strange hat with a red, white and blue cockade that had settled over his eyebrows and pushed out the tops of his ears. Barnabas glowered at Flintlock and stuck out his tongue.

"Mount up, boys," O'Rourke said. "We'll head back to the Circle-O. I don't want to leave my wife with that crazy Chinaman for too long."

"He's a crazy Englishman, actually," Flintlock said. But he was talking to the ass of O'Rourke's horse.

After the others had gone and Stump Wilson had disappeared behind the ranch house again, Flintlock rode closer to Barnabas.

"What have you got on your head?" he said.

"It's called a bicorn, you ignoramus," Barnabas said. "Napoleon loaned it to me."

"It's too big for you."

"I know that. Boney is just a little feller but he'd got a head like a nail keg. All them brains, I guess." Barnabas shook his head, but the hat stayed in place. "He's always playin' with them tin soldiers of his. Of course, they melt pretty soon, but he somehow always finds more."

"Why are you here, Barnabas?"

"Your ma is in Louisiana."

"I know. You already told me that."

"There's a rich Coonass down that way who plans to get rid of folks living along the bayous, especially the swamp witches that the folks look up to and respect. Your ma is one o' them, boy."

"When I'm all through here, I'll head that way."

"And you'll be too late by then," Barnabas said.

The old mountain man removed Napoleon's hat, scowled at it, then placed it back on his head. He looked like a bearded toadstool. "You split-ass down there, boy, and quit being an idiot," he said.

Wilson reappeared and stared hard at Flintlock. "Who are you taking to?" he said.

"Myself," Flintlock said. "I do that by times."

There was no one on the roof.

"Hell, it smells like hell around here," Wilson said, making a face. "Stinks like the sulfur poultice my ma used to put on my chest when I was a younker."

"Yeah, that's what I was just talking to myself about," Flintlock said.

CHAPTER FIFTY-ONE

His face stricken, Lucian Tweddle couldn't believe what he was hearing. It was just too much to grasp all at once. Then, after a struggle, "You killed Beau Hunt?" he said.

Steve McCord grinned. "I sure did. He drew down on me and I plugged him square."

"Oh my God," Tweddle groaned. He buried his face in his hands and sobbed into his be-ringed, chubby fingers. "All my plans . . . destroyed. This is so unfair, so unmerited. I deserve better than this."

"Hell, don't worry about it, Mr. Tweddle." The young man grinned. "You've still got me, and I'm all you need. I'm what folks will call a gunfighter."

Tweddle stared at McCord through his open fingers, saliva on his thick lips. "You fool. Your pa, Frisco Maddox, Flintlock, even Tom Lithgow, any one of them can eat you alive."

McCord's grin slipped. "Yeah? Well, tell that to Beau Hunt."

"You shot him in the back, didn't you?"

"No."

"You're a damned liar."

Tweddle saw the truth in McCord's face. "Beau was worth a hundred of you," he said. "No, a thousand of you." He shook his head. "You damned little pipsqueak you may have done for me."

"Hell, when the word spreads that I killed Hunt, I'll be the big man around town," McCord said. He had an angry red pimple on his chin. "I'll be the cock of the walk and the likes of Flintlock and Lithgow will be too scared to brace me." He leaned forward in his chair. "With me at your side with my gun, you'll be able to do anything you want in Open Sky, Mr. Tweddle. Don't you see that?"

"There's no range war, damn you," Tweddle said. "Without a war I can do nothing."

He glanced out his office window into the bank to make sure no one was within earshot. All the clerks were bent over, their steel pens scratching across massive ledgers. "Does anyone suspect you work for me?" he said.

The skin of McCord's face tightened to

his skull. "I don't work for you," he said. "We're partners, remember?"

"A slip of the tongue. But answer my question."

"Nobody knows we're partners."

"Good. Then let's keep it that way."

Tweddle sat in silence for a while. His huge bulk looked uncomfortable in his chair. Finally he said, "Guns. Maybe I can salvage everything with hired guns, wipe out both McCord and O'Rourke and grab the land."

"You'll need an army," Steve said, smirking. "How many? Two score, three? Where are you going to find that many guns around these parts?"

Tweddle blinked, as though he realized the hopelessness of his task. There weren't that many hired guns in the Oklahoma Territory.

Steve McCord grinned. "What happens to a snake when you cut its head off? The rest of it dies, huh?"

"What's your drift?"

"If I kill my father and O'Rourke, the fight is over. Their hands will pack up and leave."

"How do you hope to accomplish that?" Tweddle said.

"Easy. I send a note to dear papa and tell him I want to turn myself in and to meet me in a certain place but to come alone. O'Rourke gets the same note, but at a different place and time." Steve sat back in his chair, a self-satisfied smile on his lips. "I kill them both on the same day, drag their bodies together and make it look like they met on the trail and shot one another."

Tweddle felt a surge of hope. "What about Flintlock? He's a meddlesome trouble-maker."

"I'm a gunfighter and faster than he'll ever be. I can take care of Flintlock and that whelp Jamie McPhee."

Tweddle sat in thought for a moment, then banged his fist on the desk.

"It just might work," he said. "With their bosses gone, why would the punchers fight?"

"They won't, not after I take over the McCord ranch —"

"And I foreclose on the Circle-O," Tweddle said, his eyes alight.

"See, the death of Beau Hunt changes nothing," Steve said. "Not when I can step into his shoes so easily."

"I've underestimated you, Steve. And since we're partners, you may call me Lucian."

McCord grinned. "Lucian, we're gonna be real cozy, you and me."

"And rich on railroad money," Tweddle said.

Steve frowned as a disturbing thought struck him.

"What's the matter?" Tweddle said.

"My pa is arrogant enough to believe the note and he'll probably have it in mind to kill me, but what about O'Rourke? He's a cagey old coot."

"There won't be a note," Tweddle said, smiling.

"I don't get it."

"Nancy Pocket will be our messenger. She's an actress, that one."

"No note?"

"That's what I said."

"Explain it to me."

Tweddle affected a woman's voice. "*Oh, Mr. McCord, I am with child and I will be undone if you do not reconcile with your son. He wants to turn himself in so we can wed. But he's so frightened that you must meet him alone* . . . Do you savvy?"

"Damn, that's good, Lucian. Real good. Will Nancy do it?"

Tweddle's grin was nasty. "I'll beat her to a bloody pulp if she doesn't."

"Lucian, I don't want to do that," Nancy Pocket said.

"Why not, my dear?" Lucian Tweddle said. His voice was soft, silky, like the purr of a hearthside cat.

"They won't believe me. Brendan O'Rourke certainly won't."

"You can act, Nancy. A whore acts all the time."

"Lucian, it won't work."

"It will work. Pad your belly out with a pillow or something, look like you're far gone with child. Men get all tongue-tied around pregnant women. They'll listen."

"Trace McCord has bedded me before. He won't believe that his spineless, poetry-writing son could knock me up."

"Then, like father, like son. He'll believe you if you act well enough."

"And O'Rourke?"

"Did he ever bed you?"

"No. But he's a grim old sourpuss, drinks prune juice and reads his Bible."

"From what I can tell about him, he's an old-school gentleman. Just get his sympathy, Nancy. Plenty of salty tears."

The woman poured herself a drink and the crystal decanter clinked as she settled it back in the rack. "No, I won't do it, Lucian," she said.

"Oh, but you will, my dear."

"And if I don't?"

"Then I will beat you severely and drag you by the hair to Marshal Lithgow and tell him you tried to murder me like you did Frank Constable."

Tweddle steepled his fingers in front of his smiling face. "Who will Lithgow believe? A respectable banker who helps pay his wages or a two-dollar-a-bang whore whose been had by every man and boy in town?"

The girl looked stricken. "Lucian, I killed the lawyer for you. It was all for you."

"You murdered Constable to save your own skin. So make up your mind. Do you act the part of an undone female or hang? Answer me you damned slut."

Nancy spat words like venom. "Lucian, sometimes I hate your guts."

"I'm happy with that so long as you fear me. Now, for the last time, will you do as I say?"

The woman nodded, tears bright in her eyes. "I'll be gone all day and into the night," she said.

"Do you expect me to care?"

Nancy made no answer.

"Good, then it's settled. Now go find a pillow and ride out to the McCord and O'Rourke spreads," Tweddle said. "I'll tell you what to say."

CHAPTER FIFTY-TWO

Brendan O'Rourke read the words for the dead from the Book, then the people who stood around Beau Hunt's grave sang "Shall We Gather at the River?" led by the rancher's strong baritone.

Ruth Ward didn't know the words, but her soft sobs provided a poignant counterpoint to the male voices.

Flintlock considered the hymn a cracker-jack send-off for Beau and later thanked O'Rourke for choosing it. But as he stood beside the grave in a summer rain, Flintlock figured he'd buried a lot of folks since he'd arrived in the Oklahoma Territory and there were more to come. When he got to Louisiana he'd strip buck-naked and jump into a bayou and wash the stench of death off him.

"The death shadows are gone from Mrs. O'Rourke's face," Sir Arthur Ward told him after they'd all gone inside for coffee and breakfast. "I think she'll recover just fine."

"Good to hear," Flintlock said. "We take up the search for Steve McCord later today."

"Do you think you'll find him?"

"He's a needle in a haystack. This is a open, wild country."

"You need a native guide," Ward said.

"The Apaches are all gone and ol' Geronimo is penned up in a Florida swamp where he'll probably die of fever." Flintlock considered that, then, "I wonder if O'Hara is still around."

"I haven't a clue, old chap. He's an element of nature that native, and he comes and goes with the wind. God knows where he is." He looked toward the cabin, then said, "I thought the funeral went well, all things considered."

"Seems like. I reckon Beau would say that we did our best for him."

"Ruth said even in death he was very handsome."

"Yeah, he was all of that."

"It's too bad."

"Man who lives by the gun knows the odds," Flintlock said. "Beau Hunt's luck ran out is all. It happens to all of us sooner or later."

O'Rourke had been spending time with his wife, now he stepped out of the ranch house door and called out, "You'll ride with us today, Flintlock?"

"Sure I will. I wouldn't miss it."

"How is Mrs. O'Rourke?" Sir Arthur said.

"She seems much better. I'm sure she recognized me this morning. She smiled at me."

"Glad to hear it," Flintlock said.

"Finish your breakfast, then saddle up," O'Rourke said. Then to Ward, "Will you stay a few days, see my wife through?"

"Of course I will."

"Then I'm beholden to you, Chinaman," O'Rourke said.

"Let me ride with you," Sir Arthur said. "Mrs. O'Rourke will be just fine until I get back."

"Can you shoot?" the rancher said.

"Yes, I can shoot. I have a Martini-Henry in my wagon, but I'll need to borrow a horse."

"I never met a Chinaman who could ride."

"Well, you've met one now."

"All right, pick out a mount from the corral. But be quick, now."

It was one o'clock in the afternoon when Sam Flintlock rode out with Brendan O'Rourke and the others. The old rancher said they'd hunt until it grew dark and then return, hopefully with a captive Steve Mc-Cord.

Jamie McPhee said he felt well enough to go, but Flintlock persuaded him to stay behind and guard the womenfolk. "If it comes down to it, let McCord get real close and then gut-shoot him with the 10-gauge, one barrel and then t'other," Flintlock said. "On no account get into a revolver duel. He'll kill you."

McPhee saw the logic in that, and staying close to the exotic and beautiful Ruth Ward had its appeal. But as far as the shotgun was concerned, how close was real close?

The rain that had begun in the morning settled in for the day and by four in the afternoon was a steady downpour. A thin mist hung around the trees and ashen clouds loomed above the hill where Beau Hunt's grave was marked by a simple wooden cross.

Ruth and Isa Mae, clearing the way for women's talk, had chased Jamie McPhee out of the house and he consoled himself by working around the barn.

But after an hour of sweeping and hanging horse tack back in place, he saw a rider come out of the trees and stay close to the shelter of the rise before angling toward the ranch house.

McPhee grabbed the Greener and stepped to the open door of the barn. Lightning flashed among the clouds but there was no sound of thunder. The gray day was as dark as twilight.

As the rider drew closer, McPhee realized it was a woman riding a bay horse. She wore a hooded black cape against the rain but he saw no sign of a rifle. Warily he left the barn and walked closer, the shotgun ready.

Then McPhee recognized the pretty, angular face of Nancy Pocket. With only a couple yards' distance between them, the woman drew rein.

"Miss Pocket, what are you doing here?" McPhee said.

"I might ask you the same question," Nancy said. "Is Brendan O'Rourke to home?"

"No. He's out scouting for Steve McCord. Him and Sam Flintlock."

"That's what I wanted to talk to him about."

"Can I help?"

"I have a message for him," Nancy said.

"You can give it to me and I'll deliver it for you."

The house door opened and Ruth stood looking out into the rain. "Who is it, Jamie?"

she said.

"Her name is Nancy Pocket and she has a message for Mr. O'Rourke."

"Don't stand out there in the rain, Nancy," Ruth said. "Come inside at once and have a nice cup of tea and a scone."

"No thanks, honey," Nancy said. "I'll deliver my message and then be on my way."

She opened her cloak and revealed a swollen belly. "This is part of it," she said.

"You're . . . you're with child," McPhee said.

"Aren't you a clever boy? Yeah, I'm pregnant, that's a natural fact. Bad news for a whore, huh?"

McPhee had no answer for that and let the hiss of the rain fill in the silence.

"Well, it ain't bad news after all," Nancy said. "The baby's father is Steve McCord and he wants to turn himself in and then make a life for me and his child."

"Then he can come here and surrender," McPhee said.

"No, he can't. Steve is frightened, scared of what might happen to him. He'll give himself up to Brendan O'Rourke but only if he meets him alone."

"I don't quite understand," McPhee said. "Meet Mr. O'Rourke where? When?"

"Tomorrow morning at sunup. He should

be at the ruined trading post near Court-house Gap. O'Rourke will know where it is and I'll be there to make sure Steve gets a fair shake. I want a husband, not a dead man."

Nancy swung her horse away, an unlikely Madonna in the rain. "That's the message, McPhee," she said. "Make sure O'Rourke comes alone or Steve will light a shuck and none of us will ever see him again."

Nancy Pocket was pleased. Things had gone very well.

Despite the objections of Frisco Maddox, Trace McCord had readily agreed to a meeting in Red Oak, where he would accept his son's surrender.

But he was skeptical that Steve had had the cojones to sire Nancy's baby.

"Someone else fill your belly and you decided to blame it on the boy?" he said.

Nancy shrugged. "A lucky shot, Trace."

"Steve doesn't have it in him," McCord said. "You know I'm cutting him off without a penny, don't you? If he doesn't hang, that is."

"I don't care about money. I love Steve and I want to marry him."

McCord laughed out loud. "Nancy, the

391

only thing you've ever loved in your life is the dollar bill. Where will you live?"

"I don't know. After the baby is born, Albuquerque maybe."

"And become a dutiful little wife and mother with a picket fence and your hands in the bread dough?"

"Yeah, something like that."

Both McCord and Maddox laughed. Then Maddox said, "Why doesn't Steve just ride into Open Sky and give himself up to Tom Lithgow?"

"Because Steve is terrified. He told me that when Lithgow hears about how he accidentally shot Mrs. O'Rourke, the marshal will string him up without a trial."

"He could be right about that," Trace McCord said, grinning.

"Will you meet him, Trace?" Nancy said. "Steve means the whole world to me and I want to be his wife."

Still grinning, McCord turned to Maddox. "Frisco, did you ever think you'd hear a whore talk that way about Steve?" he said.

"Never. I didn't think I'd hear any woman talk that way about Steve."

The whole thing was so bizarre, so ridiculous, that Trace McCord was highly amused.

"All right, tell him I'll be at the stage stop in Red Oak at one tomorrow," he said. "If

I'm still in a good mood, I may even let him live."

"Trace, if I tell Steve that, he won't show up," Nancy said.

"Hell, woman, I'm only joking," Trace McCord said.

But Nancy didn't believe him.

CHAPTER FIFTY-THREE

The rain continued as Nancy Pocket rode into Open Sky just as the clock in the spire above city hall chimed midnight. Lamps glowed in the Rocking Horse but the saloon seemed empty and quiet. Nancy couldn't remember if this was the night the chess club met, but if it was, that explained the silence.

She put up her horse at the livery and paid fifty cents to have the bay rubbed down and another two bits for oats.

Pulling her hood over her head again, Nancy walked through the teeming night toward Lucian Tweddle's house. She never made it. Herm Holloway was hunting for a woman.

A huge man, made terrible by darkness and rain, he watched Nancy leave the livery stable and walk purposely, her skirt and white petticoats hiked up above her ankle boots as she picked her way through mud and puddles.

Standing in the shadow of a shop doorway, Holloway touched his tongue to suddenly dry lips. He recognized the woman. She was the whore Nancy Pocket who'd sold herself to Tweddle, the fat man. Holloway grinned. Well, Tweddle wouldn't grudge him a little taste.

He stepped off the boardwalk and angled toward Nancy who walked with her head lowered against the downpour. But when the woman glanced up and saw Holloway she stopped, her face registering alarm.

"Good evening, missy," Holloway said.

"What do you want?" Nancy said.

"You know what I want. The question is — am I gonna get it?"

"Not tonight, I'm busy. Now, will you step aside and give me the road."

"Just a few minutes of your time. A knee-trembler against a wall, huh? I'll give you three dollars."

"You're drunk," Nancy said. "Get out of my way."

"Pretty, pretty girl. You're going nowhere until I finish with you."

"I swear to God I'll scream," Nancy said.

Her hand reached inside the pocket of her riding dress and closed on her derringer.

"You'll scream all right, missy, but for

another reason," Holloway said.

He reached out and grabbed the woman by the shoulders.

"You come with me, little lady," he said. "We got to attend to business."

Herm Holloway stood three inches over six feet and weighed two hundred and fifty pounds and the bullet he took to the belly didn't drop him.

The derringer's .41 rimfire in his guts would kill him eventually, but way too late for Nancy Pocket.

Knowing he had his death wound, Holloway roared like a great wounded bear and pulled the ax from his belt. Nancy saw the danger, took a step back and brought up the belly gun again.

She fired. A second hit. But to Holloway's left shoulder.

He shrugged off the wound and swung the ax with tremendous, skull-splitting force.

Her head cleaved in twain, Nancy died instantly. She made no sound.

She dropped to the ground, her face a frozen mask of terror, the pearl-handed derringer still in her hand. Her hand, slim and white, slowly opened and the little pistol dropped into the mud.

Herm Holloway stood over Nancy's lifeless body for a moment, a tic working in his left eye. He'd seen gut-shot men take agonized days to die and knew what horrors lay in store for him.

Holloway tossed the bloody ax away. He drew his Colt, shoved the muzzle into his mouth and pulled the trigger.

CHAPTER FIFTY-FOUR

Lucian Tweddle heard the shots, loud in the midnight silence.

Two sharp reports separated by a couple of seconds, possibly the venomous *crack! crack!* of a derringer. Then seconds later the unmistakable boom of a heavy revolver.

Tweddle shook his head, his blue jowls jiggling.

No, it couldn't be Nancy's gun he'd heard. Or could it? Had she been followed?

Tweddle laid his brandy glass on the table beside him and listened into the night.

Moments passed, then he heard the yells of men and among them he thought he recognized the marshal's voice.

He struggled to his feet. Worried now. If it was Nancy, was she still alive? She was a tough whore. She could live long enough to tell him what had happened at the McCord and O'Rourke ranches.

Tweddle waddled to the door then peered

outside. Damn this incessant rain. He saw a man in the distance, a shadow in the darkness. "You there!" he called out.

The man turned his head, saw who hailed him and walked in Tweddle's direction.

"What happened?" the fat man said. "I heard shots and I fear they've made me very afraid."

"The whore Nancy Pocket has been killed, Mr. Tweddle."

The banker almost reeled in shock. "Is she dead?"

"Head split wide open with an ax."

"Who did it?"

"The marshal says it was the outlaw Herm Holloway did for her and Nancy done for him. Holloway has been hanging around town recent, him and Hank Stannic."

"Are you sure Nancy is dead?" Tweddle said, his mind working. "Say she yet breathes."

Oh please, let her live long enough to talk. This is so unfair, so inconsiderate and so typical of the cheap little tramp.

"I don't know how dead she is, Mr. Tweddle. Marshal Lithgow has sent for Doc Thorne."

"Quickly now. Tell Tom Lithgow to bring Nancy here. The poor little thing shouldn't lie out in the rain. Dr. Thorne can examine her here."

"I sure will, Mr. Tweddle. You're a very kind man."

The man walked quickly away but Tweddle remained at the door.

"Live," he whispered into the rain-needled darkness. "Give me two minutes . . . just one . . . live, you damned slut . . ."

Moments later dark shapes moved toward Tweddle in the gloom, splashing through mud as they carried a blanket-draped burden. "Bring her in here!" Tweddle yelled. Then, "Please tell me poor Nancy is still alive?"

No one answered that question. There was little need as the soaked blanket slid from Nancy's body as they carried her through the parlor door. Tweddle stifled the shriek that sprang to his lips when he saw the dead woman's head. It had been split open like a ripe watermelon.

"Where do you want her, Mr. Tweddle?" Tom Lithgow said.

Tweddle was horrified.

Not on my Persian rug . . . not in my kitchen . . . not on my beautiful Italian couch . . . not in my bed . . . not anywhere in my house!

The marshal saw the banker's confusion, put it down to shock, then said, "On the floor, boys."

"Wait!" Tweddle said. He kicked the Persian rug aside. "Now put her down."

The floor was oak, but he could always replace a few bloodstained floorboards later if he had to. After Nancy was placed on her back and the blanket covered her face, Tweddle said, "Did she say anything before she died? Did she ask for me?"

Lithgow shook his head. "She was dead when we got there. The way I see it, Herm Holloway tried to rape her and Nancy shot him. After he murdered her, he was so horrified by what he'd done, he put his gun in his mouth and scattered his brains."

"The damned, low-down piece of trash," Tweddle said. His face was black with anger. "I hope he roasts in hell."

"I don't reckon there's any doubt about that," the marshal said.

Dr. Isaac Thorne arrived dripping rain. He wore a vast, black oilskin with the words *SS Daisy* in yellow on the back.

"Marshal, the dead man was shot in the belly," he said. "I believe he realized what suffering was in store for him and decided to destroy himself. Now, let's see here . . ."

Thorne took a knee beside the body and pulled the blanket away from Nancy's face. "Oh my God," he whispered, aghast. He examined the massive head wound with a trembling hand. "Split open by a sharp-bladed instrument," he said. "Death would have been instantaneous."

"Would this do the job?" Lithgow asked, showing the ax Holloway had used. "There's still blood where the handle meets the blade."

Dr. Thorne gave the weapon a cursory glance. "Yes, that's obviously what killed this poor, unfortunate night creature."

He looked up at Tweddle, his lips white. "Sir, for the love of God, a glass of brandy, pray you."

Despite his inner turmoil Tweddle played gracious host. He poured brandy while Lithgow helped the portly and shaken physician to his feet.

"Thankee most kindly," Thorne said as he accepted the drink. He met Tweddle's eyes. "She did not suffer. Her vile murderer killed her with one mighty blow."

The banker's face did not change expression. Impassive as the Sphinx, he said, "Marshal Lithgow, now you must remove the body."

A cold statement, the lawman thought. Made by a man who didn't give a damn for the girl, his only apparent interest was in what Nancy might have said before she died.

"We'll keep her and Holloway at the Rocking Horse icehouse overnight and I'll see to the burials tomorrow morning," Lithgow said.

"Take her now, if you please," Tweddle said. "I feel faint at the dreadful sight of her."

After everyone had gone Lucian Tweddle lit a cigar and collapsed into his chair, his face troubled. This was a pretty kettle o' fish and no mistake. What damned messages had Nancy delivered? Both? None?

Had she done the dirty on him and gone into cahoots with McCord and O'Rourke to save her own neck? Or had she faithfully delivered both invites to a murder like a good little whore?

Tweddle had questions with no answers and that troubled him.

It was time to talk with Steve McCord again. Together they'd work something out.

Tears dampened the fat man's eyes. Everybody wanted to frustrate him, keep him down, believing him too uppity for a man of humble origins. Well, he'd show them, by God. This was only a temporary setback. He'd rise up again.

Then a sudden thought, like scum drift-

403

ing to the surface of a pond, made him
smile.

CHAPTER FIFTY-FIVE

"Why does he want to surrender to you, O'Rourke?" Sam Flintlock said. "Why not Trace McCord?"

"Because he's afraid of his father," the rancher said. "I can think of no other reason."

"And with good cause, I imagine," Jamie McPhee said.

"It's likely a trap," Flintlock said. "If young Steve McCord is in cahoots with Lucian Tweddle they've got together and laid plans to gun you."

"I aim to go, Flintlock," O'Rourke said. "If he shows up, I'll bring him in."

"I can't talk you out of it?"

"Not a chance."

"Go with him, Flintlock," Sir Arthur Ward said.

"He said to be there alone and unarmed and that's what I'll do," O'Rourke said. "I don't want McCord to cut and run."

Flintlock smiled. "He's too bullheaded to listen, Arthur. Mr. O'Rourke will go his own way."

"Damn right," the rancher said.

Flintlock rose to his feet and stretched. "I'm going to turn in," he said. He glared at O'Rourke. "Tomorrow promises to be a busy day."

"Ruth, we should also retire to our wagon," Sir Arthur said.

"Isa Mae, did you make up the bed in the spare room?" O'Rourke said.

"I sure did, Mr. O'Rourke," the girl said, pausing with tray in hand.

"Miss Ruth, you're welcome to the room," the rancher said.

"I'm sure my daughter would appreciate a real bed," Sir Arthur said.

"Thank you, Mr. O'Rourke," the girl said. "It's very kind of you and I gladly accept your offer."

"Isa Mae will see to you," the rancher said, brushing off the compliment. He needed no thanks for what he considered was simply Western hospitality.

Sam Flintlock headed for the barn, deciding to forgo the bunkhouse with its smells of soiled clothing, ancient sweat and dead men. He made himself comfortable enough in the hayloft and lulled by the tick-tick-tick of rain on the roof was asleep within minutes.

He woke hours later with a knife blade at his throat and a whisper in his ear.

"I could have carved out a chunk of the thunderbird real easy, Flintlock."

Flintlock's eyes flew open and his hand groped for the Colt he'd laid at his side.

"Is this what you're looking for?" O'Hara said. The revolver he held up gleamed in the darkness.

"Damn you, O'Hara," Flintlock said. "I'm gonna put a bullet in you for sure."

"Empty talk, Flintlock, to a man who's got a knife at your throat and a pistol pointed at your gut."

"Give me a shave while you're there, O'Hara. I could use one. Not too close now."

The breed flashed a rare smile and got to his feet. He slid the knife back into the sheath and tossed Flintlock's Colt onto the hay beside him.

"You're an easy man to kill, Flintlock," he said. "I think you're in the wrong line of work."

"It's because you're a damned Injun," Flintlock said. "Injuns are forever sneaking up on folks. What the hell time is it?"

"It's about four. In the morning, that is."

Flintlock was irritated. Damn, the breed could have cut his throat easily. "Why are you here, scaring the hell out of good white Christians?"

"Got news from Open Sky."

"About Steve McCord maybe? Or is it Tweddle?"

"McCord is on the brag, calls himself a gunfighter. Says he's going to kill you next, which, all things considered, he shouldn't find too difficult."

"One creak of the ladder, O'Hara, and I'd have scattered your brains."

"Injuns, even half-Injuns, don't creak ladders."

Flintlock's fingers strayed to the pocket of his buckskin shirt. It was empty.

"Damn," he said.

O'Hara threw down a Bull Durham sack and papers.

"Your tobacco is damp," Flintlock said, head bent, as he built a cigarette.

"Been riding all night in rain."

Flintlock handed the makings back and O'Hara said, "Nancy Pocket was killed in the night by Herm Holloway. She got two bullets into him, one in his gut and then he killed himself."

"She was here earlier today," Flintlock

408

said, stunned. "Delivered a message from Steve McCord."

"What kind of message?"

In the dark O'Hara looked like something wild blown in from the Great Plains on the wind, more Indian than white man, more savage than civilized.

Flintlock told him about the arranged meeting with O'Rourke and the breed considered that for a while, his black eyes intent. Finally he said, "Steve McCord got drunk in the saloon last night, told Maisie May he's going to be filthy rich soon. Him and his partner."

"Lucian Tweddle?"

"He didn't say."

"How do you know this? Were you in the saloon?"

"I don't drink with white men. Maisie herself told me."

O'Hara smiled his fleeting smile. "People don't know it, but Maisie is part Cherokee."

"You redskins have got to hang together, huh?" Flintlock said.

"Nobody else will hang with us, even you Flintlock."

"Hell, I don't mind Indians, a few of my worst enemies were Indians. They're all dead now, but you catch my drift."

O'Hara stepped to the ladder. "Don't let

O'Rourke go to the meeting place this morning. Steve McCord will kill him."

"His mind's set on it and he's a mighty stubborn man."

"Then you be there too, Flintlock. And don't let anybody sneak up on you." He shook his head. "I thought old Barnabas taught you better than that."

"Why are you doing this, O'Hara? You're not beholden to me."

"Strangely enough, I like you, Flintlock. Though why you've lived this long is a mystery to me. Barnabas tried to explain it to me. He says the Great Spirit appointed special angels to look after idiots."

"Why don't the old coot stay in hades where he belongs?" Flintlock said, even more irritated. "He's always wandering around, him and his cronies."

"Let me tell you something, Flintlock. The devil has ten thousand buffalo, each one as big as a steam locomotive," O'Hara said. "They have eyes like green emeralds and wherever they tread the ground trembles and grass flames under their hooves." O'Hara took a couple of steps down the ladder until only his head and shoulders showed. "Barnabas herds them."

After O'Hara disappeared into darkness,

Sam Flintlock thought long and hard.

Lucian Tweddle and Steve McCord had forged a relationship from hell and their plan was diabolically simple. Gun two ranch owners, take over their ranges and sell the right-of-way across the land to the railroad. Millions of dollars would be involved. Even split two ways, Tweddle and Steve McCord could live like kings for years.

But how to prove all this? How to prove any of it?

Flintlock believed Steve was the weakest link. He could make him talk.

In the past Flintlock had seen the remains of men who'd been worked over by Apaches. Good ol' Geronimo was a master of the art. He could keep a man alive for days, burning and cutting just enough to draw out the torment. The lessons Flintlock had learned from the old reprobate could be applied to Steve McCord. First he'd tell what he knew and then beg for a merciful death.

But would a confession obtained by unspeakable torture hold up in court?

No. A judge would frown on it for sure, pat Lucian Tweddle on the back and set him free.

Flintlock peered through the rain-beaded glass of the skylight window at a rectangle of black sky. The night seemed endless.

411

Restless rats rustled in the corners and shared their lodging with eight-eyed spiders.

A thought crept up on Flintlock like a dark assassin. He considered its implications.

There was a way he could end it and only the guilty would suffer. It was a risk, but then any bold endeavor was associated with risk. Flintlock smiled to himself.

And it was what Barnabas would do.

CHAPTER FIFTY-SIX

Half drunk, Steve McCord stood on Lucian Tweddle's doorstep, rivulets of rain running from the shoulders of his slicker. Behind him lightning shimmered inside the clouds and thunder growled low and angry, like an aggressive hound dog.

When Tweddle answered, McCord said, "You heard?"

"Come in, you fool," the banker said. He let McCord inside then stuck his head out the door. Open Sky was shrouded in darkness. Nothing moved and only the hissing downpour and the distant thunder made any sound.

Tweddle closed the door and said, "Yes, I heard. They brought Nancy's body here and she bled all over my damned floor."

He told McCord to hang his slicker in the hallway then ushered him into the parlor.

"What do we do now?" the youngster said. He toed a dark stain in the floorboards. "Is

413

that where she lay?"

"Yes. Drink?"

"Sure, Lucian. I could use one. It's a miserable night out."

Tweddle poured whiskey, handed a glass to McCord and sat in his chair. "Nothing has changed," he said.

"We don't even know if Nancy delivered the messages. I can't kill men who ain't there."

"She delivered them, all right."

"How do you know?"

"Because the whore was scared I'd tell Tom Lithgow that she killed Frank Constable. She knew she'd hang. She spoke to your pa and O'Rourke, depend on it. She wouldn't have shown her face in town otherwise."

"Why did big Herm chop her, do you know?"

"He tried to get something for free that he could have bought for two dollars."

"I never done her," McCord said. "Ah well, it's too late now."

"You didn't miss much." Tweddle squeezed his cigar. "Drink up, then go find Hank Stannic. As far as I know he's still in town."

"He's lost both his boys," McCord said. "Makes him kinda shorthanded, don't it?

And besides, I'm not your messenger boy, Lucian."

"No, Steve, you're not my servant. But I've been feeling a trifle unwell recently and don't want to venture outdoors on such a rainy night."

"What do you want Stannic for? I can handle any gun work that comes along."

"I know. However, I'm prepared to lose Stannic, but not you, Steve."

As Tweddle expected, his words mollified McCord.

"I'll find him if he's in town," he said. He drained his glass and stood. "Why Stannic?" he asked again.

"He's good with a gun," Tweddle said.

"Not as good as me," McCord said. He looked defiant, like a callow boy boasting in the company of belted men.

"Of course he's not, Steve. After all, you're the man who killed Beau Hunt."

"And don't you forget it, Lucian."

"I won't," the fat man said. "I will never forget it."

After Steve McCord stepped back into the rain, Lucian Tweddle stubbed out his cigar and walked to his bedroom. He unlocked the lid of the large, dome-topped steamer trunk that stood at the bottom of his bed and opened the lid. After rummaging through a pile of worn-out nightshirts, he extracted an oilskin-wrapped bundle tied with string.

Tweddle laid the package on the bed and untied the string.

He unwrapped a pair of beautiful 1851 model Navy Colts in .36 caliber, both adorned with yellowed ivory handles. Tweddle smiled as men always do when they fondle a fine firearm, then, with marvelous speed and dexterity, he spun the big revolvers and let the butts slap back into his hands.

The banker believed he'd killed eighteen white men with the Colts, though Bloody Bill himself once told him that in his estimation he'd gunned two score. Eighteen or forty, it didn't matter. The main thing was that Tweddle planned to add a few more very soon.

He stepped back to the trunk, checked his supply of powder, ball and caps, then replaced the Colts. There were two belts and holsters with the revolvers, but Tweddle didn't even try them. He'd been as lean as a lobo wolf during the war and knew they wouldn't meet around his middle as they once did.

The banker sighed. Eating too much rich

food made a man fat . . . yet another example of the unfairness of his life.

Tweddle closed the lid and stepped back to the parlor, where he lit another cigar and poured himself a whiskey.

Come the daylight, he'd take matters into his own hands and resolve this problem once and for all.

Chapter Fifty-Seven

The next day, just before sunup, three men rode separate trails through morning mists.

One was Lucian Tweddle. The second Brendan O'Rourke. The third, at a discreet distance behind the old rancher, Sam Flintlock reined in his eager buckskin to a walk.

Tweddle was determined. O'Rourke was wary. Sam Flintlock was both those things.

Steve McCord had not found Hank Stannic and when Tweddle entered the young man's hotel room he found him too stinking drunk to ride that morning. Tweddle had some long riding to do and in his present state McCord would only have slowed him down.

His plan was to meet O'Rourke at the old trading post near Courthouse Gap and kill him. Then head for Red Oak and do for Trace McCord. To meet the men in fair fight did not enter Tweddle's thinking. Somehow he'd find a way to kill them both without any real risk to himself.

Damn! He'd not ridden a horse in quite some time and the saddle galled him. Steve McCord galled him too.

But these were minor discomforts compared to the money that was at stake. Two quick kills and then he'd be on easy street.

The thought pleased Tweddle so much, he felt like singing.

Brendan O'Rourke genuinely believed that Steve McCord would surrender and take the consequence for his actions. The Chinaman said Audrey would not die, and O'Rourke felt more inclined to be charitable. Fair was fair, and he'd settle for a sentence of thirty or forty years behind bars for McCord. He'd explain his change of heart to the young man and was sure he'd jump at the chance.

After all, a spell in prison was a hell of a lot better than the rope.

Flintlock was relieved that O'Rourke never checked his back trail and the rain had laid the dust. But the downpour showed no sign of slacking and for the first time since it had begun, thunder banged closer. A keening wind stirred the pines and once he passed a small cattle herd huddled among their trunks, their shaggy brown and white shapes almost invisible in the mist.

Courthouse Gap lay in hill country two miles north of Blue Mountain.

According to O'Rourke an Irishman named Kelly, with more faith in Apaches than good sense, had built a post near the gap and for a while traded peacefully with the warlike local tribes.

But in those times it didn't take much to irritate an Apache and Kelly's thumb on the scale was more than enough. The post was burned down with Kelly inside and the consensus among the Indians was *good riddance.*

That had been in the early 1870s and now all that remained of the Kelly store was a scorched fieldstone fireplace and a few charred logs.

But in a remote wilderness of mountains and forest it was an excellent spot to meet — and to commit murder.

Lucian Tweddle had forgotten how heavy a pair of Colts were. After an hour of riding the big revolvers dragged down the pockets of his caped greatcoat and added to his discomfort. As a young man he'd carried two or even three brace of revolvers, but those days were long gone.

His rented grade horse had a rough gate and its McClellan saddle was designed to favor the mount, not the man. Tweddle's great buttocks bounced so hard his jowls juddered and the teeming rain added to his misery, dripping off the brim of his derby hat.

Angry that circumstances had forced a man in his position to such a ridiculous course, Tweddle rode with grim, enduring determination. He knew the stakes were high and he was about to play his last hand. And by God, he would make sure it was a winner.

The black and silver rosary in Brendan O'Rourke's left hand clicked with each whispered Hail Mary as he neared Courthouse Gap, riding through a rainy half-light before the dawn.

Half a mile to his north wound the tortuous course of Fourche Maline Creek, where a tribe of warlike Old Ones once prospered then disappeared hundreds of years before the Caddo moved into the area. It was said that if a man was quiet he could hear the battle chants of ancient warriors in the wind, but O'Rourke heard nothing but the fall of the rain and the steady plod of his horse.

He admitted to himself that he was scared, a ridiculous emotion for a man of his years. But suddenly he valued his life highly, not for himself but for his wife. Audrey would need a lot of care and he wanted to be around to give it to her.

The wind had picked up and drove the rain among the trees with a sound like a forlorn whisper. The sky was as black as spilled ink and every now and then a fork of lightning cracked and the air smelled of electricity.

His eyes on the trail ahead, Sam Flintlock listened to the wind and his thoughts strayed to what O'Hara had told him about Barnabas and the devil's buffalo herd. He guessed Ol' Scratch liked his buffalo meat. Roasted of course, the only way it could be served in hell.

A volley of revolver shots rang through the solemn silence of the dawn.

O'Rourke was in trouble!

Flintlock drew the Colt from his waistband and kicked the buckskin into a gallop. The destroyed post swung into his vision, then fleeting images he tried to take in at a glance . . . a horse standing head-down near the ruin . . . a gray-haired man sprawled at its feet . . . a drift of gray gun smoke.

Flintlock heard the departing beat of a

running horse, but reluctantly drew rein. His first duty must be to O'Rourke. But when he took a knee beside him he saw that the old man was dead, his chest shattered by bullets. A black rosary lay in his outstretched left hand.

Sam Flintlock was stunned. It seemed that he had badly underestimated Steve McCord's skill with a gun.

From what he could put together from the rain-smeared tracks, McCord had fired from horseback and at least six rounds had hit O'Rourke's chest dead center. By any measure it was excellent shooting by a man who knew his trade.

McCord called himself a gunfighter and it seemed that's what he was — a natural-born shootist. Flintlock had seldom seen the like in a man so young. Bill Bonney maybe? Or Beau Hunt? McCord could be their equal, or even better than either of them.

Flintlock didn't know the how or the why of the thing, but Steve McCord had transformed himself into an elite shootist who could take his place among the most dangerous men on earth.

He rose to his feet. The hoof beats had faded into distance and he stared into the rain and made up his mind that tracking the killer was both dangerous and useless.

Steve McCord had grown up in this country and probably knew it like the back of his hand. He could lose a pursuer easily among the rugged hills and tree-lined valleys.

And if he chose, set an ambush.

Despite being raised by mountain men who'd taught him the ways of the rifle, Flintlock was a draw fighter. In a saloon or in the street a fast gun had its advantages. But in a wilderness like the one that surrounded him, it was a skill that counted less than a dog turd on an ant nest.

Flintlock shoved the Colt back into his waistband. A man who carries a gun has to know his limits, and Sam Flintlock had just discovered his.

CHAPTER FIFTY-EIGHT

Someone once told Lucian Tweddle that shooting was a perishable skill. But he didn't believe it, not any longer. His mounted charge at the gallop, a bucking Colt in each hand, had gone splendidly, just like in the good old days when he rode with Bloody Bill and them.

O'Rourke, the stupid, trusting old coot, was dead when he hit the ground.

Hell, he'd actually arrived unarmed, some popish bauble in his hand instead of a gun.

Tweddle smiled. Well, more fool him. He should have put his trust in Sam Colt, not God.

Now on to Red Oak and take care of another fool.

The fat man had little doubt that Trace McCord would be just as stupid and trusting as O'Rourke. And why wouldn't he be? Were they not cut from the same cloth? Arrogant men who believed themselves too rich and powerful to die?

The thought pleased Tweddle as he drew rein under a wild oak and struggled out of the saddle. He sighed as he pissed a hot stream against the tree then recharged his revolvers.

Remounting was a painful chore but when he regained the saddle he tilted back his head and opened his mouth wide to the rain. Refreshed, Tweddle lit a cigar, then urged his horse in the direction of the Red Oak settlement.

With all the contentment of a rich man who knows he's soon going to be richer, Tweddle rode and smoked in a leisurely fashion.

Things were going well and he had plenty of time, all the time in the world.

It was not yet noon when Lucian Tweddle arrived in Red Oak. A nerveless man, confident of his own ability, he felt a little niggle of hunger and decided he had plenty of time to eat lunch.

As he had O'Rourke, he planned a mounted attack on Trace McCord followed by a fast getaway. But he'd take care of all that after luncheon.

There were a couple of men in the saloon when Tweddle entered, miners by the look of them. The owner, the man named Slaton, came from behind the grocery counter and asked the fat man to name his poison.

"Lunch," Tweddle said.

Slaton had met amiable, even jolly fat men before, but when he looked into Tweddle's pale, direct eyes he realized this man was neither.

"I got some roast beef," Slaton said. "And corn bread."

"That's all?" Tweddle said, disappointed.

"Cheese. Do you like cheese?"

"I'll have the beef and I want coffee."

"Oh, and I got apple pie," Slaton said.

"Is it any good?"

"My wife baked it."

"I asked you if it's any good?"

"Yeah, it's real good."

"Then cut me a wedge."

Tweddle nodded in the direction of a vacant corner table. "I'll eat over there."

As Tweddle waddled across the floor the two miners exchanged glances but offered no pleasantries. The front pockets of the fat man's expensive greatcoat were weighed down by heavy loads, obviously pistols, and judging by his conversation with Slaton he was not inclined to be an affable gent. Such men were better avoided.

"How was it, mister?" Slaton said.

Tweddle stared at the man, his piggy little eyes mean. "The beef was tough, the corn bread tasted as though it was salted through with broken glass, the coffee was like mud and tell your wife she should quit baking. Anything else you want to know?"

Slaton shook his head. "No, mister, I reckon you summed it up for me."

"Then take the damned plates away, makes me sick to look at them," Tweddle said.

He stood, brushed past Slaton and stepped to the flyspecked window.

The rain fell heavier and the sky looked like curled sheets of lead. Thunder beat a bass drum to the north over the Sans Bois. Tweddle glanced at his watch then snapped it shut. It was ten minutes until one.

Would Trace McCord show? He shook his head, annoyed by his own negative thought. Of course he would show. He had to.

Then the fat man saw a sight that made his heart sink. Four tall men rode through the rain, stopped opposite the saloon and looked around them. Despite the upturned collar of his slicker and lowered hat brim,

428

Tweddle recognized Trace McCord. Beside him sitting a rawboned gray was Frisco Maddox. The other two men he didn't know.

Bitterly, the fat man abandoned his plan to kill McCord. Even he couldn't buck those odds. The rancher and his three gun-slick riders would be too much to handle.

He saw McCord turn his head and say something to Maddox.

The big man nodded and kneed his horse to the hitching rail, where he dismounted and then stepped into the saloon. He and Tweddle saw each other at the same time.

"Mr. Tweddle, what are you doing here?" Maddox said.

"On my way to the Gentleman's Retreat cathouse," Tweddle said.

"A tad off the trail, ain't you?"

Tweddle shrugged. "I enjoy riding in the rain."

"I don't," Maddox said. Then, "We're supposed to meet young Steve McCord here. Have you seen him?"

Tweddle shook his head. "Can't say as I have." He smiled. "Is that young scamp in trouble?"

"You could put it that way," Maddox said, an infuriatingly tight-lipped man.

He turned and walked out the door, his

spurs ringing in the quiet.

Tweddle considered a move. A quick shot into Maddox's back then a rush out the door, guns blazing.

He dropped the idea as soon as it occurred to him. Those boys outside would take their hits and shoot back. It was way too risky. Tweddle's face tightened. Why did these things always happen to him? His carefully laid plan was ruined. He should have known a treacherous lowlife like Trace McCord wouldn't keep his word and come alone.

Maddox led his horse to the others and spoke to McCord again. After they swung into the saddle, the four riders separated and began a search.

Tweddle smiled to himself.

Good luck with that, McCord. Your no-good son is lying drunk in Open Sky.

He stayed at the window like an innocent traveler waiting for the rain to subside, but Tweddle continued to observe McCord's every move. Damn him, the rogue was never isolated, always within hailing distance of his men. A quick strike was totally out of the question.

Finally, the four riders huddled together. They talked for a while then left.

Frustrated, Tweddle saw no alternative but

to head back to town and try again when the odds were more in his favor. He stepped to the door and behind him Slaton said, "Excuse me, mister, you haven't paid your score."

"Go to hell," Lucian Tweddle said. "I don't pay for pig swill."

CHAPTER FIFTY-NINE

The Circle-O was a dark, lonely and haunted place.

For a week the ranch had been plunged into mourning, first for Brendan O'Rourke then, two days later for his wife. When Flintlock had broken the news to her of her husband's murder, she had thanked him kindly then turned her face to the wall and willed herself to die.

Now the two lay together on a hill above a treed valley, side by side in death as they'd been in life. There were no heirs. Audrey had a sister in Philadelphia but since nobody had heard from her in years, it was supposed that she'd passed away.

After the O'Rourke funerals, Sam Flintlock slipped into a black depression and blamed himself and his moral weakness for all that had happened. He told himself he should have acted sooner, settled matters with a gun and then rode away.

A man who stepped lightly from one side of the law to the other, he'd allowed himself to be governed by legal principles and that had led only to disaster and the deaths of men he liked.

The old Sam Flintlock knew only one law . . . the law of the Colt . . . and to that code and to the life it represented he planned to return.

Sir Arthur Ward and his daughter, Ruth, both badly scarred by the death of Audrey, left the ranch and Jamie McPhee went with them.

"Ruth has made me no promises," he told Flintlock. "But I live in hope."

"Then good luck to you, both of you," Flintlock said. After a while he said, "The murder of Polly Mallory will always dog your back trail, McPhee. But there's nothing I can do about that."

"Time will pass. It will be forgotten."

"I sure hope so."

McPhee stuck out his hand. "It's been an honor, Sam. You taught me much, including what it takes to be a man."

Flintlock smiled and shook hands, but said nothing. But finally he said, "The Ward wagon is leaving. You'd better go."

"I'd guess I'd better."

The young man swung into the saddle.

His pale clerk's face never tanned, but he was brick red. McPhee said, "Good-bye, Sam Flintlock," then turned his horse away.

Flintlock watched him leave for a few moments then called after him: "Jamie! Good luck."

The young man waved, smiling, then rode at a gallop after the wagon.

Flintlock locked up the ranch house and bunked with the hands.

Brendan O'Rourke's will stated that on his death the ranch must go to Audrey, but it seemed that now it belonged to no one.

Taking advantage of the situation, Trace McCord had already moved cattle onto the Circle-O range, but that was not Flintlock's battle to fight and he ignored it.

Then came the news that the rancher planned to wed Miss Maisie May, the New Orleans Nightingale, and Flintlock and the Circle-O hands were invited to their engagement shindig.

Flintlock declined, as did the Circle-O punchers.

Two weeks to the day after Audrey O'Rourke's death, Marshal Tom Lithgow rode up to the ranch house, a paper in his hand, and his face solemn. The lawman sat his horse. Sweat leaked from under his hat and stained the armpits of his shirt. He didn't need this damned grief and it showed.

Flintlock had been wielding an ax, adding to the woodpile stacked beside the cook-house. Now he buried the blade in the stump that served as a block, shoved his Colt into his waistband and stepped in front of the big lawman. His face showed open dislike without even a trace of a compromising smile.

"What can I do for you, Lithgow?" he said. His voice was flat, cold as steel.

"Well, you can say howdy for a start," the marshal said.

"Consider it said. Now, what can I do for you?"

"Got me a notice of foreclosure here, Flintlock. But I got no one to serve it to. Unless you're aiming to take over as owner."

"Lucian Tweddle?"

"He says old man O'Rourke took out a five-thousand-dollar loan and never repaid a dime. Now he's foreclosing on the delin-quent loan."

Flintlock's anger spiked at him. "Tweddle is a damned liar. Brendan O'Rourke never borrowed money in his life."

Color flushed into Lithgow's face and

neck. "It's all legal and signed by witnesses," he said. "All I can do is serve it. You've got three days to vacate, Flintlock."

"I don't live here. There's three punchers who do, at least they were still living here earlier this morning."

Lithgow swung out of the saddle. He was ill at ease and Flintlock smelled his sweat. "Then I'll tack it to the ranch house door," he said.

The marshal seemed to have prepared for this eventuality. He took a hammer and some nails from his saddlebags and stepped to the door. *Tack, tack, tack.* The noise of the hammer was loud in the silence.

"There," Lithgow said, stepping back like an artist admiring his work. "It's done." He spoke without turning to look at Flintlock. "Railroaders in town. Well-fed men in black broadcloth and gold watch chains." Flintlock said nothing and the lawman said, "The rails are coming right enough and so is the money."

"What about Trace McCord? What about his share?"

Lithgow looked puzzled. "You mean you didn't hear?"

"Hear what?"

"Three days ago Trace McCord and Miss Maisie May were murdered on the wagon road a mile west of Open Sky. They were headed into town to buy Maisie's wedding trousseau when it happened."

Flintlock felt as though he'd been punched in the gut. "Who did it?"

"Bushwhacked by person or persons unknown is how it stands. Trace didn't even get a chance to draw his gun."

"And the ranch?"

"Young Steve McCord is the new owner. He's all grown up now since he gunned Beau Hunt. He struts. I guess that's the word."

"He murdered Beau Hunt," Flintlock said.

"That's not how folks see it. Local boy does good, shoots down notorious desperado. That's how they sum it up."

"How do you see it, Lithgow?" Flintlock said.

"I don't see anything." The lawman mounted, then touched his hat brim. "So long, Flintlock. Maybe we'll meet again in some other town."

"Tweddle murdered Polly Mallory. You know that, don't you?"

Lithgow didn't answer right away. Then he said, "I'm a tough lawman with a reputation and you're a famous bounty hunter and draw fighter. Right, Flintlock?"

"If you say so."

The marshal looked like he'd just sucked on a lemon. "Flintlock, the fact is we're nothing. We're just two little men in a world grown too big for us. Right now the real power isn't this Colt on my hip, it's back in Open Sky, where fat men are smoking Cuban cigars, planning a railroad and talking in millions."

Flintlock said nothing, still waiting for an answer to his question about Tweddle.

"All right, Flintlock, if I knew for a fact that Lucian Tweddle strangled Polly Mallory, there's not a damned thing I could do about it," Lithgow said.

"His smart lawyers would tie the court in knots, huh? Is that how you see it?"

"Tweddle would walk and he'd see to it that I never again worked as a lawman. I need my seventy-five dollars a month, Flintlock. I don't want to end up old and destitute, begging for my bread in some dung-heap town."

"Did he murder Polly Mallory? Tell me what you believe."

"Yeah. I believe he did. And many more beside."

"Trace McCord?"

"Yes, I think so. But there's not a damned thing I can do about it."

Lithgow kneed his horse forward, but

Flintlock grabbed its bridle. "Even for little men like us, there is a way," he said.

"There is no way. We're done, Flintlock, you and me. Tweddle has beaten us and you're too damned stubborn to accept it."

"And I won't accept it. Very soon I plan to step over the line, Lithgow. Just don't be waiting for me on the other side."

"If you commit murder I'll do my duty by the town, Flintlock, and go through the motions of earning my salary. That's how it's going to be with me."

"I don't want to kill you, Tom."

Lithgow smiled. "Then that's a chance I got to take, isn't it?"

"Some towns just aren't worth dying for, Marshal."

Lithgow shook his head. "Hell, Flintlock, what do you believe in?"

"I believe in what old Barnabas taught me. Justice. Honor among men. And most of all that for every evil deed there must be a reckoning." Flintlock let go of the horse's bridle. "I am the reckoning," he said.

Lithgow's eyes opened wide. "Damn it, I could swear the big bird on your throat just spread its wings."

Flintlock smiled. "Maybe it did. The Ojibwa say when the thunderbird gets angry and spreads its wings it means it will bring thunder and violent death."

Lithgow stared into Sam Flintlock's eyes, but shocked, he quickly looked away.

"God help us all," he whispered.

Chapter Sixty

"You did a fine job, Steve," Lucian Tweddle said, smiling. "I mean I couldn't have asked for anything better."

"It was easier than I thought it would be," Steve McCord said. "After I shot dear papa, his wife-to-be begged for mercy. What a stupid sow."

"But from what I heard you didn't feel inclined to extend it to her, of course."

McCord grinned and made a gun of his fingers. "Dropped her as she tried to run away. Pop! Pop! Pop! She went down like a ton of bricks."

The young man wore his gun low, almost on his thigh, and the cartridge belt slanted across his lean belly at a rakish angle. He looked ten years older than his twenty-one years.

Tweddle smiled and squeezed his cigar. "Did your pa give you any trouble?"

"He said he was in a good mood because

of his upcoming marriage and offered me money to leave the territory and never come back."

"What did you say?"

"Nothing. I just shot him. Boy, was he surprised. He looked down at the bullet hole in his chest and you should have seen the look on his face. *How could you do this to me?* Yeah, right, daddy, and here's another, smack between the eyes."

Tweddle changed the subject, the image of the dying McCord troubling him. "So, how does it feel to be a rich ranch owner?" he said.

"Just fine. I'm riding out there later today."

"Frisco Maddox could give you trouble. He set store by your pa."

McCord slapped his Colt. "He's nothing. I can take care of him."

"Stay alive, gunfighter. I can't afford to lose my partner."

The young man grinned. "Frisco can't shade me and he knows it."

"The railroad talks went well," Tweddle said. His piggy eyes were greedy.

"How much?"

"Nothing will be settled until my foreclosure of the O'Rourke property is finalized. Say, two, three days."

"How much, Lucian?"

"Enough to make us both very wealthy men. And I'm pushing for shares in the railroad as a bonus."

A clerk tapped on the door and stepped inside. "Marshal Lithgow wishes to talk with you, Mr. Tweddle."

"What the hell does he want?" the banker said, scowling. "Oh, very well, show him in."

Lithgow's huge presence seemed to fill Tweddle's office.

"What can I do for you, Marshal?" the banker said.

"Just a word of warning," Lithgow said.

Tweddle frowned. "*You* are warning *me*? Come now, that's a bit, shall we say, impertinent? You're acting above your station, Marshal."

The big lawman ignored that. "I believe Sam Flintlock means to kill you," he said.

Tweddle almost swallowed his cigar. "That's preposterous," he said. "Did you arrest him?"

"No I didn't."

"Why not? Flintlock is a violent, dangerous thug."

"I can't arrest a man for making a threat."

"If he comes this way I'll make him eat his threats," McCord said. "I'll gut shoot then watch him kick."

Lithgow, already on a short fuse, rounded on the young man. "You damned, lily-livered cretin, the only way you could shade a man like Sam Flintlock is to shoot him in the back like you did Beau Hunt."

"Swallow that, Lithgow," McCord said. His face was livid. "Swallow that down and then you go to hell."

McCord cursed and dived for his gun. But as he cleared leather, the big marshal's left hand shot out as fast as a striking rattler and grabbed McCord by the wrist. At the same instant he delivered a crashing back-hand that slammed into the man's face.

Spraying blood from his mouth and nose, McCord staggered. His head and shoulders hit hard against the picture window that gave Tweddle his view of the street. The glass shattered as McCord went through it backward. He came to rest with his upper body on the boardwalk, his legs still inside the office.

Lithgow picked up the young man's fallen revolver and tossed it, bouncing, onto Tweddle's desk. "Chain up your dog, Tweddle," he said.

The fat man was furious. "By God, Lithgow, you'll pay for this," he said.

A clerk opened the door and stuck a timid head into the office. His eyes flicked to the shattered window and the unconscious Steve McCord.

"Are you all right, sir?" he said to Tweddle.

The banker ignored him. "Get out of here, Lithgow," he said. "You're finished in this town, and any other town."

"Tweddle," the marshal said, "you're nothing but a piece of murdering filth and I hope I see you hang."

Tweddle's smile was unpleasant. "You won't live long enough to see anyone hang," he said.

A couple of clerks helped Steve McCord back into Tweddle's office.

The young man dripped blood from his swollen nose and mouth and his rage was a snarling, dangerous thing, strands of pink saliva stretching between his teeth.

"Give me my gun," he said. "I'm gonna kill that son of a bitch."

"No, you're not," Tweddle said. The fat man picked up the revolver and struggled to his feet. "You're coming home with me to have a drink and calm down," he said. He smiled. "Maybe write a poem."

"The hell with you. I'm through with poems. I want my gun."

Suddenly Tweddle was angry. He looked like a fat, belligerent pumpkin.

"You fool, you're a respectable rancher now and soon you'll be part owner of a railroad," he said. "You can't go around shooting lawmen, at least not in daylight, you can't."

McCord visibly struggled to calm himself. Finally he wiped blood away from his mouth with the back of his hand and said, "You're right. I'll kill him later."

After McCord cleaned up, Tweddle handed him a brandy and bade him sit in a parlor chair. "Feel better?" he said.

"Yeah, I do, but I still aim to kill Lithgow," Steve McCord said. "The son of a bitch split my lip."

"Yes, yes, I know. But you can do that in a few days. First things first, my boy."

"I'm not your boy, Lucian. I'm not anybody's boy."

"I'm aware of that now. Hell, I saw you grow up real fast after you shot Beau Hunt."

"And the others."

"Of course, of course, you're man grown and no mistake. How old are you now, Steve?"

"I was twenty-one a week ago."

Tweddle gave the appearance of being crestfallen. "And I didn't get you a twenty-first-birthday present! Don't worry, your forgetful friend will remedy that just as soon as he can."

McCord built a cigarette, a recently acquired habit. He thought it made him look tough, like Frisco Maddox and the Texas punchers. Behind curling blue smoke he said, "Where do we go from here?"

"You ride out to your ranch and take possession. Move right into the ranch house and sleep in your pa's bedroom. Too bad you can't take over his woman. That would be so . . . elegant."

"Well, too late for that. I shot her, didn't I?"

"Yes, you did. But no harm done."

McCord drained his glass and rose to his feet. "All right, I'm heading out to the ranch."

"Stay the night, then report back to me tomorrow, Steve."

"Report! I have to report?"

"Just a slip of the tongue. I should have said, consult with me tomorrow."

"Don't make too many more of those slips, Lucian. I don't like them."

"Of course not, dear fellow." Tweddle squeezed his cigar and looked worried. "Steve, you're a firebrand and you're always on the prod. Don't antagonize Frisco Maddox."

"I'd say that's up to him, isn't it?" McCord said.

After McCord left, Tweddle locked his doors and windows and pulled the curtains together. He placed one of his Navy Colts under his pillow, the other in the parlor.

Sam Flintlock was not a man to be taken lightly.

But then neither was Lucian Tweddle.

CHAPTER SIXTY-ONE

Frisco Maddox stood outside the McCord ranch house in cobalt blue twilight. The glow of lamps made orange rectangles of the windows and smoke rose from the chimney of the bunkhouse. The air smelled of fried bacon and of the surrounding pines.

Maddox smiled and touched his hat. "Howdy, Steve. It's good to see you again."

Steve McCord sat motionless on his horse for long moments. Then he said, "Shouldn't that be *boss*?"

"You ain't my boss, Steve," Maddox said.

"I own this ranch."

"No, you don't. You never did and you never will."

"Damn you, Frisco, are you trying to steal what's rightfully mine?"

"Nope, on account of how this spread isn't rightfully yours no more."

Several hands had drifted from the bunkhouse. Like Maddox they carried guns and their faces were less than friendly.

McCord tried to look tough, his right hand close to the iron, but he knew he was running a bluff that impressed nobody.

Then Maddox shook him to the core. "You could have let Maisie live, Steve. You had no call to kill her. Hell, she had friends and admirers here."

"Damn right," a man said, his face in shadow. "Purty little gal like that and she could sing like a nightingale."

"Hell, I didn't kill them."

"Yeah, you did."

McCord swallowed hard. "Whoever told you that is a damned liar!"

"You can tell him to his face, Steve." He turned his head. "O'Hara!"

The tall figure of a man detached itself from the shadows and glided forward like a ghost. O'Hara stood and stared silently at McCord, his black eyes glittering.

"Steve says you're a damned liar, O'Hara."

"I heard," the breed said.

"O'Hara says he was headed back from hunting when he saw you kill Trace and Maisie," Maddox said. He smiled. "Though how come the belly of the deer he shot was stuffed full of newly minted double eagles, he hasn't rightfully explained."

O'Hara shrugged his shoulder high, an

expressive Indian gesture. "Maybe the deer was hungry and got them from a Butterfield stage," he said.

"Yup. Maybe so, it being hungry an' all," Maddox said.

"Are you going to take the word of a dirty half-breed over mine?" McCord said, his anger peaking.

"Any day of the week," Maddox said.

"I saw you through a long glass, McCord," O'Hara said. "You shot the man called Trace and then the woman. And then you rode away. I speak the truth."

"Yeah, sure you do, breed. And a jury of white men is likely to believe you, huh?" McCord said.

"God calls down a terrible curse on those who commit patricide," a gray-haired puncher said from the gloom. "It is among the very worst of mortal sins."

McCord was furious. His slightly slanted eyes narrowed and his face, a pale oval of hate, picked up dull red highlights on his nose and cheekbones from the oil lamps inside.

"All right, that's enough!" he yelled. "My talking is done. I want all of you off my property. Now!"

Maddox smiled without humor. "Steve, I told you, this is no longer your property."

He reached into his canvas coat and produced a folded paper. "Know what this is, Steve?"

McCord didn't answer.

"Well, apparently you don't. It's a will your pa made a year ago, before he decided to marry again. I don't need to read it, because I've pretty much memorized the thing."

"Cut to the chase, Frisco." McCord said.

"It says that if he dies without further issue, ownership of the McCord ranch passes to James Charles Maddox. That's my legal name, like."

"You forged the will, damn you."

"No, Steve, it's legal, all signed and witnessed. Mind you, your pa told me he planned to change the will again in favor of a son born of himself and Maisie May. But he never got the chance, did he?"

Steve McCord's mouth opened but no words came out. Finally, his face bitter, he said, "He cut me off —"

"Without a penny," Maddox said.

The big man slid the will back into his coat. "Steve, I watched you grow up and always I tried to tell myself that you were not a bad seed, that you'd break through one day. I was wrong. You're just sorry, murdering trash."

Maddox drew, his gun coming up faster than Steve McCord could ever have imagined. It made something sick lurch in his gut.

"Now get off my property," Maddox said. "This once, for old times' sake, I'm letting you live, Steve. The next time I see you, anywhere, anytime, I'll kill you."

Two realizations hit Steve McCord that evening, both of them unpleasant.

The first was that all he could do was ride away with his tail between his legs. Empty threats would not impress Maddox and the dozen or so hard cases that faced him. The second, and this tore at him, was that he called himself a gunfighter but the speed of Frisco Maddox's draw had shown him that he wasn't in a real shootist's class.

He'd killed Beau Hunt, but that was murder and meant nothing, just an empty thing to impress folks when he was on the brag.

Frisco Maddox had demonstrated a harsh reality.

"I'll be back, Frisco," he said, trying to make it sound thin, menacing.

But as he swung his horse away a hard ball of horse dung hit the back of his neck and Steve McCord's face burned with shame and defeat as hard men laughed.

Chapter Sixty-Two

Lucian Tweddle was concerned. A real man had just spanked his protégé and he saw a major part of his plan and maybe even his future empire crumbling. Somehow he had to salvage this disaster.

As for Steve McCord, he'd lost most of his swagger and somehow the gun he wore no longer looked intimidating.

"Damn it, I told you not to brace Maddox," Tweddle said. "He's a man-killer from way back."

"It was him who braced me and then he showed me pa's will. What was I supposed to do?"

"Did you examine the will?"

"No. It was dark, remember?"

"It's no matter, we can challenge it in court, Steve. Maybe a judge will allow you to take possession until the matter is settled."

"Frisco said he'd kill me on sight."

"You can shade him. Your timing was off, just a little."

"No, I can't shade him. He's too fast."

"Then, if Maddox needs killing, I'll do it myself."

"You kill Maddox? That I have to see."

"Don't underestimate me, Steve. Don't ever do that at your peril."

"Then what about Flintlock? He's probably even faster than Frisco on the draw."

"My concern right now is the McCord ranch. We can deal with saddle tramps like Flintlock later. Still, you'd better stay the night here as a precaution."

"I need a drink," McCord said. "Damn, I need a drink bad."

"Help yourself. You know where the whiskey is."

Tweddle, his massive belly a huge mound under his bathrobe, sat in his chair and considered his options.

Have Steve contest the will?

No. It could take months, maybe years, and the railroad wouldn't wait.

Kill Frisco Maddox?

Risky, but it was a way if all else failed.

Offer Maddox a partnership with the O'Rourke range as bait?

Now that was a real possibility.

Of course, Tweddle realized he'd need to

dispose of Steve McCord, a small matter that he could settle tonight.

But he instantly dismissed that idea.

No, he must talk with Frisco Maddox first and settle the deal. Then get rid of Steve.

The fat man smiled to himself.

Yes, that was the way to handle this difficult situation.

He'd ride out to the McCord ranch tomorrow.

Maddox was a pragmatic man. He'd see reason.

Steve McCord was surly.

A full glass of whiskey in hand, he scowled at Tweddle.

"What are you hatching in that brain of yours, Lucian?"

"I will ride out to your ranch" — *your* ranch, such a nice touch — "and demand to see your father's will."

"And if it's legal?"

"I will tell Maddox we're disputing the content of the will and that he must vacate the property until the matter is settled in court."

"Will he go for it?"

"He won't have any choice. Not when I threaten him with a battery of out-of-town lawyers."

Steve McCord's face regained some of its

viciousness. "There's treed rises all around the ranch house," he said. "I could lay for him and kill him the first chance I get."

"That remains a viable possibility, Steve. But let's try it legally first."

"Whatever you say, Lucian."

McCord knew that his standing with the fat man had slipped since Frisco had put the crawl on him. It would take time, and maybe a killing or two, to regain his previous status.

Flintlock! Yeah, that was it! If he gunned Sam Flintlock, Tweddle would be impressed. How could he fail to be?

That was the answer.

CHAPTER SIXTY-THREE

In the thin gray of dusk, Sam Flintlock strapped his blanket roll in place behind the saddle and slid his Winchester and Hawken into their boots.

His few possessions were in his saddlebags along with clean socks and underwear.

He mounted and looked around him at what had been Brendan O'Rourke's Circle-O, now a place of the hurting dead, empty, echoing with a dreadful silence. Superstitious as all cowboys were, the hands had decided to leave and winter on the grub line rather than remain where ghosts walked, and Flintlock did not blame them.

He mounted and sat his horse for a while, head bowed, thinking.

Frank Constable's place must look just like this ranch. It too lay abandoned and desolate, his barn and infernal machine destroyed, and all the old man's dreams of journeying to the moon on a steamship with

Jules Verne had died with him.

Deep in his gut, Flintlock believed he could have prevented all this death and desolation. But he'd laid back. Let it happen. He tilted his head and looked at the amber sky where the first sentinel stars were posted, a vast, empty space inside him.

"God forgive me," he whispered aloud.

Old Barnabas perched on top of a hayrick beside the ranch house, knitting needles click-click-clicking in his hands and a ball of bright green yarn at his feet.

"Lookee, boy," he said. He held up about five feet of the knitting. "I'm making me a winter muffler fer ol' Genghis Khan. He's an ornery cuss, always wanting to massacree folks, but he feels the cold something terrible."

"There ain't any winter in hell, Barnabas," Flintlock said.

"So you say, but I say different."

Barnabas paused his needles. "Didn't do so good this time around, did you, boy?" he said.

"I reckon not. A lot of fine people dead."

"And you let it happen, Sammy."

"I could have done better. I was dealt a lousy hand but I could have played my cards better. I think that."

"And now you're going to make amends, right?"

"That's the plan, Barnabas."

"Shoot straight and fast, boy, like I teached you, even though you were an idiot and couldn't remember anything."

"I'll try to remember this time."

"Afterward, like a good boy, you go help your mama down there in the bayou and have her give you your name. You hear what I'm saying, boy?"

"I will, Barnabas. You can depend on it."

"I asked that heathen Injun O'Hara to help you, but I don't know if he will. He don't like you much, says you're too easy to kill, even for a white man. Well, I got to go."

Now Flintlock saw only a hayrick in the gloom . . . then the ball of green yarn came bouncing toward him. He leaned from the saddle, picked it up and shoved it into his saddlebags.

"For your ma," Barnabas said. His hollow voice seemed to come from the far end of a long tunnel. "Tell her I think about her every now and then."

Flintlock kneed his buckskin into motion and rode through shadows under a somber sky that brought him no comfort.

Sam Flintlock planned to be in Open Sky

just before dawn.

Taking his time, he spent the witching hours when the night was at its darkest hunched over a small fire near a stream that ran brown from silt. But the coffee tasted just fine.

Flintlock's head nodded, but he woke with a start when a man's voice rang out from the darkness. "Hello, the camp!"

He recognized the voice immediately. "Dave Glover, what the hell are you doing out here?" he yelled.

"Is that you, Sam'l Flintlock?"

"Yeah, it's me."

"You got coffee and smoking tobacco?"

"I got both."

"Then I'll come in."

Glover led his mule into the glow of the firelight. The man looked older, as though his years had suddenly caught up with him.

"What are you doing wandering around at this time of night?" Flintlock said.

"I could ask you the same question."

Flintlock smiled faintly. "I'm a lost soul, I guess."

"Me too, Sam'l. My house fell down. The whole thing just crashed to the ground."

"Where's your woman?"

"The house fell down on top of her. I buried her a two-week ago."

461

"Damn, I'm sorry to hear that. She was a real nice lady, comfortable if you catch my drift." Flintlock shook his head. "You're a crazy old coot an' no mistake. I told you not to build a house where there was never a house before. Help yourself to coffee."

"You got the makings?"

Flintlock tossed over tobacco and papers and after Glover had settled, he said, "Sorry about your loss, Dave. I truly am."

"Thank'ee kindly. I can always build another house, but I'll never find another Miss Maybelline Bell. She was one of a kind."

"Hard thing to lose a good woman."

"Ah, well, she made me happy fer a spell. You ever been happy fer even a little while, Sam'l?"

"Looking back, no. Can't say as I have. Not happy like feeling good about everything happy."

"I didn't think so. It's left a mark on you. Lines on your face, scars on your soul."

Glover smoked and drank coffee for a while, studying Flintlock with shrewd eyes. Then he said, "Got your hair tied back."

"My hair is as it's always been."

"No, it ain't, Sammy. It's tied back."

"Whatever you say."

"What I mean is, I reckon you got revolver

462

fighting in mind."

"I've got killings in mind, Dave."

"You lost your way, Sam. For a while you did. You tried to ride a more peaceful trail, but in our world there ain't any of those, not fer rannies like us."

"It was that obvious, huh?"

Glover said nothing. He stared into the fire where the embers glowed red.

"I plan to even things out this morning," Flintlock said. "Make it right."

"I recollect Billy said that, said it right afore he shot Sheriff William Brady in Lincoln back in '78."

"Yeah, I guess he did. But we all had a hand in that killing, Dave. Our hearts were bad that day because we were hurting over John Tunstall."

"I had no hand in that killing. My Henry jammed. You recollect?"

"No. I reckon I don't recollect that."

Glover drained his cup then threw the butt of his cigarette into the fire. He rose to his feet.

"I got to be moving on, Sam'l," he said. "I'm headed into the Sans Bois, do some trappin' and a little prospecting, maybe."

"Bide awhile, Dave. Spread your blankets by the fire and warm them old bones of your'n."

The old man shook his head. "You reckon you're on a high lonesome, boy, but you're not, you're surrounded by ghosts. They tell me I'm not welcome here and that I got to line out."

Flintlock nodded. "Then so long, Dave."

"Yeah, you too, Sam. So long."

Glover gathered the reins of his mule and without another word stepped into the crowding darkness.

The fire crackled and flames danced as a wind rustled in the trees. Sam Flintlock pulled his knees to his chest, bowed his head and became one with the night.

CHAPTER SIXTY-FOUR

Sam Flintlock rode into Open Sky after dawn. The sky was ablaze with scarlet and the air was clear, the morning coming in clean.

A stray dog skulked along the boardwalk past the darkened stores then stopped and studied Flintlock for a moment before deciding he was of no interest and moved on.

The false front of the Rocking Horse saloon was draped in black bunting for the death of Maisie May and the town had a drab, weatherworn appearance in the harsh light of morning like a tired old whore gazing into a cruel mirror. A north wind blew strong and lifted skeins of dust from the street and the hanging store signs banged back and forth on their chains.

Lucian Tweddle's house was the biggest in town, built on a shallow hill with shade trees along the driveway. For a fat man it was an easy downhill walk to the bank, slightly more strenuous on the return.

Flintlock led his horse along the driveway to the front door.

He listened for a while and heard activity inside, the low hum of men's voices interrupted by a cigar smoker's rumbling cough. Tweddle was to home all right, but the other man's identity was a mystery.

Flintlock hoped it was Steve McCord. His presence would make things a lot simpler.

He tried the door handle. Locked. And maybe bolted. No doubt the same with the windows.

On cat feet, Flintlock walked wide around the house, intending to try the back door. But he stopped at a large flagstone patio flanked by a pair of marble statues of Greek nymphs with small breasts and generous hips and thighs.

The ornate French doors that opened onto the patio were locked, behind them a large formal dining room. As far as Flintlock could tell only one lock closed the doors from the inside, unless there were bolts he couldn't see. There was only one way to find out.

He pulled his Colt, measured his kick then struck out with his booted right foot.

The doors, manufactured for show not

security, crashed open. Glass shattered and splintered wood flew in every direction.

Flintlock stepped through the wreckage, tossed aside a door that angled on one hinge across his path, and quickly crossed the dining room.

He almost collided with Steve McCord.

Shocked, the man took a step back. He had shaving soap on one side of his face and a razor in his right hand. He wore only his hat, underwear and his holstered Colt.

"Flintlock!" he yelled. Then his hands dropped to the buckle of his gun belt. He let belt and holster thud to the floor, and shrieked, "I'm out of it!"

"Way too late for that," Flintlock said. He fired twice into McCord's chest and didn't wait to see the man drop.

Flintlock stepped into the hallway and yelled, "Tweddle!"

"In here, Mr. Flintlock," the fat man called out, his tone calm. "Join me for coffee and pastries and a man-to-man talk in the parlor."

Flintlock followed Tweddle's voice and stopped at the partially opened parlor door.

"Come in, come in, Mr. Flintlock, and welcome," the fat man said. "I am unarmed."

Flintlock pushed the door all the way open

467

with the muzzle of his revolver and warily stepped inside. Tweddle sat in a leather armchair like an obese, smiling toad. He was fully dressed and wore English riding boots as though he planned to take to the trail that morning.

"I take it young McCord is dead?" he said.

Flintlock nodded. "Dead as he's ever gonna be."

"Good. He was a bad apple, take my word for that. Coffee? Pastry?"

Flintlock shook his head. "Not today, Tweddle."

"Well, don't stand on formality, man, take a seat. We have business to discuss. Fortunes to be made with you at my side."

"The only business I have with you is in my right hand, Tweddle."

"Oh, let's not be tiresome, Mr. Flintlock. I plan to make you a rich man." He slapped his hands together. "What do you think of that, my buck?"

But Tweddle had made a fatal mistake that morning. He should have armed himself.

The man who faced him was what Sam Flintlock had trained himself to be . . . a cold, efficient and soulless man-killer.

And he demonstrated that now. "Tweddle, I still got three unspent cartridges in this gun. One is for Beau Hunt, one for Brendan

O'Rourke and the third for his wife. You're gonna get all three in your fat gut."

Tweddle was afraid, but he retreated into bluster. "I'm unarmed, Flintlock. Kill me and you'll hang."

"I'll take my chances," Flintlock said.

He fired three times.

The morning was bright and the sun beamed, happy to create a brand-new day.

Sam Flintlock carefully closed the front door of the house behind him and swung into the saddle. A crowd of people had gathered, whispering to one another, as they stared at the house and the approaching rider.

Among them stood the tall figure of Marshal Tom Lithgow.

As Flintlock rode close, he touched his hat brim. "Morning, Marshal," he said.

Smiling, Lithgow returned the courtesy. "It's over, isn't it?" he said.

Flintlock drew rein. "It's over. Play it any way you like, Tom."

"Thieves fell out over the spoils and killed one another. That's the truth of it as far as I'm concerned."

"I'm moving on now, Tom," Flintlock said. "Headed down Louisiana way."

"Ride easy, Sam," Lithgow said.
"You too, Tom. Ride easy."

CHAPTER SIXTY-FIVE

Sam Flintlock camped by a shallow playa in the rugged, remote timber country south of Horseshoe Mountain. He'd killed a deer the day before and now broiled a venison steak over the fire, the last of his coffee on the bile among the coals.

When he heard a rustle in the brush behind him he didn't look up.

"Come on in, O'Hara. I'm not easy to kill today."

The breed led his horse into camp. "It seems that Barnabas managed to teach you something."

"He taught me how to scout an Injun who's been dogging my back trail for days." He passed a hunk of scorched, dripping meat to O'Hara. "Eat," he said. "I'm a lousy cook."

The breed squatted, the reins of his horse trailing behind him.

Flintlock stuck another steak on the stick

and said, "Why are you following me?"

O'Hara bit into the venison and chewed. After a while he said, "I heard about what happened in Open Sky."

"I killed two men. Is that what you heard?"

"They needed killing."

"I reckon so. I'll ask again, why are you following me?"

"And I ask you: Why are you here, Flintlock?"

"Headed down Louisiana way. Why are you here?"

"Following you."

"Damn you for a cigar store Indian, O'Hara. Speak plain, white man American."

"I was bored. When I'm around you, stuff happens."

"Hold this." Flintlock handed the venison stick to O'Hara. "Don't burn it."

He pulled over his saddlebags and took out a folded paper. "I picked this up at a stage station back a ways. It's a year old, but what the hell, I'm riding that way anyhow."

O'Hara opened the paper, a reward dodger, yellowed and ripped at the corners where it was torn from a wall. The breed whistled between his teeth. "Zack Hawk. Flintlock, you aim high."

"Look at the reward."

"Ten thousand dollars."

"Dead or alive."

"For the murder of a Texas Ranger and two deputy United States marshals in El Paso," O'Hara said.

"From what I heard, after the killings Hawk rode clear across Texas and skipped over the border into Louisiana. He might still be there."

"That's five thousand each," O'Hara said.

"Suppose I say I like to work alone," Flintlock said.

"I promised old Barnabas I'd look out for you," the breed said. "I aim to keep my promise."

"Old Barnabas! Hell, O'Hara, you're even crazier than I am, seeing things."

"Is that a fact?"

"Yeah, it's a natural fact."

Flintlock chewed on his steak, then said, "My ma is in trouble down in the bayou country."

"I know. Barnabas told me."

"Well, maybe after all you could help. You're real good at sneaking up on folks."

"Glad to be of help," O'Hara said.

"Is Zack Hawk as good with a gun as they say?" Flintlock said.

"Wes Hardin stepped around him, called him 'Sir.' "

"Then I'm right glad to have you along," Sam Flintlock said.